A VICIOUS PROPOSAL

THE
FALLEN KINGS
OF EDEN

KRISTY MARIE

For Papa.
My father. My friend. My teacher.
The man who always showed up with a hug and shovel when I needed them.
You are my ride or die.

This novel is a work of fiction. Names, characters, businesses, places, events, and incidents are either the product of the author's imagination or used in a fictitious manner. Any resemblance to actual persons, living or dead, or actual events, places, and companies is purely coincidental.

First Line Editor: The Ryter's Proof
Proofing: K&K Edits and VJF
Object Cover Design: TRC Designs by Cat
Model Cover Design: Bitter Sage Designs
Interior Formatting: Champagne Book Design

Copyright © 2024 by Kristy Marie
Published by Kristy Marie Books, LLC
All rights reserved.

No part of this book may be reproduced in any form or by any electronic or mechanical means, including artificial intelligence software, information storage and retrieval systems, without written permission from the author, except for the use of brief quotations in a book review.

AUTHOR'S NOTE

A Vicious Proposal contains villainous government officials. These men and women are entirely fictitious and do not represent or resemble anyone who has been or currently holds positions in the United States Judicial System.

This is a fictitious story and in no way represents the feelings or personal opinions of the author on the men and women who serve and protect our country. We thank you for your service and daily sacrifices for our safety—except for you evil ones. We prefer you not work with the public if you can't act right.

It should also be noted that *A Vicious Proposal* contains sensitive themes in portions of the story. Use your best judgment when choosing to read this novel, as it contains foul language, the mention of past abuse, alleged rape, parental death, and descriptive sexual encounters. If any of these things unsettle you, proceed with caution or slide this book back onto the shelf.

As always, please put your mental health before fictional stories.

Buckle up, loves. This story is one wild ride.

Come unto me, all ye that labour and are heavy laden, and I will give you rest. Matthew 11:28 (KJV)

Vincent Van Gogh once said, *"I put my heart and my soul into my work and have lost my mind in the process."*

There's freedom in losing one's mind—especially to his passions.

My obsession is much darker than art, but in the shadows of the night, I am still an artist.

I don't paint landscapes or beautiful sunflowers. My twisted works engulf the towns of corrupt leaders with flames and ash, reminding each of them that I'm coming.

Through their fear, I will keep her memory alive.

I am the arsonist known as a soulless judge, and in my courtroom, no one escapes my creative passion for justice.

A VICIOUS PROPOSAL

PROLOGUE

Van

Many Fires Ago…

"I BEG YOU! DON'T DO THIS!" THE RESPECTED MAYOR OF Orange Grove, South Carolina, trembles in his designer suit when I step forward.

"Now isn't the time for begging, Mayor Williams," I scold. "That part comes later"—I offer him a threatening smile—"when the smoke is thick, and the roar of the flames drowns out your cries for help."

The ever-present knot lodged in my chest stirs as his frightened gaze flicks to the angry flames behind me, burning brightly within the metal trash can.

My mother felt this fear. She stood at the window, armed with a brave smile and empty assurances, as the fire breached our doorway, atop our painted ceilings.

"As you can see, Mayor, the flames are contained, but if you don't tell me what I need to know"—I grab the glass of Cognac off the table and take a drink—"I'll feed the flames with your finest spirits and paint your corrupted town with the ashes of your lounge."

To emphasize my point, I toss the tumbler of alcohol into the fire and step back, admiring how the flames rise from the ground, begging for more.

"As you know, I have quite the hard-on for the contemporary arts."

And modern, but I doubt the mayor is in the mood to discuss my artistic preferences.

"I've already told you, I don't know who he is!"

The bitter hatred in his words amuses me. "Now, now, Mayor. Didn't anyone ever tell you that shouting is rude?"

He lets out a vicious growl. "You don't know who you're fucking with, boy!"

And here I was, growing bored with the lack of threats.

Without blinking, I leap forward and grab him around the neck. "I know exactly who I'm fucking with, Mayor—a *murderer*."

A tear streaks down his cheek, but any remorse I might've possessed died long ago.

"I won't ask you again. Tell me his name, or you will wear the ashes of your precious lounge like a scarlet letter."

"Please," Williams begs through trembling lips. "I only kept *him* out of the papers. I had nothing to do with the fire."

Lies. Lies. Lies.

"Come on, Mayor," I chide. "You did more than keep his secret." Squeezing harder, I lean in and whisper, "You helped him get away with *murder*."

He shakes his head, remaining dedicated to his lies. "He never told me his plans to set the fire. I swear."

My eyebrows rise mockingly. "You swear?" Who does he think I am? A second grader? "Well, if you *swear*, then this has all been a terrible misunderstanding."

He nods densely, sniffing through his congested nose. "I would never protect a murderer."

I tilt my head, my voice lowering to a deadly whisper. "I don't believe you."

Mayor Williams shakes his head from side to side, and my hands tightening around his neck before he can utter another lie.

"By not bringing *him* to justice, you may as well have lit the match that killed those women—that killed my mother." He starts to wheeze, but I don't stop. Instead, I watch his veins turn a nasty shade of blue. "But you can make this right, Williams. You can have absolution by giving me *his* name."

Exhaling into the stale stench of cigar smoke, I demand once more. "Tell me *his* name, Mayor, and this will all be over."

"I—"

The back door to the employee entrance opens and slams against the wall.

"Oh, sorry. I forgot my purse."

I know that voice all too well.

Hope fills the mayor's eyes. "Reese, my darling! Call the police!"

Never looking back, I cluck my tongue at the naïve man. "Haven't you heard, Williams? Ms. Employee of the Decade isn't going to call the police. Not when she's been stealing from your customers for the last three months."

Employers these days… they equate beauty with innocence.

"You should start doing background checks on your employees." Chuckling, I drop my hands and stand tall, still not bothering to face the woman in the doorway. "You'd be surprised to learn of their many skills."

Mayor Williams's lips part, his shocked gaze locked on the woman behind me.

"Isn't this your day off, stalker boy?" The pain in the ass pushes off the doorway and stands just out of reach. "I thought you haunted someone else on Tuesday nights?"

A genuine smile tugs at the edge of my mouth. "How would you know? You have Tuesdays off."

Reese, the innocent-looking thief, blows out a frustrated breath. "I forgot my purse."

I shrug, fully grinning at her lie. "I forgot the mayor. Guess we're both having an off day."

If Reese Carmichael fears me, she hides it well. But then again, she's good at hiding a lot of things.

"I don't think you can call it an off day when you planned to break into the cigar lounge and torture the owner." Her laugh rings throughout the bar—a far better sound than the mayor's gurgling cries.

"I would never torture the mayor of Orange Grove," I lie, flashing concern at the man tied to the chair and clutching my chest. "Tell her, Mayor. You and I were just chatting in front of a cozy fire."

Finally, I turn around and face my golden-haired muse. Her emerald-green eyes sparkle under the lamplight, glistening like morning dew on a blade of grass.

Her mouth twitches, fighting a smile. "So, you're telling me you're just here to see your friend and are not about to burn down his lounge?"

"Absolutely not! I'm appalled you would insinuate such a thing."

Even I don't believe myself—not that I am putting on my best performance here.

Reese Carmichael is much more intelligent than her employer. She knew I was up to no good the first time she saw me watching from the lot across the street.

"You should be appalled by your lack of tact. Any idiot could figure out what you were up to, *Van Gogh*."

"There's no need for name-calling," I scold, turning back toward the mayor, who has since tuckered out and is indulging in a quick nap. "He's learned from his mistakes and promises to be more aware of his surroundings in the future."

I must admit, I will miss this back-and-forth with her. My cock and I rather enjoy beating off to the memory of her calling me by my street name.

If there is one good thing about Mayor Williams, it is that he hires the most exciting and observant staff. Not that I was hiding my presence, but when Reese first spotted me at the lounge, she came outside with a drink and a sandwich, claiming that if I was going to case the place, I should at least tip her for not reporting my sorry ass.

I knew then that Mayor Williams's punishment would be different—and much longer than the others.

"As much as the mayor deserves it," Reese finally says with an air of regret, "I can't let you hurt him."

"Good thing I wasn't asking for your permission," I snap back, allowing the rage to bubble to the surface as I step closer. "Don't let my fascination with your mouth confuse you, Flower. No one comes between me and justice." My gaze lowers, taking in the soft curves of her body, covered by a black tank top and ripped jeans. "Not even you."

I do not make mistakes, but I did with Reese. I watched her for months. I let her consume my time more than my revenge. She amuses me to the point of laughter, but I won't let her destroy my purpose.

"Hurting someone is different than simply destroying his property," she argues. "I can't allow you to harm him. His family would miss him."

I doubt that, but I no longer feel like arguing with her. "And you would miss your source of income."

She and I both know I'm not talking about her hourly wage. "You can't scam his wealthy friends if they no longer have a place to puff their chests and cheat on their wives."

"That's not true." She shakes her head and steps back toward the door as if considering running.

"Interesting," I muse, stalking forward, noticing her shoulders tightening. "Are you scared of me, Flower?"

If she wonders why I call her Flower, she doesn't ask. Instead, she bravely rolls her eyes. "If I say no, will you choke me, too?"

"Only if you're a good girl."

Her breath hitches. "Don't be crude."

"Shall I be mean, then?" I prompt. "You particularly enjoy those nights more than the others."

Tonight isn't the first time she wasn't in the mood for my company—especially when I fucked with her marks.

You can't fault a man for flirting.

"What do you want, Van Gogh? Mayor Williams won't give up his friends if that's what you're after. He'll take his secrets to the grave."

"I can live with that. Do you think he prefers oak or pine for his casket?"

Reese drops her head to her chest, and I'm all too happy to lift her eyes back to mine with one finger under her chin. "Don't get all righteous on me now, love. He's not a good man."

"And you're not a killer."

"So you say," I whisper, stroking her supple skin with my thumb before being completely honest. "He must pay for his crimes."

"And what about us, huh? Will you make us pay for ours?"

She means it as a rhetorical question, but I answer it anyway. "Everyone must pay for their transgressions—even you and me."

I swear I can see flames dancing in the gold flecks of her eyes when she slips her arms between us, revealing a stainless-steel lighter. "But what if I told you I am more than just a thief?"

"I'd believe you."

She pushes the lighter into my chest. "Would you believe that I want to leave here?" She swallows harshly. "To get away from this town—"

I don't let her finish.

"Foolish little sunflower," I snap, flipping open the lighter and igniting a flame. "I know the truth you hide, and the only thing I'm interested in with you is punishment."

With that, I drop the lighter.

CHAPTER ONE

Reese
Present Day

"What did I say, Reese?" The giant asshole named Blake grabs me by the upper arm, squeezing to the point of pain. "Act like you're enjoying it."

It's a sad day when your boyfriend needs to remind you to pretend to *enjoy* him. Then again, most boyfriends aren't blackmailing their girlfriends. Blake, however, is. He's super romantic like that.

Not that I'm girlfriend material or even want to be Blake's girlfriend.

The only reason I'm allowing Blake to pretend that I am his forever love is because he caught me, a teacher's aide, hacking into his roommate's computer a few weeks ago and decided that instead of turning me into his father, the dean, my computer skills would be of better use to him. You see, Blake is a social pariah that most students want to poison but don't—again, his daddy is the dean. Instead, they merely talk shit about him behind his back like the cowards they are. Anyway, all those mean and nasty comments make my poor, sweet boyfriend cry himself to sleep at night, and he's tired of it.

Thanks to my financial prowess, it's their turn to feel pain as they watch their bank accounts dwindle to nothing when I hack their phones at parties, just like now. Except, this party is a kegger in the middle of the woods with no cell service, but try explaining that to Blake, who thinks a D- is a passing grade. So, yeah, it's been hard for me to act like I'm enjoying his company when there are no accounts to hack.

"My apologies, darling," I coo. "The alcohol and fresh air aren't the best combination."

But the bonfire is. It reminds me of freedom and bittersweet mistakes.

Blake makes this sound that is supposed to be intimidating, but like his golf game, it's simply pitiful. "You think this is funny? You're here for one reason, and it's not your sarcasm."

I can't help myself. "It's for my ass, isn't it? I knew I shouldn't have worn these shorts."

Before I can laugh at my witty remark, Blake yanks me against his chest, moving the hand on my arm to my ass cheeks, gripping so hard it feels they may bruise. "Watch yourself, Reese. You may have everyone else fooled, but I know who you *really* are." He levels me with a wicked smile. "You aren't the only one who can break through a firewall."

I should probably clarify that he's right. I'm no Mother Theresa. Hacking dickbags's bank accounts isn't the worst thing I've done. But unlike them, I did it out of necessity, not for pleasure. I'm not a bad person. I've just been in very bad situations where even I questioned my morality.

"Bullshit. You can't even work the vending machine, much less find any dirt on me."

There are only two people in this world who know what I've done, and this fucker isn't one of them.

"You bitch. You think you're so smart, don't you?"

Actually, I know I'm smart. I don't need a man to say it so I can believe it. I'm quite confident all on my own.

I cock my head to the side and flash my boyfriend the fakest smile I can manage. "If you wanted to talk sweet, you should have led with that." I make a show of batting my eyelashes like a total fool.

"Reese," Blake drawls, his voice developing a hard edge.

Immediately, my fake smile drops and matches the tight line of his mouth. I might be a novice at pretending I like him, but I'm a pro at hating him.

"Get your fucking ass back to the bonfire, or you won't have to worry about your shorts giving the wrong impression. Do I make myself clear?"

I almost say no and ask him to repeat it, but then I'd have to talk to him longer, and, well, no one needs more of that torture. I already know the little tattletale will turn me in to his daddy, who will turn me in to the police, who will then investigate my past and find a secret I'd rather keep buried, even though it eats away at my soul to hide it.

"Yeah, crystal."

Fucker.

Blake nods, as if I've just told him he is the prettiest boy in the whole wide world and handed him a cookie. It makes me sick, but not enough to punch him. That would really make waves in the rumor mill, and we can't have that. Blake is already a tease away from turning me in anyway. If I want to keep my little hacking gig a secret, I have to keep Blake happy—at least until I can figure a way out that doesn't require jail time.

"Reese?" Blake snaps. "Did you hear me?"

My eyes focus back on Abercrombie and Evil. "Yes. You love me.

I get it. Let's get back to your friends so they don't get jealous that you spend so much time with me."

I have no idea what he was saying. I'm sure it was stupid.

Before Blake can do one more thing, I yank away and walk backward, never taking my eyes off him. "Are you coming, or do you need me to moan and cry out how amazing you are?"

I'm so being sarcastic. He might require that I pretend to enjoy his kiss, but I draw the line at pretending he has a nice dick. Everyone would know I was lying then.

"Watch it, Reese. You're getting brave."

Never taking my eyes off him, I smile. "I've been brave."

He doesn't know me. He thinks I'm a coward because I don't want to go to jail. I agree, orange is not my color, but I would wear it proudly if I had to. After all, we are all prisoners at some point.

In a mock salute, I flash Blake the most extensive eat-shit look I can. "Don't worry, sweetheart; you'll have no more trouble out of me tonight."

Tomorrow is a different story. I haven't given up on finding a faster solution to rid myself of Blake and his heavy hand. His father might have impressive encryptions on his accounts, but somewhere, someone—likely Blake—has reused a password that will open a virtual door.

And that's all I need—an opening to buy back my freedom.

When Blake and I approach the tents where his friends huddle around the fire, they look up, grinning.

"Do we even want to know what you two have been up to in the woods?" The blonde, I think her name is Ashley, flashes me a wink like I'm the luckiest girl in the world. She's here with one of Blake's jock friends. And when I say jock, I mean golf. They are on the golf team at the university, not something hot, like football.

Anyway, Ashley isn't the worst of the bunch. If I weren't here against my will, I might actually talk to her.

A VICIOUS PROPOSAL

Blake's laugh rumbles from behind me, much closer than I remember him being. "Tsk, tsk, Ash. Nice guys never kiss and tell."

There's so much wrong with that statement that I don't even know where to start. But you know what? It doesn't matter. Like me, Blake lives a lie. Let Ashley think he's a decent human. With one conversation, she'll realize quickly that he's Satan's number one toe sucker.

"I need a drink." I groan. "Maybe several."

I had way more than several drinks.

I couldn't endure one more sober second of Blake's bullshit stories about playing the back nine or sandbox—whatever that means.

It was socialized torture.

And I was done.

The first three beers went down like water. Blake's friends clapped and cheered for my lack of gag reflex on drinks four and five. By drink six, Blake tried picking me up and carrying me to the tent so I could sleep it off. I responded with an uncoordinated kick to his balls that sent him into a rage, claiming I could sleep outside with the bears.

I don't know about the other women at this party, but that didn't sound like a horrible idea. It was better than waking up to Blake's long-ass fingernails digging into my back.

Honestly, I prefer the outdoors anyway. I've always found it to be my sanctuary.

I wasn't like most kids. The boogeyman or monsters that lurked under the bed didn't scare me. I felt at home with them. Like them, people steered clear of me. I could never master the fake smile and crafted persona. I wasn't from a prominent family or even a notable one. I was simply a runaway—a girl that didn't listen to her parents, or so they said. The truth is, I hid in the dark with monsters because I am one. And I miss the peace it offered.

The leaves rustle beside me, and I sit up quickly, scanning the darkness for threats. Monsters may accept me as one of them, but that doesn't mean they won't kill me all the same.

It's survival of the fittest, and that's not me right now.

"Blake?" I scan the tree line, knowing good and damn well Blake isn't out there taking a midnight pee. "Listen, if you want money, I have none." I shrug into the darkness, trying to find my bravery, and add, "And, if you're looking for your next victim, I'm not your girl. I've outrun the devil himself."

A deep rumbling comes from behind me, and I'm on my feet in seconds.

"And here I thought you had forgotten me."

My voice takes on a whisper. "Van Gogh?"

When I said that I have never been afraid of monsters, I wasn't kidding.

Van Gogh and I were friends.

We had a mutual understanding.

We kept each other company in the dark silence.

We shared no stories.

No hopes or dreams.

Only the parable that we all eventually become prisoners.

"Were you expecting Tiger Woods?"

I roll my eyes—definitely Van Gogh. No one else has a level of sarcasm that makes you want to punch him in the face every time he opens his mouth.

"Don't tell me," I say, my eyes darting around the woods, "you forgot something."

The man I only know as Van Gogh chuckles. "You could say that."

I step back, wishing the fire was still roaring so I could see. "I hate to be the one to break the news, but I don't have anything of yours."

But he has something of mine—my heart.

"Hmm," he answers, which is an improvement. "I disagree."

Of course, he does. When has he ever agreed with me? Never, that's when, and Van Gogh is the longest relationship I've ever had. Sure, I don't know his real name, but I loved his psychotic ass for one magical summer—until he left me without a word.

I was trying to get over it, but you know what? Fuck him. I'm still bitter.

"Why are you here?" I narrow my gaze into the woods, hoping he can see how not excited I am to hear from him after nine years.

A rustling comes from behind me. "The same reason you're here."

I flip around, trying to get a glimpse of the man who has haunted my dreams since I was a teenager. "You were blackmailed, too?" I pitch my voice to sound ditsy like we're discussing our mutual love of a pair of Jimmy Choos. "Samesies!"

This time, I don't hear his deep chuckle.

"Aww. Don't tell me you've forgotten how to laugh, Van. I'm disappointed."

Honestly, I could count on two fingers how many times I've heard him laugh, but I'm still pretty drunk and happy to spar with the man who used to make me come alive.

The keywords here are *used to*.

"Are you going to ignore me or say hello?"

Still, nothing.

Sighing, I flop down onto the ground next to the firepit. I'm sure it looked super sexy, considering I only have one shoe. I don't even want to pretend to figure out how that happened. All I can hope is that I find it before I have to hike back to the car barefoot. Don't think for a second that Blake will offer to carry me.

Van Gogh, either.

That's not how he works.

Romance is dead to him.

So are people and anything that breathes.

But he used to tolerate me. He was there for me, and that's more than I can say for anyone else.

Then again, fuck him.

"It's awful to see you again, Van. If you'll excuse me, I must return to the titty baby in my tent who thinks he's a supermodel."

Standing, I dust off my pants and ignore the whole one-shoe mystery. "You know how to get back home, don't you?"

Like the serial killer Van longs to be, he says nothing. "It's straight down through the earth's center," I remind him. "I heard Satan even put out a welcome sign for you."

I pause, waiting for any reaction, but I get nothing but the chilly feeling of loneliness.

My moody stalker, the bane of Orange Grove, South Carolina, disappears, just as he always has.

Fucker.

Ugh. Why is my heart suddenly beating like I ran a 5K in fifteen minutes? Who cares about Van Gogh? Not me. He is so yesterday.

The only thing I need to focus on is the here and now and the giant-sized twat likely lying on my sleeping bag.

I need Blake out of my life. Hell, *I* need out of my life. As thrilling as some claim college to be, I think it could use fewer pricks and more average people. At Havemeyer University, everyone has something to prove. No one can be an average Joe and finish with a C.

No, they must be the best—everyone competes, and failure is not an option. Perfection is a must, and it spreads like a sickness.

And I'm tired of being sick. I'm tired of feeling like I'm never enough. Where are the small wins? Where are the victories when there's never an end—never an attainable goal?

It's brainwashing at its finest—a fear that my sister's boyfriend instilled in me from a young age. You can never fail. Girls who can't be the best end up on the streets—like my sister and me.

The thought of Julia sends a chill down my spine. I'd never been good at making friends, but Julia could charm anyone. She was my parents' pride and joy.

She was my everything.

Until she wasn't.

Maybe I was always drawn to Van Gogh because he was everything I wanted to be. He lived behind a cloud of darkness. No one told him what to do. He lived by his own rules.

He was truly free.

Something I would never be.

Even now, a state away from my past, I'm a prisoner who can't fail, or Blake the Snake will expose me and send me to prison. I will lose everything and end up just like my sister.

Looking around the woods, I don't see Van, but I know he's there, watching, waiting for me to close my eyes like before.

Van Gogh may not care about me anymore, but luckily for him, it doesn't matter.

I keep my promises—I just deliver on them a little shittier than I used to.

Grabbing a marker from my bag, minding Blake's obnoxious snoring, I take the protein bar out and scribble *Coward* on the wrapper.

CHAPTER TWO

Reese

I WAKE TO SCREAMS, AND NOT THE DRAMATIC KIND, LIKE A BUG flying into someone's tent, either.

These screams are blood-curdling panic.

"Help us!"

I jump to my feet and find the tent empty and the door open. Blake is gone, and from the sound of his distant screaming, he is in someone else's tent.

I told you he was a real sweetheart.

Crawling out, I'm met with a face full of smoke and a blazing fire circling Ashley's tent. But it's not the screams or the raging fire preventing their escape; it's the fear from the words painted in ash on the ground: *Betrayer*.

I didn't need to look down at my feet—at the spot where I left the protein bar. I knew this was Van Gogh's handiwork. The ash lettering is his signature, but it's not *the one* he uses when punishing those who wronged him.

For that, he leaves a sunflower burnt into the ground—where the protein bar lies in the center, right next to my missing shoe.

It's a warning—one he's never used on me.

He's coming for me, and I better be ready.

For what, I don't know. All I've ever done is protect Van. Undoubtedly, last night's encounter upset his moody ass, but surely not enough to kill me. I was joking, after all. Van should be used to my humor, even if we haven't seen each other in years.

But seriously, what did he expect me to do? Hug him? Fall to my knees and kiss his tight ass for finally gracing me with his presence after he up and disappeared, leaving me waiting at our meet-up point like a total idiot? Uh, yeah. I might have been happy to see him, but not that much.

"Reese! What the fuck are you doing? Help us!"

I tear my eyes from the protein bar and look at Blake's panicked face. The fire isn't that tall, nor is it thick. Blake could easily throw his blanket on it and get out, but Blake didn't spend a summer watching the silent arsonist paint the town he loathed with fire. Van Gogh controlled the flames as if they owed him a debt. He fanned them until the screams started, but it wasn't until his victims cried out for help with their guilty tears that he allowed their escape.

He always left them a way out, but to take it, they would lose everything else. As soon as they were free, their most prized possession would go up in flames.

It was their punishment—though I never knew for what, but each of Van Gogh's victims escaped with their lives.

This fire—the one he set for me—is my punishment. I have wronged him somehow, and as soon as I put out this fire and get myself to safety, I will lose everything that matters.

But then again, so will Blake.

And I might be okay with him losing his designer camping gear and thin, ribbed condoms.

I feel a smile creep up my cheeks. "You didn't think this through, lover!" I shout out into the open air, knowing Van can hear me, then slip on my shoe like a psycho princess and kick out the fire. "You think I'm scared? You think I care if you destroy my life?" Van Gogh wants to threaten me and call me the betrayer? Please.

"Go ahead, love. Destroy me. But remember, I'm not like *them*. I have nothing left to destroy."

"Are you fucking crazy?" Blake whips his head around, taking in his friends' curious yet fearful faces. "Do you really want to have this conversation now?"

Blake. Blake. Blake. You narcissist. Not only am I not talking to you, but I don't care enough about you to set a fire around your tent for cheating.

"Fine. Okay. It was wrong of me to betray you, but—" He throws his hands in the air "Look, I'm sorry. I promise to make it up to you, but please help us."

What a pompous prick.

"Look. I know you're hurt, but no one needs to die here."

Oh, how the mighty have fallen.

Was he not threatening to destroy me mere hours ago? Did he not see my crazy shine then? Well, to his credit, this is not my crazy. It's Van Gogh's. He's always been more of a show-off. He likes to make an entrance and leave you with a lasting impression of real fear.

I scoff. "No one is dying, Blake."

I take a step toward the flames circling Ashley's tent, and he backs up. "Stay back! I've already called the police. Help is on the way."

Perfect. "So, you don't want me to help you? You want me to let the fire spread until the tent goes up in flames?"

Blake swallows and looks at Ashley for a decision.

"I mean, your friends are welcome to help, too. It's not just me who has shoes on to stomp out this little campfire."

Let this teach Blake a lesson. His friends are just as shallow as he is.

They give zero shits if he dies. Fine. Maybe they care about his demise, but not enough to risk scorching their perfect hair and expensive spray tans.

Like Blake just realized other people have the potential to help, he yells, "Parker! Get over here and help us!"

Parker doesn't move.

"I'd try Trent," I suggest. "He hasn't been dating Ashley since freshman year. He's likely feeling a bit more hospitable than Parker."

"Shut up!" Blake points at me, a vein pulsing in his forehead.

Uh-oh. Someone needs a Botox touch-up.

"This is all your fault!"

Sheesh. I'm so over this.

"You know what, Blake?" I clear the remaining space between us, inwardly smiling as Blake steps behind Ashley, using her as a shield. "You are a self-righteous bastard."

I grab the small cooler outside their tent and pop open the lid. "And I'd love to see you burn, but I'm a better person than that."

Revealing the water left from the melted ice, I douse the flames at his feet and walk through the woods until I get to the road and hitch a ride in the back seat of a cop car.

"Okay, let's go over this again."

I let out a dramatic sigh and slump down in the cold metal chair. "Why is it so hard for you to believe that I don't care that my boyfriend was cheating?"

Detective Lee doesn't need to know that Blake isn't my actual boyfriend since Blake had some sense and didn't admit he was only using me to hack his enemies' bank accounts. I'm impressed he realized confessing would implicate him, as well. Sure, I could come clean and loop him in, but in doing so, I'd only provide Detective Lee with more charges to book me on.

I have to give it to Blake. It was a good move to blame me for the fire.

"Detective Lee?" I match his folded hands on the table. "You've spoken to Blake, right?"

"I have."

I nod. "Then you know Blake is an arrogant prick with small-dick syndrome. Anyone could have wanted to torch his ass, not just me. We've only been dating for a little while, and honestly, I only dated him for the money."

It's not my best excuse, but everyone knows I'm broke as fuck. I can barely afford a combo meal at the drive-thru.

"So, you're saying you didn't want to harm Blake for cheating on you?"

I offer him a smile. "I would have pulled the covers back for them if they'd asked. I one thousand percent support Blake sticking his dick in shallow places."

Disappointingly, Detective Lee doesn't buy my happiness for the couple.

"Come on, Reese. This would go much faster if you were honest with me."

Can't a girl catch a break?

"I don't understand why you don't believe me."

Surely, Detective Lee has dated someone just for the hell of it.

Well, maybe not, judging by the ring on his finger and his hand-pressed suit. Detective Lee is likely a good guy who follows the rules. Not like me, who hacks social media accounts to avenge a friend or gets passwords to a jerk's Cash App to send a few charitable donations in their honor.

My actions are technically a crime, I get that. But I never take a dime of the money for myself. I help those like me—charity cases—go up against influential people like Blake. Everyone deserves justice, even the wealthy.

I'm sure Detective Lee could understand that, but he would suggest leaving it in the hands of the legal system. And I've tried that.

It didn't work.

So, I took a page out of Van—

"If you didn't set the fire, Ms. Carmichael, who did? Who would write the word *betrayer* in front of Blake's tent if not you? Who else did Blake betray?"

It's at this very moment that it all hits me.

Vengeance.

Van Gogh spared me the wrath of his flames. Instead, he's taking everything I have in a different manner. Detective Lee would have done the same if he knew the truth. Van is handing me over to the law—allowing them to seek justice instead.

Fucking Van Gogh changed his trademark.

He won't watch me burn.

Instead, he will frame me—punish me by the very thing that betrayed him.

The law.

My eyes fill with tears, but I don't allow them to fall. Instead, I sit straight, clear my throat, and say, "I want a lawyer."

CHAPTER THREE

Reese

I DIDN'T CALL MY LAWYER.

Instead, I left a message on my voicemail and told Detective Lee I was sure he would be on his way.

I can only hope that Blake or Van Gogh show some mercy and clear things up before I really need to call an attorney. Detective Lee hasn't arrested me yet—which, I suppose, is a good thing, but then again, Van Gogh is no amateur when it comes punishment and criminalizing, if that's an actual word. If he wants me locked up and charged, it will happen. No one escapes Van Gogh's wrath—not even his muse.

"Ms. Carmichael." The door to the interrogation room opens, revealing a tired and suddenly irritated Detective Lee. "Your 'attorney' is here."

I don't know if someone switched off the air conditioner or if the cold sweat that breaks out over my body is from the icy chill coming from the imposing figure in the doorway.

Van Gogh is here.

He's not in the shadows or waiting behind the flames. He's here in the light, donning his trademark black attire. Unlike years ago, he isn't wearing a hoodie and jeans. My dark vigilante sports an expensive-looking three-piece suit tailor-made for his body.

But what's most noticeable—other than his definitive scowl and his haughty disposition—are his brilliant green eyes swirling with flakes of gold. He looks otherworldly—like simmering coal ready to spark into flames.

"If you're done jerking off to my client's tasteless attire"—Van Gogh pushes through the door, frowning at my tank top and lack of bra—"we'll be leaving. Unless Blake Worthington wants to cry a little more. My client seems to enjoy lies as much as she does frat boys."

Oh, hell no.

I jump from the chair and level Van Gogh with a look that doesn't scare him.

"Yes, Ms. Carmichael?" The fucker tilts his head, daring me to say something stupid. "Did you have something to add? Surely, Detective Lee hasn't convinced you to talk when you know to remain silent."

Fuck him.

Right in the armpit.

Who does he think he is, barging in here like a real attorney?

You know what? It doesn't matter. Clearly, Van is in the mood for games.

"Actually," I say sweetly, "I just wanted to hug you."

Immediately, Van Gogh's posture stiffens.

"Thank you for coming so quickly." Detective Lee's gaze volleys between Van and me as I step toward Van. "No one here would believe me. But you do, don't you?"

Van's gaze is ice cold. If I didn't know him, I'd be fearful that he would shove me away before setting the entire precinct on fire for hugging him. But I do know him, and he won't do shit in front of witnesses.

"Uh." Detective Lee shuffles back as I take hold of Van's forearms and squeeze.

For so long, I felt like Van was a dream—a figment of my imagination—but here he is, still an asshole.

"Thank you, Mr...."

I pull Van closer until there's merely a breath between us, holding his angry stare in a challenge.

"Cain," he clips out, as if the surname disgusts him.

I tilt my head and offer him a smile. "Mr. Cain," I repeat, rolling the name around momentarily. I'm not dense enough to think he's given Lee or me his real name. After all, he's still a wanted criminal in South Carolina.

"Well, Mr. Cain, thank you for coming to my rescue." With one last warning look, I pull the boy I once promised to run away with into my arms, and just like back then, he makes me regret it.

"Are you finished copping a feel, Ms. Carmichael, or should I ask the good detective here to turn off the cameras?"

Van Gogh or Mr. Cain—whatever the hell his name is—can go straight back to hell, where he came from.

Pulling back, I let the bastard go and face Lee. "If you have any more questions, please call my attorney." Lest I be the only one to suffer by having to speak to him.

Detective Lee nods. "Stay local, Ms. Carmichael."

Stay local.

Where the hell would I go? No one would believe this insanity or have the power to help me. I'm literally at the mercy of three shitty men.

"Wouldn't dream of it."

But I *would* dream of socking Mr. Cain in the stomach as I pass by his hateful ass. Oh, wait, I didn't dream it. I fucking punched his ass, and he didn't so much as grunt.

Maybe someone will run him over in the parking lot. Miracles have occurred in this town, but apparently not for me since as soon as I'm out of the drafty interrogation room, I'm jerked to a stop. "Oh, for heaven's sake, will this day never end?"

Van Gogh or Cain—I'm going to call him fucking Bob just to be annoying—doesn't answer. Instead, he steps in front of me like the true asshole he is and pulls me behind him.

"If you wanted to kill me, I could think of a million other places with fewer witnesses." I make a tsking noise as he leads us out of the precinct and down a back alley. "You're losing your criminal touch, lover. I could give you a few pointers, but it'll cost you."

And the angels of heaven gasped in wonder as the demon himself chuckles. "I'm not the one who just spent hours in an interrogation room after fleeing the scene of a crime. Perhaps you should lay off the Hot Cheetos and crime shows. Maybe then you won't get caught setting your boyfriend on fire next time."

This asshole. If I had something sharp, I would stab him right in thigh.

"We all know who caused that fire."

He tsks me like I'm a child. "We do, and I'm ashamed of your technique. You were taught better."

This is why he hides in the shadows. Everyone wants to kill him for being a giant pain in the ass.

"Well, we can't all be lonely psychos who stalk their marks for years. Sometimes, we have to balance our days with a little thing called a job."

He snorts, and it's so not sexy.

Fine. I'm lying. It's *very* sexy.

"You call what you do a job?" His head turns enough to catch me flipping him off.

"I make an honest living. It's more than I can say for you."

"Grading papers for the rich pricks of Havemeyer isn't an honest living. Not when you're stealing their personal information to access their bank accounts and give yourself a generous tip for the effort."

Well, well. Look who has been doing more than just stalking me.

"I don't keep the money," I explain. "I donate it to the local animal shelter."

"I don't care if you choke your precious boyfriend with it—just call it what it is. You're no more honest than your prick of a jailer."

I smile at his term. He still refers to people as jailers.

"You were sloppy at the frat house. You deserved for Blake to catch you."

Alrighty, then. This reunion is over.

I pull to a stop, jerking his hand back. "Don't act like you fucking know me or that we're somehow back in South Carolina with that giant stick still shoved up your ass. I've moved on with my life, which doesn't include you."

The corners of his mouth tip up into a predatory smile. "I've missed your naïveté, Flower."

In one smooth motion, I'm up against his heaving chest, the smell of bergamot and smoke scalding my senses, begging me to draw closer to the familiar.

"I've missed it like I've missed the wretched stench of cancerous plastic assaulting my delicate senses."

My head jerks back, but only because he wanted me to see the hate swirling with the golden flecks in his eyes. Hate that's never been there before.

"Wow." I breathe out a burst of air. "And here I thought the stench was your sour-ass attitude."

My lip quivers with the snarky remark. It isn't the first time someone has hurt my feelings, but it is the first time Van Gogh has.

And that's... heartbreaking.

"Don't cry, Flower. Eventually, we all must pay for our sins."

He tips my chin, and like a psycho, he leans forward and licks the tear that streaks down my face.

"Why are you doing this?"

I don't bother trying to stop the tears that follow. It's been an exhausting few months with Blake, and now someone I've missed is treating me like he does everyone else—shitty.

"Why?" he repeats, licking his lips as if he's hungry for more of my pain. "Because you begged me."

I cock my head to the side, sifting through the dozens of memories I shared with Van that summer when I was eighteen. I come up empty, only remembering his watchful gaze as he sat outside the lounge's window like a sentry.

He was my dark protector.

The artist who displayed his betrayal with flames and ashes.

My silent punisher—a true...

Vigilante.

My blood runs cold as soon as the word pops into my head. I try pulling back, but it's no use. The punishing smile that scared even the monsters emerges.

"You wanted to run away with me once upon a time."

I swallow, remembering when I begged to go with him—to leave South Carolina and the scorched town behind me forever.

"You never showed," I plead, knowing that whatever Van Gogh believes is fact in his eyes.

"I showed," he clarifies, "at 2:02 a.m., the exact time I wrote on the ground in ash."

"No." I shake my head. "You wrote 3:03."

Those strong muscles twitch in his jaw as his smile fades into a sharp, angry line.

"I showed," he clarifies. "I showed up with a backpack." He touches a stray tear but doesn't lick it this time. Instead, he presses his thumb to my mouth, quieting any more excuses.

"And I met the cops you sent for me."

CHAPTER FOUR

Van

I HATE EXCUSES ABOUT AS MUCH AS I HATE PEOPLE.

"I never would have betrayed you!"

I roll my eyes, ignoring the tears trickling down Reese's cheeks. Someone lied to my sunflower and promised to protect her if she turned me in. Unfortunately, she believed them.

"Don't worry, my love," I coo. "I don't plan to kill you."

A whimper escapes her, which doesn't feel as delightful as it should.

"What do you plan to do with me, then?"

One thing about my flower is that I don't need to scare her with threats. She's seen what I'm capable of—and she knows my threats are nothing compared to my punishments.

"Did you know they sentenced me to six years." My heart kicks up just thinking about the time I spent behind bars, in seclusion, with nothing but memories and betrayal keeping me company.

"I didn't betray—"

I press my finger harder against her lips. "Now, now. There's plenty of time for apologies."

I lock eyes with the only person who has ever made me believe in the goodness of this world. "For the crime of betrayal, Reese Carmichael, I sentence you to six years as my prisoner." I flash her a wink and a smile. "I believe society calls that a marriage."

She scoffs, and I add, "Or I can help Detective Lee convict you for attempted murder and fraud when he finds out you've stolen nearly half a million dollars from university students."

Something in my chest tightens when her face drops.

"I helped you," she cries, "I gave—"

My hands are in her hair before I realize I've tipped her head up, my lips hovering over hers. "You gave me nothing but a conviction. Those innocent eyes might have fooled me before, but they don't anymore."

Her lips quiver as she squeezes her eyes shut, blessedly saving us both from any more lies.

I step back and inhale, unclenching my hands and calming the rage burning under my skin. Van Gogh would set everything she loved on fire, but Alistair Cain would make her pay for the life she took in a more boring way—legally.

All who wrong me pay for their actions—even those I once loved.

Calmer, I level my gaze with her now-tearless eyes. If we were still friends, I would be proud that she's standing here, facing down the devil as if she alone can defeat him.

My determined little sunflower, always fighting for the pinhole of light in her dark world. We made the perfect duo: her goodness, a soothing balm to my darkness.

But like everyone else, she feared the hungry demon inside me—the one who was scarred and broken. Her salve never stood a chance with him. So, she did what everyone else did—she saved herself at my expense.

And for that, I will punish her as they did me.

She'll have to choose: save the life she knew and face the consequences of her crime or serve her time by my hand and let everything she gained by her betrayal burn.

I only offer two options: run or burn.

Fortunately for Reese, she knows the truth. Wherever she runs, I will find her, and my fire will grow bigger each time until I've burned entire cities in her name. It's a simple decision for those who care about the lives of others—even fuckers like Blake.

"What's it going to be, love? Should Blake and those idiot friends of his burn tonight? Detective Moron would love a jelly doughnut in the morning for solving a case."

I grin and make a tsking noise as I reach for a wayward strand of her golden hair. "After all, most crimes are born from passion."

She slaps my hand away, glaring defiantly. "They will know it wasn't me."

Her faith in humanity is adorable.

"I think you're giving Detective Dumbass too much credit. When he finds proof that you've been scamming Blake and his friends, he'll have no problem accepting the theory that after you failed to kill Blake in the woods, you went home, grabbed a can of gasoline, and came back to finish the job. You'll spend the rest of your life in prison."

I shrug and slip my hands into my pockets. "No one would blame you, you know? Detective Lee would do the same if he were in your position. After all, humans are notorious for valuing their lives above others. Setting fire to Blake's frat house would save you. No evidence. No Blake. No witnesses.

"The question is, Flower, will you sacrifice Blake's future for yours?" *Like you did mine?* "Or will you own your crimes and pay the price?"

I didn't expect the sting to my cheek that followed my question, but I appreciated it as much as my cock did.

"Did that make you feel better, love?"

I don't bother touching the heat where her palm landed. "If not, I'll turn the other cheek, and you can have one more go, but let me remind you, those strikes come at a price."

The mouth that used to captivate me for hours tips at the corner mockingly. "Let me spare your brain from thinking up these threats." Like earlier in the interrogation room, she leans in, eliminating any space between us, knowing it makes me uncomfortable. "You didn't scare me before, and you certainly don't scare me now"—she presses her lips chastely against mine and chuckles—"Husband, or is it guard?"

It's this behavior, this fearless spirit, that I've always admired. Too bad I'll have to break it.

Reaching into my back pocket, I pull out a match—something she's seen me do many times—and hold it between us.

"Speaking won't be necessary," I say, flipping the match between my tattooed fingers. "Forbidden even."

She jerks back at the rule. "And if I disobey?"

Faster than her gaze can track, I strike the match against my belt buckle and hold it to her face. She doesn't even flinch at the heat licking her skin.

"You know what happens to those who disobey me, love."

With my eyes still trained on hers, I lean forward, parting my lips just wide enough.

And then I close them over the flame, snuffing out its light forever.

"I told you to shut the fucking door!" She rakes her hands through her hair and slowly spins in the middle of her bedroom.

I distinctly remember telling her that talking was forbidden, yet...

"If something happens to Biscuit because you can't follow simple instructions, I will kill you."

She'll kill me.

I fight the urge to laugh and manage to ask with a straight face, "What the fuck is a biscuit?"

"A 'Biscuit' is my half-blind cat that likes to escape when the door is left open." She glares at me and tips her chin to the open door behind me. "I told you to shut it behind you. I swear if my cat slipped out while you were bitching about having no elevator, I will slit your throat with my disposable razor."

That sharp tongue of hers is going to get her bound and gagged if she isn't careful.

"I'd watch your threats, Flower, or I might throw out a few of my own." Ones that I will enjoy far too much.

"Oh, shut up." She puffs out an exaggerated breath and wipes the sweat from her forehead. "I am already so over you talking."

Ditto.

"I liked it better when you just stared at me and set fires."

And I liked it better when I thought she had a code. She might have been stealing from wealthy men, but she never kept the money. It was all funneled into different battered women's shelters along the East Coast. She wasn't like any criminal I had ever met. I thought she was different, but then she proved me wrong. That won't happen again.

"You have ten minutes to find your fucking cat and finish packing before I burn this place down."

I'm not fucking joking, and she knows it.

"You know," she muses, dropping to her knees and shimming under the bed, "you could just ask me to hurry. Most fiancés don't need to threaten one another."

Did she not threaten me first?

"I'm not your fucking fiancé," I clarify. "I'm your warden."

She slides out from under the bed and faces me. "Eh. It's not a common pet name, but I'll roll with it if that tickles your taint."

Six years with this woman is just asking for a murder charge.

"You have eight minutes." I take out a match and twirl it between my fingers. "Ask yourself what exactly your priority is: taunting me or preventing the untimely demise of a family pet."

"You're an asshole."

"And you're down to seven minutes." Turning around, I strike the match against the door frame and toss it behind me.

"Are you fucking serious?" she screams. "Put it out!"

The muffled tears that seem clogged in her throat do nothing but bring on a migraine. That's the only reason I stomp out the flame before it can do more than blacken a spot on the tile floor.

"You have five minutes. I won't warn you again."

Leaving her, I lumber down the staircase of the apartment complex and ignore a few curious onlookers as I settle against the side of my car and wait for Reese to find her fucking cat.

I click the lock on my key fob a few minutes later when she steps outside. "You're not putting that cat in my car."

"You told me I was your prisoner for the next six years. I can't just leave her and hope she survives."

"She's a wild animal, not an infant. She'll be fine."

"No. I'm not leaving without her."

For fuck's sakes. "Give it to someone in the building."

"No. Either Biscuit accompanies me, or you can call Detective Lee and turn me in. But I'm not leaving without my cat."

I roll my eyes. "You realize the prison system won't allow Biscuit to come with you either?"

She shrugs. "They also wouldn't demand I marry them, so if you want to punish me yourself, then you'll open the car door and shut up. Otherwise, I have Detective Lee's number if you need it."

Fuck her and Biscuit.

"If it scratches the leather, you'll suffer for it," I warn, not bothering to open the door just because she told me to.

"Looking forward to it, husband."

And like the pain in the ass she is, Reese drops her duffle bag at my feet and smiles. "If you break anything in my bag, just know you will suffer, too."

She walks past me, stopping at the back door, a slow smile drawing on her face. Immediately, my stomach clenches.

I know that look.

It's the same one I make right before I unleash havoc.

CHAPTER FIVE

Reese

BISCUIT'S CLAWS ARE LIKE TINY RAZORS AGAINST MY ARM, A painful reminder that I'm once again leaving another place I consider home. Granted, Georgia has never felt like my real home, the one I had with my sister, but it's all I've known for the past five years.

Here, I've been able to obtain my bachelor's degree in computer science and secure a job as a teacher's aide while I obtain my master's. No one is chasing me here or trying to use me to get to my sister.

Here, I am simply Reese, the girl who prays for her sister's safety every night before bed, and the woman who feels a deep connection to those who lie down penniless and afraid. This town has given me something to fight for—a place where I feel needed. I've helped fund so many women's shelters from men like Blake and his friends. So many women are trapped in awful situations. My funding and connections have given them options, and now, I'm leaving it all behind to become an unwanted wife for a crime I didn't commit.

"Whatever you're thinking, I urge you to consider the consequences."

Van's voice pulls me from my depressive thoughts and back to my depressing situation sitting next to me in the driver's seat.

"I'd hate to ruin our wedding photos with tears."

My head snaps to attention. "First, shut up. No one is scared of your hateful ass. Second, fuck your wedding photos. They're nothing but an expensive mug shot."

I'm so going flip him off in every photo. See if he frames those gems.

Van cocks an eyebrow. "I hope you stay this feisty. It'll make the next six years sufferable."

Sufferable?

I startle Biscuit with a high-pitched voice on the brink of tears. "Why are you doing this? I've done nothing but help you. You were the one who disappeared on me!"

Van's jaw clenches so hard I worry he might crack a tooth.

Well, I take that back. I don't *worry* so much as I *hope* he cracks a tooth.

Van Gogh is a demon; no one survives him.

Except me.

But that was long before he left me standing in an empty parking lot—alone.

He used me, then left me—just like he always intended.

The question is, why come back now? Why blackmail me into becoming his wife? Unless…

"You need something from me, don't you?"

I shake my head and open the back door. "You are such a piece of shit. I should have known this was just an elaborate excuse." I set Biscuit on the floorboard, and she immediately has enough sense to hide under the devil's seat.

"Your fucking cat better not shit in my car," he says hatefully, with all of his six-foot-two frame.

Wow. "After everything I just said, you choose to worry about the possibility of my cat shitting on your precious leather interior?"

I am such an idiot. How did I become this guy's friend, much less find him psychotically attractive? I should have minded my damn business and ignored him lurking outside my work all those years ago.

But nooo...

He and his many tattoos intrigued me. I wanted to know every scary detail about him—which was wishful thinking. I made him who I wanted him to be, and he let me.

Because he needed something from me.

"Just so you know, Biscuit doesn't go around shitting in cars regularly, but if there were ever an appropriate time for her to hack up a hairball, now would be it."

Van cocks his head to the side, his lips twitching. "I had forgotten how charming you could be."

"And I had forgotten how delusional you could be. If you think for one minute that you will manipulate me into helping you with one of your punishment games, then you are sadly mistaken."

As soon as I get into the car, Van's signature scent of bergamot hits me straight in the face. Damn, he smells so fucking good. What does he bathe in, the tears of newborns?

"You might have evidence against me that requires my compliance, but just know, I'll make sure we both suffer for my mistake."

"Get out."

I don't.

"Ask me like you love me and can't wait to say 'I do.'"

Come to find out, we're getting married right now. No engagement parties. No wedding showers. Just a quick ride to the courthouse.

I might have shouted several four-letter words that will shame me later, but at least I didn't sit quietly and give Van peace for his last ten minutes of being single.

Van sighs and reaches into the center console. I should have known he wasn't pulling out a wedding gift or anything. "Flower," he croons in a voice I've never heard him use, "if you don't get the fuck out of my car—" He holds a match between us in warning.

"Yeah, yeah. I know. You'll burn down the courthouse. I thought you might have become more creative with your threats by now. Guess not."

Like I've said something impressive, he smiles. "Okay. Let me rephrase."

He leans in and strikes the match against the dashboard, causing us to go silent. If there was anything Van and I bonded over, it was fire. I loved it, and, well, so did he. Fire kept my sister and me warm when we were on the run, and fire destroyed Van's enemies.

We were weird and a little psycho.

"Flower," he begins softly, "you have two seconds to get the fuck out of my car before I toss this match into the back seat, ensuring your fucking cat doesn't shit in my car while you marry me."

I mean, seriously. Is Van not the most romantic man in the universe?

I flash him a grin. "Jeez, who knew you were that excited to marry me? Next time, just say *I love you* like most men."

But he isn't most men—that much is evident when he holds my gaze, daring me to defy him as the flame dances between us.

Hesitation isn't in Van's wheelhouse. If he threatens you with a fire, you best believe he'll stay until the last ash falls—even if he must sacrifice his car.

Van Gogh doesn't cherish material things. I suppose that's one thing I used to admire about him. He didn't form attachments to wealth or money. He despised both, yet…

"Go ahead," I say. "I'm sure you've wanted to set this car ablaze for a while now."

Don't worry. Van would never set the car on fire with us in it. He might be vengeful, but he's not suicidal. Existing in this shitty world is Van's purpose. The world needs a punisher, and his mean ass is it.

"I'm surprised you picked such a flashy car." I cross my arms over my chest, letting him know that the only way he's burning my cat is to burn me, too.

And he won't do that.

Not yet anyway.

He still needs to punish me.

A frightful grin crosses his face. "And here I thought you had forgotten me, Flower. You're right; this car is dreadful, but a bride should have something, old, new, borrowed, and blue."

He shrugs, sending a fleet of panic coursing through my stomach.

"I was only keeping with tradition."

Van Gogh is anything but traditional.

"Are you saying this car is your way of giving me all those things?"

He nods almost proudly as the flame burns lower between his pinched fingers. "You know I like to be efficient, and while this car isn't what I would have picked for myself, it was perfect for you." He chuckles like it's hard not to lose himself to the laughter. "I understand you might not love the idea of a used car, but the nice man at the police impound insisted."

I gasp as fear grabs me by the throat. "You stole someone's car?"

At least he's stopped laughing as his face turns serious again. "I borrowed it, but don't worry. I know you still need something new, so I put new plates on it."

He chucks me under the chin. "Anything to make your wedding dreams come true, sweetheart."

This bastard. He thinks his humor is charming. "I'd hate to seem ungrateful, but I believe the tradition is for the bride to wear the items, and unless this thoughtful gift can park itself on my wrist, I'm afraid we'll have to be just like all the other rich people and be nontraditional."

I should have known his smile held more than a stolen car. "That's what the match is for, my love. If I remember, you always loved wearing the ashes of my enemies."

The number one rule of dating a criminal is never to show them how attractive they are when they do bad-boy things. Van Gogh has never had a problem with confidence. He knows he's brighter than most and more skilled with flames than firefighters.

His arrogance knows no bounds.

So, why not play his game and indulge me in his vigilante ways? Because. There's more to Van Gogh than flames and a lousy attitude. I don't blame him for seeking justice for his mother, but I hoped it wouldn't define him.

I wanted him to know that I loved him more than the fear and match he held in his hands. He was kind, protective, and full of compassion. I've never seen anyone more selfless than Van Gogh. It isn't the reason I wanted to run away with him, but it is the reason I've always waited for him to return.

He's more than a villain, but that doesn't mean I don't get wet when he reminds me how much I love his brand of justice. Clearly, I've always had a kink, and a dark-haired smartass with a penchant for arson is it.

Van notices the flush settling in my cheeks. "There's my flower."

With the back of his hand, he brushes along the heat. "In the shadows of the west, she grows stronger at night…" Opening his mouth, he holds my gaze and lifts the match to his lips—something I've seen him do a million times, but this time, he hesitates, finishing his sentence. "To follow her true love east, knowing the price of his warmth, is her soul."

I'm unsure if I'm turned on or terrified, but then he opens his mouth and places the burning match onto his tongue, snuffing out its light with his venom.

CHAPTER SIX

Van

I THRIVE ON THE DISCOMFORT OF OTHERS.
    Those are the moments where I find peace and justice. "Should I ask you again, Flower, or drag you out of the car?"

There is no escape. Reese Carmichael will marry me this instant, or she will spend the next six years in prison. If she were smart, she'd choose prison. At least there, they have rules. In my prison, the only rules that govern me are the ones that work to my benefit.

Those curious emerald eyes blink slowly and cautiously. "This is a courthouse—a place of law. If you drag me out of this car, they'll arrest you immediately."

Her naïveté is sweet.

"You seem to have a lot of faith in the judicial system when less than twenty-four hours ago, Detective Dumbass accused you of a crime you didn't commit."

I flash her a wink. "But hey, maybe the public servants here will be smarter and recognize your distress for what it is—guilt."

She scoffs. "You're insane."

"And you're out of time."

As soon as I reach for the door handle, Reese goes for hers and is out of the car, running down the sidewalk like an escapee. Her golden hair whips behind her in the wind, seeking the warmth of the eastern sun.

"Flower," I call, not bothering to run but leisurely walking behind her, "don't make this harder than it needs to be."

Her steps falter, and her pace slows, but it's not because she's scared. She's out of breath.

"It's quite a shame, really," I scold, closing in on her. "You might have had a real chance at escaping if you'd scammed the track team instead of a lazy frat house."

I give her about two seconds before I sprint the remaining distance between us.

"Ahh!" she screams, her weak hits doing nothing as I wrap my arms around her and toss her over my shoulder.

"I hate you!" She tries again, attempting to kick me instead.

She's the worst criminal I've ever seen. What criminal resorts to kicking? I might as well marry a sexy toddler who enjoys playing on everyone's cell phone.

"You only think you hate me now," I add, holding her tighter. "Just wait until we spend our first night together as husband and wife."

She doesn't know what hate is. She should be grateful I'm leaving the car running for her fucking cat.

"The joke is on you, asshole. Married or not, I will never sleep with you."

I laugh at the finality of her voice. "Oh, thank goodness. I was worried I'd have to keep the cuffs on you all day."

Her body might appeal to my baser nature, but the rest of her I detest. I have no space in my life for anyone other than a prisoner. Reese taught me that many years ago. I'm not like other men. I don't get the joys of a woman's love and body. That's not my purpose. My purpose is to punish the guilty for the innocent. The judicial system has many holes that I fill with evil souls who thought they could escape my wrath.

I might not have the love of a woman, but I damn sure have a passion for vengeance, and that's enough to keep me satiated.

"Cuffs?" She stops kicking and goes still. "You're going to put me in handcuffs?"

Finally, a little fear works its way into her brain. "Since when do you use cuffs?"

Since never, but she doesn't need to know that.

"I'm not the same man you betrayed, Flower."

I walk back toward the courthouse.

"Oh, well, that's certainly something to brag about." She lowers the pitch of her tone and mocks me. "Don't fuck with me, Flower. Like a true serial killer, I've evolved."

My mouth twitches, but I fight off the smile. "I think you're mixing up your criminals, darling. You need to kill to be a serial killer." I smack her on the ass just for getting on my fucking nerves and making me laugh. "I've never killed anyone, unlike you."

Something drew Reese and me together all those years ago. We both carried a weight of guilt deep in our dark souls.

Reese was better at hiding her darkness than I was.

"Van," she whispers, turning her head to face me. "I swear it wasn't me who betrayed you."

My, how the sound of her lying makes my dick rock-fucking-solid.

"Tell you what, love… Since I enjoy a good mystery, if you can prove who set me up that night, I will pardon your crime and release you with time served."

She lets out this girly sniffle that stops me cold. "But if you cry during this marriage, I will add time to your sentence."

I might as well have threatened her cat again.

"Let me go, you bastard!"

She thrashes against me, and I nearly go feral. My heart races, and sweat beads at my temple. It's all I can do to keep my hands on her while my cock strains against my zipper.

I bite her.

I sink my teeth into the soft flesh of her side, relishing the sound of her returning scream as she kicks angrily against the wind. The only thing making contact is her shoes as they fall to the ground.

"Okay!" she screams. "I'll stop fighting."

Is it wild that I feel disappointed she gave up?

"Do you hear me, Van? I'll behave."

Fuck her for ruining the moment. I haven't enjoyed myself like this in years—decades, even.

"Stop biting me!"

I do. Slowly and a little pissed off, I ease my teeth off her skin and place a kiss on the reddened mark.

"That was your one free pass," I warn, straightening and hitching her higher on my shoulder. "The next time you induce an ache in my back, you will relieve it on your knees with nothing but tears in your eyes and my cock down your throat."

I would have been wrong if I thought my threat would settle her sassiness.

"Do you even hear yourself?" She laughs. "You're an arsonist, not a mafia boss."

With a mischievous glint in her eyes, she raises her hand like she plans to take a swing at me, but then she grins and lowers all her fingers except for the middle one. "Get my fucking shoes, dear husband, and let's get this punishment over with."

I want to shake her. Maybe even toss her into the car's trunk and slam on the brakes a few times, but she'd enjoy seeing me lose control. Reese Carmichael is an intelligent woman. This whole moment was a test to see where my weaknesses lie. Unfortunately, I might be rusty, but I'm never weak.

I walk up the sidewalk again, sending her a clear signal that I don't plan to pick up her shoes. Not now or ever. I'm not her mother, and I'm certainly not a caring husband. I will let her walk on the courthouse's disgusting tile floor if she wants to go barefoot.

After all, it's essential she understands just how much I don't give a fuck about her comfort level. This is her prison sentence, not a fairytale with the boy she wanted to run away with.

She laughs as we approach the courthouse doors. "You want to embarrass me, don't you?" Her long lashes blink up at my face, and I hope she finds a severe look of annoyance. "Guess what, lover? I don't get embarrassed. You, on the other hand, with your fancy suit and expensive cologne, speak otherwise."

Fuck, I hate her.

Without answering, I shift her off my shoulder, sending her scrambling to catch her balance awkwardly.

"My expensive suit isn't made of Velcro," I state while smoothing the wrinkles from my coat. "Maybe you'll remember that the next time you want to insult me."

I couldn't give two shits about her comment. Everything she said is true. The suit I'm marrying her in cost me eight grand, and the cologne was a gift. I don't know how much it cost, but my embarrassment at her bare feet and sweatpants is nonexistent.

No one is stupid enough to look at me when I walk through these halls. They know the warning I carry in my eyes. I am not their friend or their colleague. I am the assistant district attorney.

"Wow, threatening innocent people now. You have evolved." She holds my gaze just as I do hers, waiting to deliver the final blow. Dare I say, I yearn to feel the stab of her knifed tongue. At least this time, I'll see it coming.

"You've become one of them."

She could have said anything else to get under my skin, but she didn't. She used the words she knew would bring out the devil inside.

She wants a war.

CHAPTER SEVEN

Reese

HE'S THE ASSISTANT DISTRICT ATTORNEY!

His title shouldn't have surprised me. I've always known Van Gogh to seek justice, but I never thought he would do it legally, not when the system he works for was the very system that failed him.

At least, that's what he led me to believe. Now, though, seeing him move through the courthouse halls like a worshipped tool, I'm not so sure.

Van Gogh looks very much like he belongs here—with these men who deal with the wicked.

"Make him look at you again, and his family will spend their evening gathered in the morgue instead of at the dinner table."

I'd grown so used to Van's grip on my arm as he dragged me down the hall of his admirers that I didn't realize he had stopped walking, let alone had caught me scrutinizing his coworkers.

"I beg your pardon?" I tear my gaze away from the man lingering in the doorway. His nearly black eyes follow our every step, directed at my soon-to-be husband.

Like most criminals, Van has mastered the psychotic look and doesn't withhold it from our curious onlooker. "My pardon you have. Though, I encourage you to save your begging for the next man that draws your attention."

Have you ever just been so fucking confused that you need to stop and stand still so you can properly digest the mess you've heard? That's precisely what I do.

"Are you mad?" I finally ask, not bothering to keep my voice down. These people need to know the demon they employ here. "Are you seriously threatening to kill the next man"—I shake my head in disbelief before I say the next part—"that looks at me?"

Van's face is stoic. He doesn't even seem ruffled that I'm being loud, but I suppose arrogance and a box of matches taught him confidence. He knows no one here will dare question him. Somehow, he's instilled fear in the fearless, and I'm so over it. Van Gogh may set fires to appease his sense of justice, but he's not a killer—no matter how much he'd like me to believe he is.

"I'll tell you what, Van," I snap when he chooses not to answer. "I'll look at whomever I want. And you won't do a damn thing about it. You want to know why?"

I'm playing a dangerous game when I stand on my tiptoes, drawing in the very air he breathes through his parted lips. "Because, Mr. Cain, you don't know what it's like to see the life drain from a man's eyes, but I do."

His cheek twitches and everything inside me rejoices. The infamous Van Gogh likes to be the baddest motherfucker in our demented relationship, but unfortunately, that title belongs to me, whether he likes it or not.

"I'm not like the other prisoners, darling." With a smile that shouts *fuck you*, I lean in and plant a rough kiss on his lips. "Your empty threats won't work on me."

My body is humming with adrenaline at provoking the devil. How many times have I dreamed of lashing out at this man who pretended to be my friend, only to leave me waiting like some sad little girl?

Well, I'm not that same girl anymore. I learned who valued me, and it damn sure wasn't Van. "I don't know who betrayed you, and I don't care, but when you finally figure out it wasn't me, I'll be waiting for you with more than an empty threat."

Fuck him.

Van doesn't know what I've been through. We all have bad memories and crappy childhoods. He's not the only one. "You should have stayed away, Van. Because I won't forget this."

Heaven help me, the man smiles. No frown, no annoyed squint, just a raw and genuine smile that sends real fear into my spine before he even responds.

"While I loathe being threatened, I am a man who can admit when he's wrong."

I scoff. "Since when?"

Those dark brows arch with amusement, but I can't share the sentiment.

"Oh, darling, don't be so quick to judge. Men can change."

Not him. I've never seen Van Gogh admit he was wrong or even apologize. He lives his life by cause and effect. I issued him a threat, and he will call me on it, no matter what.

Van Gogh doesn't lose, and I will never follow through on my threat. I didn't plot it for years like he did. I just reacted, but Van doesn't know that. He believes I'm a killer, and if I'm going to make it through this marriage, I need to think it, too.

A featherlight touch lifts my chin until I'm staring through the depthless eyes of the man who made me feel strong when other men told me I was weak.

"You, my love, are right. You aren't like the other prisoners."

My mouth dries at his dangerous tone.

"You're different." He grins for half a second before he drops it, letting the real Van Gogh shine through his façade. "You'll be my wife—my brutal sunflower."

The light touch to my chin turns rough as his fingers hold me still while his mouth descends to mine, hovering, delivering the final blow in our war. "For great suffering comes from the crypts of my prison," he warns, "and death from the tomb of my vengeful heart."

At that moment, I realized that everything Van promised was a lie. He wouldn't burn my apartment or my clothes. Those things don't matter to me; freedom does.

The old Van Gogh would have required six years of marriage, but the man before me isn't Van Gogh. In his fancy suit, this man isn't the orphaned boy I fed night after night when he returned from painting our town in ash and flames.

This man is a powerful attorney who gets vengeance with loopholes and case law. I won't be his wife for just six years.

"No," I warn. "I'll turn myself in."

His wickedness knows no mercy. "If that's what you prefer... But just know, if you confess to your little hacking hobby, it will force me to share the financial reports of where you funneled the money."

The confidence in his tone makes my stomach clench. He knows. "Please, no. Don't do this."

Van grins. "I don't need your idiot boyfriend," he whispers, "because I have your sister."

A sob bursts out of me, and I don't even care who he pretends to murder because of it. "Please, Van. Please—"

"Please, what, darling? Please don't drag your sister back to South Carolina so the police can discover what really happened to her boyfriend?"

He clucks his tongue. "The DA will have no problem charging her with murder after he parades you—the only witness—in front of the jury. Tell me, love, will you tell the whole truth and nothing but the truth, or will you let the darkness take you and perjure yourself to save your sister?"

"You bastard." My chin quivers as tears stream down my cheeks.

"I might be, but then again, so are you."

With every single bone in my body, I hate him. "Fuck you."

"Flower," he chides, ignoring my tears, "I am growing tired of indulging you. You have two options: Own up to your crimes and serve your time with me." He shrugs. "Or confess to Detective Lee and risk sharing a cell beside your sister. I honestly don't care, as long as you suffer."

I don't even realize I've tried to slap him until he stops my hand with his, merely inches from his face. "My wife will only strike me when I command it."

I'm nothing if not stubborn. I won't go down without a fight. "I'm not your wife—yet."

Yet.

That word, that three-letter word, released the vigilante he kept trapped in an expensive suit.

"Well," he coos almost sweetly, "let's fix that."

I don't even have the chance to run or pull away before he has me by the wrist and pulls me into an office where an older man in a black robe sits behind the desk.

"Do it, Enoch," Van barks. "Do it now, and yes, I'm fucking sure."

I'm pretty sure Van Gogh is about to be dragged off to the nearest jail cell, especially when the gentleman pulls his gaze from the document in his hand to Van's.

"Alistair," he greets dryly, sparing him only a moment's look before his gaze drifts toward me. "And you are?"

I swear Van—or Alistair, what the fuck ever—growls. "You know who she is."

The man's face hardens. "And you know who I am," he snaps. "Or do you need a reminder?" The words are ominous, and neither Van nor I miss them.

"A reminder will not be necessary, Your Honor," Van replies, that attitude still there, waiting for the opportunity to jump back into this conversation.

"Good." He smiles like he didn't just intimidate the shit out of the room. "Now, introduce me to the future Mrs. Cain."

My stomach does this girly flutter for some odd reason, like she enjoys the sound of such an atrocity. We only want to be the future Mrs. Cain if we can remove that giant stick from Mr. Cain's ass and beat him with it.

"Reese Carmichael, Your Honor."

I don't wait for Van to say something shitty or make this situation even more awkward. "It's very nice to meet you."

Van makes a choking noise beside me, but I ignore it. I don't have time to deal with him and his bullshit. The judge looks to be in no mood for delays, especially since Van busted into his office for an impromptu wedding. Van truly brings out the worst in people.

"The pleasure is all mine." Enoch, as Van called him, stands and rounds his oak desk. "I have to say, Alistair failed to accurately portray your beauty."

"Well,"—I smile, unable to help myself—"Alistair fails at being a decent human, too, but we're working on it."

Working on burying him where no one will find his ripped-ass body.

A boisterous laugh belts out of the judge. "You're right, Alistair. She's definitely the one."

I stop breathing. Did he just say Van was right? That I'm *the one*?

Surely, he doesn't mean it like I'm his one true love. It's probably something crappy, like, the one he can get away with blackmailing into being his wife, or something even crazier like, I'm perfect for his next victim. You never know about people. Van could have grown tired of fires and resorted to murder.

I'm about to bring it up, too, but Van snatches me against his hard chest, knocking the breath from me.

"Do it, Enoch—I mean, Your Honor. Or do you plan on going back on your word?"

Damn them and their cryptic conversations. Does the good judge know the truth of what's happening? Did he agree to help this monster? If so, I'm just as screwed with the judicial system as I am with Van. The man knows how to keep people in his pocket.

"You know I am a man of my word; if you do this, you will be, too."

His eyes find mine in a warning. "No matter the circumstances, once you recite these vows, there is no turning back. The sanctity of marriage will forever bind you."

Sweat beads on the back of my neck. I try pulling away to look into Van's eyes. Does he hear this man? Judge Gadot knows this is a sham, and he's warning us of the repercussions of violating something holy with blackmail.

"We understand," Van snaps above my head, holding me close so I can't see his eyes.

Gadot smiles, and it makes me nervous—very nervous. "And do you also understand that your marriage is forever?"

Oh, hell no.

I hold up a finger, stopping the honorable judge, but Van's warm hand quickly covers it, answering for us both.

"We will remain as one," he warns, "until death do us part."

CHAPTER EIGHT

Reese

I DON'T KNOW IF THE WHOLE *UNTIL DEATH DO US PART* THING rooted my feet to the floor or the finality in Van Gogh's words did. Either way, it paralyzed me with fear—something that never happens.

Being scared is for people with something to lose, which I have always lacked.

But this feels different. I'm not losing my house or even six years of my life.

I'm losing forever.

My entire life is gone, committed to the man I once loved.

He made no threats and gave me no warnings about what would come if I didn't follow through with our vows. Not that I needed them.

Van had warned me enough, but there was something different when we were before Judge Gadot.

There was no hate or bitterness between us. Instead, the weighted promise of forever felt less like punishment and more like freedom. There had to be something in the air that relaxed me enough to recite the vows and hold Alistair's eyes. Granted, the words didn't sound loving or even caring. They were simply cold promises that harbored no love.

But no one ever claimed Van Gogh to be loving. He is simply an artist who expresses himself through his actions.

Each canvas is his story.

Each brushstroke is his apology, and each smear with his fingers is a promise.

I never needed Van Gogh to promise to take care of me or protect me. He simply was there when I needed him.

Until he wasn't.

Until he claimed I betrayed him.

Our relationship may never be the same, but after hearing Van Gogh promise to love and honor me with his words, I know he still yearns for me.

Even if he's hated me all these years, somehow, he's protected me.

Or maybe the vows sparked the romantic in me, making our relationship more than it truly is.

"Alistair," Judge Gadot's voice rips me back. "You may now kiss your bride."

I don't know what I thought would happen, that Van Gogh would jump up, wrap his arms around me, dip me to the ground, and maul me with that sharp tongue, but I most certainly didn't think he would just stand there. His eyes morph back into the man with a grudge against the world as he bites out, "No."

Pain rushes through my chest for a split second, but then heat takes over and pools in my cheeks, pissing me off.

"No?," I repeat, dropping his hands and gripping the lapels of his jacket. "You just promised me an eternity, and you won't kiss me?"

Like the asshole he is, Van doesn't respond. I don't even know why it bothers me. I should be ecstatic that I don't have to kiss this wretched man, but my ego doesn't agree.

If I'm being honest, neither does my heart.

There was a time when this man was my everything. I was ready to leave my entire life behind and go with him into the pits of the abyss where he stayed, running from the law and helping those who couldn't help themselves.

I had this whole Bonnie and Clyde fantasy, which turned out to be a big fat lie.

"Fine," I tell him after a moment. "You don't have to kiss me." I push him away, pissed off that I'm even pissed off that he won't kiss me, and take a step back. "If anyone understands you, it's me." I flash him a smirk and make eye contact with Enoch. "So, I'll save your kiss for later, my love—right on my ass."

Fuck him, and fuck embarrassment. We may have recited vows, but we both know we don't intend to keep them—sacred or not. Van Gogh doesn't play by the same rules as others.

It's then that Van Gogh smiles. It's brutal and beautiful, and it makes me fucking sick.

"Understood," he says dryly, turning and extending his hand to Enoch. "You have my word," he promises.

Enoch nods, and whatever they promised each other, I hope it gives them both a rash.

"Congratulations," Enoch says softly.

I don't even have it in me to be polite, so instead of saying thank you, I simply brush past him and open the door.

I have a cat to get to.

We've been driving for almost an hour and he's yet to speak. It's the best wedding gift he could ever give me.

Except I'm hungry and could use some caffeine, like yesterday.

"I hope we're almost to the dungeon," I tell him, staring out the window, admiring the countryside between the rolling hills and winding roads.

"Be patient."

Two words. That's what I get—two freaking words.

"And if I'm not?"

Van never takes his eyes off the road. "Then I suggest you change clothes at the next stop. The trunk can be blistering in the heat of summer."

The sad part is I'm not even shocked by his answer. I knew he would say something shitty when I baited him with the question, but the thing is, Van Gogh is a whole lot of talk and minimal action.

"I'm hungry," I say instead.

"And I am annoyed. Should we cry about it?"

I hate him.

"I hope you know that I do have to eat and sleep. You can't just lock me away in some room for the next six years."

One dark eyebrow of his arches. "Can't I? Humans can live for thirty days without food."

His lip twitches, and I know he's fighting back a smile. "I may not have completely been paying attention, but I remember promising until death do us part—particularly your death."

I can't. Engaging in conversation will only increase my blood pressure. So, instead of making that ridiculous smile of his grow more prominent, I turn back to the window and mash my lips together for the rest of the ride.

"Hopefully, you're dead, but I've never been a lucky man, so get out before I make you."

It wasn't the most romantic way to be awakened from an asshole-induced nap.

"Oh, wow," I say as soon as I focus on the sprawling grounds with extravagant water features and professional landscaping. "This is a freaking castle!" *A castle!* "What billionaire did you steal this from?"

"Welcome to Eden," Van says, eyeing the stone mansion that looks like something from the eighteenth century, "your home for the next six years."

"It sure beats the apartment." I chuckle. "It's just that insignificant fact of living here with you that's disappointing."

Van gives me a long look. "Disappointment is for the weak."

He gets out of the car—likely because he knows my hands get a little twitchy when he speaks—rounds the front, stops at my door, and pulls it open like the gentleman he is not.

"Wow," I say. "I would be impressed if all guards didn't escort the prisoners to their jail cells."

There may have been a moment I wished it could have been real in that courthouse. It wasn't. Van doesn't love me. The past that we shared has long been corrupted with lies and misconceptions. Wanting to bask in a moment where someone promises to love and honor you is every girl's dream, and I am no exception.

My mother once said love was the cure for everything. At the time, I thought she meant love had to be given to heal, but as I've grown older, I've learned that to receive love, you need to know how to give it. I fought with that concept for many years after Van. I helped and accepted him, thinking it would cure my emptiness if we left together.

But that never happened. It wasn't until a few years ago that I realized my mother meant that I needed to start with myself to give love. If I couldn't love myself, how would I truly love others?

"Keep up," Van barks, pulling me out of my thoughts. "This is not a place to be caught alone."

Abruptly, I pull to a halt and double over with fits of laughter.

"Okay," I wheeze out between breaths. "I will keep a lookout for the murderous gardener hiding behind the bushes."

Van shrugs. It's not the reaction I was expecting. "There are worse things than me around here."

What? We're standing in front of a literal castle. What could possibly be so scary?

"Wait!" I jog to catch up, stopping in front of the giant oak doors. "Are you saying there are ghosts in there?"

"Not ghosts," he corrects. "Killers."

CHAPTER NINE

Van

I N MY LINE OF WORK, IT PAYS TO BE PATIENT.

Awkward silence makes people squirm. They need to fill the space or their anxiety kicks in and their heart rate speeds up. My wife is one of the few who can stay quiet during tense situations.

"What do you mean, killers?" She pulls the door back and closes it, her hand on my arm to restrain me. It's quite comical, though I don't laugh. "Four and a half years you've been in school, don't tell me that grad school is only a farce." My gaze travels down to her black-painted fingernails against my tan skin.

"Are you calling me stupid?" Immediately, she takes her hand off my arm, which goes to her hip. She's a pint-size ball of fire.

We've always ignited when we were together. Our personalities clashed as much as they found common ground.

It's baffling, absolutely insane that I still find her attractive after everything she's done. The betrayal, the lies… and even now, she has the audacity to bear my last name, my true last name, and I'm ready to pound her on the front steps.

"Hello."

Reese waves her hand in front of me. "I asked you a question." I find her simmering eyes full of ferocity.

"How I feel about your education level doesn't matter," I answer.

She scoffs. "Just as long as I look pretty on your arm, huh?"

I arch a brow and smile. "Is that what I told you?"

"You know what?" She throws her hands in the air. "Let's go see some killers. Actually, I hope I come across a killer so that I can get rid of you."

See, there's that fire that claws its way through my barriers. I'm not an easy man to impress or manipulate. Except when it comes to her. And that weakness pisses me off.

"Be my guest," I dare, opening the door and snatching her to my chest. "But let's get one thing straight. Your life depends on your performance while we're here. I'm not Blake. I won't pout and threaten to tattle. I'll do much worse."

She leans in closer, her eyes full of fire and intrigue. "How much worse?"

My cock hardens, straining against my pants. With Reese, I break the rules. I couldn't watch while Blake blackmailed what was mine.

"I am your husband," I remind her. "The man you've loved for almost a decade."

Her brows arch mockingly.

"If you can't convince my family of such love, then I will destroy everything you love, starting with your sister."

She shoves me back in an instant. "I thought you were better than this."

"You thought wrong." I never underestimate my targets. It's my business to know what makes them comply with my needs. "And underestimated your value."

This time, I don't stop her when her palm stings my cheek.

Revenge shows no mercy, even when the heart objects.

"It would disgust your mother to know who you've become."

"I am your husband, and you better put on a much better show than you did with Blake."

This time, it's her that smiles. "Are you saying you expect me to fake it?"

There's something in the way she asks the question. It's like she's finally figured something out. "Are you saying your family thinks this is a real marriage?"

A chuckle slips past me. "Don't get your hopes up, sweetheart. My family may be killers, but they're not stupid. I could never convince them I married for love. They would be disappointed if I did."

We stand there, staring at each other, the fire in her eyes fading. Whatever we once had is long gone.

I might take my vows seriously, and Enoch may have forced me to, but that doesn't mean I don't have a lifetime to hate her. What's a better way to take revenge than make someone miserable?

Reese Carmichael will never love.

She will never have a white picket fence and children running around. She'll spend her days in a lonely house with a husband who hates her and nothing but rolling hills and awful neighbors for company. It's better than she deserves, and hopefully, it won't kill us both.

Reese Carmichael took years off my life. More importantly, she tricked me. She made me believe that there were good people in this world who truly cared.

She showed me I was right and deserved a lifetime of misery.

"Ladies first," I finally say.

She snatches out of my hold. "This is a castle. I don't know where to go."

I'd love for her to get lost here. Maybe she will find me in a few years when I've forgotten how she smelled and how her face looked when she realized I hadn't planned on kissing her.

"You know what?" she says, frustrated with my silence. "Maybe I'll just scream, and everybody will come to us."

She really is brave. "Go ahead. Their prey instinct is stronger in the evenings."

Her smile falls as she wages if I'm lying. After all, it's not that hard to believe that the man she fell in love with, an arsonist by trade, doesn't have criminal friends or family.

"I hope you know I hate you," she says after a moment.

I tip my chin but don't return the sentiment. Not because I'm a gentleman. But because I more than hate her. I loathe the very air that she breathes. And I hate myself even more for wanting to be smothered by it.

I feel Reese's hand tighten on mine as we reach the kitchen, where laughter sounds from the outside, you'd think we were a real family. Except, we are the monsters lurking in the dark, waiting for you.

"For real, all bullshit aside." She pulls us to the stop and looks at me. "Give me your word. Please. Are there really killers in there?"

I almost lie to her and make her feel better, but then I remember how much I enjoy watching her squirm. "Yes." I won't elaborate. It's the second time she's asked this question.

"Well…" She blows out of breath. "Okay. Introduce me to the killers, then. I'm ready."

She's far from ready. But I'm not giving her another opportunity to calm down. I pull her through the doors, into the massive open kitchen, where three of my brothers are standing with Magda.

Ignoring the wide eyes and curious stares, I approach the table and pull out an upholstered chair. "Sit," I demand.

She doesn't.

Instead, Reese stands frozen as my three brothers track her with predatory eyes.

"Boys," I mock curtly, moving in front of her to block their view.

"Unless you want to spend the evening cleaning blood off the kitchen tile, I suggest you avert your eyes to something that won't get you killed."

These fuckers can never act right, but neither can my wife.

Turning, I grab Reese by the shoulders and deposit her stubborn ass into a chair.

"Now, where was I?" I ask as silence and shock saturate the room. "Right, introductions.

"Reese," I announce to everyone before proceeding clockwise around the table.

"Shakespeare." I point to my youngest brother, who is still leisurely playing with the knife in his hand. His dark and frightening eyes find my wife, pinning her with a venomous smile.

I don't give him the chance to speak to her. I might enjoy taunting Reese, but I'll kill anyone else who does.

I nod curtly to the blond to the right, with scars spanning across the base of his neck. "Tennyson, my middle brother."

Moving on, I land on the man with midnight-black hair and green eyes that scream with tortured pleas. "And this is Bach." His fingers move rapidly along the table like he's playing a song on a piano—his death song.

None of them speak. They simply evaluate the situation because that's what they do. They're criminals, just like me—patient men. Bred from tragedy and filled with revenge and malice. Our past may be reconciled, but the demons still wait for a chance to finish what we started...

We are new men. The world no longer sees us as criminals. But in our darkest days, the criminal beckons, pleading to come out and play.

"Alistair." Magda, the lady of the house and whom we consider Mom, dusts her hands off on her apron and graces me with a big smile. "I am so glad you're home, and you brought a guest." She skips hugging me and goes right to Reese, who doesn't let go of my hand. "And who might you be?"

"Reese," she says truthfully. "Reese Carmichael".

Just because I'm an asshole, I kill what little progress she's made at finding comfort in Magda's smile and drop the words, "My wife."

The bottle in Tennyson's hand drops to the floor and shatters.

"What the fuck, Tennyson?" Bach yells, grabbing him by the throat. "Where are your manners?"

Tennyson ignores him. His gaze, like Shakespeare's, is on mine.

"Married," Magda says. "You're *married*?"

Shakespeare chuckles at all of us. He's the deadliest and the snarkiest. He's also the most unpredictable. He pulls out a knife, peeling an apple in his hand, and steps forward. "Now, Ma," he drawls, holding Reese's gaze. "Of course, she's his wife."

I feel a shiver go through Reese when Shakespeare approaches. At least her self-preservation instincts have kicked in. As I told her, I'm not the worst person in this house. Some wish to do more than just torch her future.

"Congratulations, brother," he says, sickeningly sweet. "I applaud the tactic."

I ignore him and look at my other two brothers, who have taken an interest in Shakespeare's theory.

"Is this her?" Tennyson asks. "Did you break the covenant?"

Bach straightens and smooths his button-down shirt. My brothers are still in their suits from work. Like me, they look wealthy and professional. No one would ever know they've been convicted of heinous crimes.

It's at that point Bach begins to clap. "My, oh my, Magda. You were right. Tonight's dinner is going to be amazing."

Magda flips around and cuts what I'm sure is a stare that promises punishment or, in reality, dishes. Magda doesn't believe in a dishwasher, and her husband does not believe in ungratefulness.

"Bach," Magda scolds, "pretend you have some manners."

Magda gives me a look that promises me a very long and most likely alcohol-needed conversation later and takes Reese's hand.

"Come. You can help me finish the lasagna. Tennyson has been absolutely no help."

Shakespeare flashes me a wink and licks his lips. "Tell me," he whispers, inhaling a breath and smelling the smoke on my clothes. "How did it feel to burn again?"

CHAPTER TEN

Reese

HOLY SHIT. Van wasn't joking when he said there were scarier things in here than him. I might as well call Van a saint. Not that he isn't scary, but these guys are freaking terrifying.

And what's with their names?

Shakespeare. Bach. Tennyson.

The greatest playwriter of all time.

The musical prodigy.

The famed poet.

They're all named, or at least known by the street names of famous artists throughout history. I can't even imagine why they call the man with chaos behind his eyes, Shakespeare. The way he looked at me was frightening.

Van has his faults, but it's not because he loves to destroy the lives of others for fun. Van needs justice to sleep at night. Albeit, he goes about it the wrong way—at least he used to—but behind the flames is a boy who loved so fiercely that he couldn't move on until he found closure. Until they paid for what they had done to her.

Van is one of a kind.

He's protective yet threatening.

Loyal but vengeful.

Loving but cold.

He's a hard man to love, but I did, even when I knew he was using me.

But I'm not that girl anymore, and Van is not that boy, though I hope his protectiveness still lurks within him since he basically chummed the shark-infested waters before tossing me overboard.

But then again, I don't know what these guys have done. Van says they are killers, but are they human killers or, like, bug killers? Van could just be playing word games.

Honestly, they don't look like criminals.

While tattoos peek out from under a few sleeves, one would never know that a thousand-dollar suit disguises a former convict. For all I know, they could really be elementary school teachers.

"Reese," Magda interrupts, pulling my attention back to the perfect lasagna causing my stomach to rumble. "When did you and Alistair meet?"

It's funny she refers to Van as Alistair, not Asshole or Demon Child.

"We met in South Carolina," I tell her vaguely, "when we were teenagers." As soon as the words leave my mouth, Van is beside me.

"We can't stay," he tells Magda, almost as if he's ashamed.

She turns slowly and faces him. There's no fear in her eyes, only the brightest look of concerned suspicion. "You can't? And who—"

"I approved it."

My head jerks back at the familiar voice and find Judge Gadot standing at the kitchen door.

"It's his wedding night," he offers as an explanation, flashing Magda an apologetic smile.

"He'll come for breakfast tomorrow instead."

I don't remember that conversation ever being discussed, but I also don't remember Van telling me that Enoch was family, either.

"All right," Magda says sternly. "But I expect you both here for breakfast in the morning. I need to get to know my new daughter-in-law."

My head snaps in Van's direction, but his hard gaze gives nothing away.

Daughter-in-law?

It's not like I didn't already know his mother was dead. After all, that's how we met, but the passion he feels about his mother is incomprehensible. I cannot imagine him ever calling someone else Mom or even allowing a person to attempt to fill that role.

"Understood." Van tips his chin at Enoch and then grabs my hand rather roughly and pulls us out of the kitchen without a single goodbye.

"Slow down," I say, short of breath. "I can't keep up."

"You'll keep up, or I'll drag you. The choice is yours."

Oh. My husband is quite romantic. Forget carrying me over the threshold like a normal person. My husband prefers to drag me through it.

"Where are we going, anyway?"

We exit the front door, where a man dressed in a black suit and white gloves awaits with Biscuit next to our car. "Mrs. Cain," he addresses me.

"Uh…"

I have no idea who this man is.

"Peter," he answers my unspoken question. "I'm the butler for The House of Enoch."

A butler? Wow. No wonder Van is an arrogant little prick. He's got a silver spoon shoved up his ass.

"Thank you, Peter," I say hesitantly, scooping Biscuit into my arms and clutching her to my chest, "for taking care of my cat." *While I deal with killers...*

I don't add that part because it looks like Peter is all too familiar with dealing with said killers. "It's my pleasure." He then looks at Van and tips his chin. "Mr. Cain."

"Peter."

Without waiting for Peter, Van opens the car door and guides me inside before rounding the front and easing behind the wheel.

"You never answered my question." I stroke Biscuit's soft fur, not bothering to acknowledge the aggravated huff I hear from my left. "Where are we going?"

"To my home."

I don't miss that he chooses not to say *our* home. Fucker.

"I assumed you lived here." The house is big enough to house several families without them passing each other in the halls.

"You assumed wrong." He pulls out of the circular driveway and heads through the peach orchards and rolling hills. But instead of getting back on the main road, he veers off to the right, to another driveway I didn't notice when we were first coming in. It runs through several acres—I'd guess, about a mile away from his family.

"Eden," Van clarifies dryly, "is my home, but the house of Enoch is not."

The House of Enoch? When did Van grow up? The 1800s?

"Enoch," he says finally, "is a man of tradition. I am the son of Enoch," he continues, like we're in biblical times. "Shakespeare, Bach, and Tennyson are my brothers. We are heirs to an undeserved throne."

"Ah," I say like it makes perfect sense and not like I'm in some parallel universe. "And Magda? Is she—?" I shake my head. "Are you also the son of Magda?"

He pauses like he didn't expect that question.

I assume he isn't going to answer, but then, as we cross the top of the hill, he whispers, "Yes."

"They must be amazing people," I say, slipping back into the past when we used to talk openly without threats.

"Yeah," he says, "they've been good to me." The *unlike you* hangs unsaid in the air between us.

I try changing the subject. "So, if you don't live in the house of Enoch—"

I'm cut off as a monstrous house, much like the house of Enoch, comes into view with its sprawling acreage, beautiful flowers, and magnificent Magnolia trees decorating the front. The loop around the driveway has a darker stone with flashes of white and red flowers, situated behind massive iron gates. It looks like a castle built from fire and ash. I don't need to even ask if this is his home. It screams Van Gogh.

"The House of Cain," I whisper, never having seen something so beautiful—so hauntingly perfect. And I've been around beauty and money, but this is something different.

This castle feels like pain and agony, yet the splashes of color are bright. Great big windows pour light through them, and suddenly it all makes sense. "Light from the east and darkness from the west," I say, just as he pulls to the front and gets out. My door opens, and I struggle to mask the shock.

"Wow," I say. "I didn't know you had it in you."

He fights back a smirk.

"I didn't want you waiting for a butler here."

I can feel my brows crunch. "You mean only The House of Enoch has staff?"

"Yes."

His clipped tone leaves no room for questions, and even if I wanted to push him on it, I doubt he would answer. He's shared enough on the mile or two over here.

Curling Biscuit to my chest, I get out and let the man of fire and brimstone lead me into his castle. It boasts nothing but deep, rich navies and golds, much like Enoch's house, but then there are black-accented walls and tarnished fittings. It looks like the whole house has been scorched, but it still shines brilliantly in the dark.

"If you're hungry, the kitchen is there." He points to a massive kitchen with black counters and glossy cabinets. A huge island sits in the middle, but it's bare, sans the vase of sunflowers, in the middle.

"What if I would like to go out? I mean, it is our wedding night and all," I push, trying to break up the awkwardness that circulates around us.

"Do you want to go out?" he questions mockingly as he descends one of the many darkened hallways.

"Well, no."

"Then I suggest you get over it."

Without another word, Van disappears, leaving me standing alone in the massive kitchen.

Suddenly, his threats and promises of punishment become very real. This house isn't alive and warm like the house of Enoch.

This house is cold, silent, and empty.

Worse than solitary confinement.

CHAPTER ELEVEN

Reese

Biscuit and I raid every cabinet we can find in the kitchen and choose the most expensive-looking bowls for her food, water, and litterbox. That'll teach Van to stay in his room and leave us alone in his kingdom.

Not that his kingdom is all that amazing, now that I take a closer look. The pantry is in desperate need of stocking, and the refrigerator looks like a garden barfed in it. Is Van seriously a vegetarian?

"Well, Biscuit," I say to the kitty at my feet, "shall we go find the best room our beast has to offer?"

Biscuit looks up at me, and the answer is clear in her wide cat eyes: *No. No, we shouldn't go roaming around dark mansions. That has never played out well for women or cats.*

"I know," I tell her, "but I'm tired, and unless we want to sleep on the tile floor, we're going to have to figure out something else. Preferably a king-sized bed."

Before Biscuit can cut me another serious look, I scoop her up, grab a bag of grapes, and head out into the *dark dungeon*, as I have deemed it.

We count five doors along the wide and expansive hallway that are locked. The sixth one, though, is a bathroom, which Biscuit uses to stretch her legs by clawing the shit out of the door frame. By the time we reach door number seven, we have a winner.

"A bed!" I say joyfully. "We have a freaking bed." A large, masculine, and empty bed, just like Van's soul.

"You want the left side or the right?" I ask Biscuit, entering the room.

I'm only slightly nervous that something might be lurking under the bed as I close and lock the door behind me.

"Never mind, I'll take the right. You can have the left." I set Biscuit down, and she wastes no time heading under the bed for safety. "Oh, under the bed is fine, too."

I don't blame her. Honestly, if I could fit under the bed, I would. It's pretty creepy in here.

I'm not silly enough to believe there are more monsters than Van in this house, but just in case, I slide one of the chairs up under the door handle so if anything tries to get in here during the night, it'll wake me up. Hopefully, long enough to scream. I'm not as proficient with fire or threats, like Van, but I can scream and hide like it's an art form. Running, as I've already said, is pretty much not an option.

I don't remember falling asleep. I don't even know what time it is. All I know is that *he's pissed*.

"Flower," he yells, his voice threatening and low, "if you wanted to play a game, darling, you should have told me. You know hide-and-seek is my favorite."

I roll my eyes. Fuck his hide-and-seek and stomping through the halls.

He'll eventually find me, but that doesn't mean I can't piss him off first.

"Flower," he calls again, his voice closer. "I'm growing impatient."

What else is new?

"Show yourself and come out now."

His voice is at the door. He knows I'm in here. If he didn't, he would have already tried the handle and moved on.

I slip out of bed and crawl to the door. "Make me."

I can picture the vindictive smile he'll try to hide.

Van has always loved playing these games with me.

"Have you taken a liking to this room, Wife? Are the accommodations up to par?"

"Not really, but it'll do."

I can hear his chuckle.

"As much as I want to please my wife, I must say, I'm a little disheartened to find her in the guest room and not where she belongs."

Fear tangles in my stomach, but I stuff it down. "Is this not the dungeon?"

"Of course not," he muses, almost sounding kind. "Your dungeon is upstairs—with me."

This night is going to get worse before it gets better.

"I'll pass, but thank you for the offer. Maybe I'll join you in the dungeon tomorrow night."

The house grows silent, but I know he's still there.

"Good night, Husband," I call, waiting for him to react, but nothing comes. Not until the sudden banging on the door sends me scrambling backward as the door disappears and my psychotic husband's body fills the empty space.

"You took it off the hinges," I cry, seeing his red face and eyes burning with fury.

He kicks the chair out of the way and steps threateningly toward me.

"Fine, fine, I'll go to the dungeon," I speak quickly, hoping he's hearing me. It's like something has taken over and possessed him. Maybe now he's going to kill me.

"I said I would go. Just lead the way."

I try redirecting him with a forward hand motion, but he doesn't stop. He just keeps moving, with those dead eyes trained on me.

Fuck this.

I sprint past him and scream as I run down the dark halls. "Help me! Someone, please help me!"

I can hear Van's footsteps growing closer.

Dammit, maybe I should become a vegetarian. "Help me," I try again, already out of breath. "Please, someone—"

His hand clamps over my mouth, and my back is yanked to his chest. "Now, now, Flower. Is that any way to treat your husband?"

I snatch my head away. "You mean my *jailer*?"

He turns me around, gripping me by the shoulders harshly. "No. Your punisher."

It's the same tired conversation we've had before.

"I don't deserve your punishment," I clip, looking him in the eyes. "I didn't do anything to you."

His jaw twitches, and I know he's close to exploding.

"Upstairs, now," he finally says.

Like a petulant child, I finally pop off. "I don't know where upstairs is. Otherwise, I would have set a fire up there earlier while you jerked off."

It was the wrong thing to say, especially when he hauls me over his shoulder, manhandling me down the hall and up a flight of stairs to a door that leaks an awfully familiar smell.

"If you want me to sleep with you," I nearly cry, freaking out that Van might not be the man I knew, "you'll have to force me."

"Don't worry, Flower. I'm not interested in your body. I'm only interested in your pain."

He kicks open the door, revealing a king-sized bed with black sheets and sunflowers on the nightstand.

"My wife," he says flatly, like the term is a curse, "sleeps in her husband's bed by commitment, not by force."

Putting me down, he turns me to face him. "You vowed to love and honor, and you will do so until death do us part."

CHAPTER TWELVE

Van

I SAW THE FEAR IN HER EYES, AND I ENJOYED EVERY FUCKING second of it.

Then she ran, and that enjoyment turned into a passionate obsession. I love when her bravery fades and survival kicks in. Reese Carmichael knows I'm no typical man. I won't love her tenderly and whisper sweet nothings in her ear. I am the man who will consume her until she's nothing but a beautiful memory.

She's always been mine to ruin and love as violently as the flames that dance between my fingers.

"I want to turn myself in!"

I find a smile as I chase her through the darkened halls of my home, the only light cascading from my lit match. She's made the rookie mistake of wanting to play hide-and-seek, so like the generous host I am, I indulge her.

"It's too late, darling. Just because you don't find the atmosphere suitable doesn't mean you get to back out of our deal."

Her voice breaks, meaning she's on the verge of tears, as she stumbles, steadying herself on the wall. "Why? Why me, Van? Why would you punish me before *him*?"

It's the first time she's acknowledged the man she was supposed to hand over. The man who started all of this, the man who created me and made me the monster I am today. He's one of the few left on my list to destroy.

"Because you failed to deliver, love," I voice, holding the match high enough that I see her golden hair whipping as she runs from me. I haven't cared to run after her. She knows she won't escape my wrath. She will endure it until her end.

"I didn't fail! I had him." She cries, slowing to a stop. "You know I wanted him to suffer just as much as you did."

"And yet," I round her front, get directly in her face, and find her dry cheeks with the light from my flame, "you let him disappear." Tsking, I add, "But I found you."

"That's because I wasn't hiding, dickbag!" She struggles against me, and I can feel my cock thicken, hardening against her stomach.

"Tell me," I say, grinding my hard cock into her, "was it always your plan to turn me in?"

This woman has always been able to pull the emotions from me. Deep-seated emotions that I thought had burned with my mother.

I didn't want a sunflower. They didn't exist in people, as my mother believed. No one could balance the light and the dark other than a flower.

"Stop struggling."

Her body seemingly molds to mine. "Look at my hands," she pleads.

"I'll pass," I say. "Now, answer the question."

She has a twitchy palm, and I'm in no mood for the sting on my cheek.

"Only if you answer a question of mine," she counters.

Any other time, I would say no, but I'm desperate when it comes to information about the man I need to destroy. More than that, I'm desperate to know if it was always her plan to betray me.

"What?"

"Did you follow me here to Georgia?" I hold there, shocked that she would ask that particular question.

"Sometimes," she adds, "I felt like I wasn't alone. It was almost like I could feel you sitting outside my window again."

She tries shrugging, but I still have her in a firm grip.

"Did you follow me here, Van?"

She's already my wife, and soon, she will have served her punishment. There's no reason to lie to her now.

"Yes," I clip. "I followed you."

She lets out of breath, digesting my words.

I knew I had been careless. Sitting outside her window, studying, plotting, planning, discovering who she had become.

"I wanted a fresh start," I lie.

"By stalking me and imprisoning me as your wife?"

I don't hide my smile. "A wife looks good on the résumé," I drawl, "and more importantly, her tears look great on my pillow."

"How could you? I loved you!" she screams. "I cried for you. Called you all the time. And you've been here all along!"

Call it a surge of emotions. Call it temporary insanity. Call it my rock-hard cock making all the decisions. But I shove my tongue deep into her mouth, taking every ounce of lies and screams she gives me. She struggles against me for a moment. I hurt her earlier today when I didn't kiss her at the courthouse. But I didn't want a fake kiss from her.

I kiss her angrily for the lies she's told and the betrayal she's caused.

I kiss her for making me think that I could be loved again.

I'm consumed by taking out my aggression on her and she lets me.

Her fingers wrap around mine, her voice soft and comforting as she says, "I'm sorry. I'm so sorry."

And just like she did us, she ruins the moment. I step back and put the match against my tongue to mask the taste of her on my lips.

"Come," I bark into the darkness. "I'm tired."

I'm also horny as fuck and would rather put eight miles between us than look at her anymore tonight.

She doesn't move. "Flower," I croon, "I would love nothing more than to spice up our wedding night with violence."

She laughs. "Your threats are not violent, and neither are you."

If she were any other woman, I would deliver on my threats to show her exactly how violent I can be when someone betrays me. But she's my wife, and violence is too sweet of a punishment for her. Reese Carmichael deserves much worse. She deserves years locked away from the life she wanted.

"I'm calling your bluff, Van Gogh. If you want me to walk through the darkness with you, you'll have to make me."

I let out a sigh. "I believe I've already proven that I will make you do as I say, but since you're struggling to catch on, I'll make it a little more interesting for you."

I fight the vengeance bubbling in my chest. I'm not this man anymore. These feelings of rage and hate shouldn't flare in her presence. I'm an assistant district attorney. I represent justice. I fight for the people, not myself. But all it took was one look at Reese with Blake, and I lost sight of all the accomplishments I gained over the last nine years.

CHAPTER THIRTEEN

Reese

I'M NOT A MORNING PERSON, NOR AM I A PERSON WHO ENJOYS waking up to people who are. (I'm looking at you, Biscuit.)

Turning my head to the sound of obnoxiously loud purring, I find my traitor of a cat pacing back and forth in front of the bathroom. The bastard didn't even bother closing the door.

"Just so you know," I tell the ball of hormones, "he isn't as charming as he seems." Like I don't even exist, Biscuit turns and sits, facing the opening that separates her from Van.

"Unbelievable," I muse to no one since Biscuit apparently hates me. "He threatened to set you on fire! Twice!"

Nothing. The traitorous cat acts like I'm an inconvenience she must endure until her daddy returns.

"Whatever. Don't come meowing back to me when he abandons you, too. He's not known for his loyalty."

And I'm angry at my cat now... How pathetic am I?

Actually, no. I have a right to be bitter. I waited on Van—helped him when I could have turned him in the night I found him with the mayor. But I didn't.

And how does he thank me?

By blackmailing me into being his wife after I've spent years being pissed off at him for breaking our deal.

I hope he drowns in that fancy bathroom.

Fucker.

Huffing, I raise up on my elbows, noting a slight breeze on my backside.

"Oh, no," I murmur, dropping face down back onto my pillow. "My ass is hanging out, isn't it?"

Damn cheeky panties. Why do they always end up in my ass crack when I sleep? I can only imagine how excited the devil was when he woke and found my shirt above my waist and my panties in my crack.

I bet the asshole took a picture.

What am I saying? No, he didn't. He probably waited until I fell asleep before he eased out of bed, sat in his fancy leather chair in the corner of the room, and plotted my death.

For as long as I've known Van, I've never seen him sleep at night. At one point, I even considered he might be a vampire.

I know. I know. He's far too mean to hang with vampires. But seriously, that summer in Orange Grove, Van and I only met under the cover of darkness. He never showed his face in the daylight—not even when I begged.

Van Gogh has always been a mystery, so seeing him now, awake with the sun, acting like he's not a serial arsonist but a regular guy getting into his morning shower irks me.

Don't ask me why.

I don't know.

Maybe it's because the man currently steaming up the bedroom is not the man I once knew.

That scares me.

I know how to deal with the Van Gogh of the night. But Alistair Cain, of the day, is a stranger and, worse, my husband.

"What did I say, Rudy?"

Van Gogh's surly voice cuts through my thoughts just as Biscuit's purring grows louder.

"Your client gives me the dealer's name, and I'll recommend minimum security."

My eyes widen when a voice answers.

"Come on, Alistair. He's a small fish. He gets his orders from Barclay, who you already have in custody."

The shower is running when it dawns on me that Van is negotiating on speakerphone while naked. And his fellow attorneys must realize it. Why doesn't he say anything or call back? It seems like a renowned assistant district attorney would have more professionalism than that.

But then again, we're talking about Van Gogh. I've never known him to give a shit about the rules or other's perceptions. The man does what he wants. Everyone else be damned.

"I do have Barclay," he confirms with a chuckle. "And I will have his boss. The question is, Rudy, will your client be safe in a maximum-security prison where rumors circulate more than STDs?"

The man on the phone goes quiet.

I look at Biscuit like she will fill me in or gossip about this scene later, but something behind me holds her attention instead.

Of course, I look.

A killer could be perched in the window from across the way, where Van's family lives. You never know the shit that can happen when you're with Van.

Immediately, Biscuit darts off as I turn around, perching her chunky self on the window ledge and watching a hummingbird flutter at the open window.

"Is that why I am so freaking hot?" I whisper to Biscuit as she follows the bird with her head. "Because you wanted to bird watch?"

"Don't threaten me, Cain, or I'll drag you before Judge Gadot."

The threat stops me cold.

No one threatens Van Gogh without consequences, but this man isn't talking to Van Gogh. He's talking to Alistair Cain.

The water stops, and dammit, I can't help but get closer. I don't know much about this man, but if I could learn, I could figure out a better way to escape my captor.

Padding across the wood floors, I press as close as I can to the wall without leaning against the door frame. The last thing I want is to fall into the bathroom and have Van Gogh realize I'm eavesdropping. He already thinks I'm a traitor. Listening in on his case would only add merit to his theory.

"Rudy." The threatening rumble of his voice sends a tingle shooting through my center.

"You know how I feel about threats."

I scoff. If he doesn't, he's about to—poor guy.

Without warning, I'm yanked inside the bathroom, facing a very wet and very naked Van Gogh.

His eyes are bright with hunger, holding me captive with the golden hues that I still dream about.

"Cain." Rudy's voice trickles in through the fog that I'm not sure is in my head or floating around me.

"Be reasonable. You don't need him."

Van's gaze drops to my chest, where the oversized sleep shirt has slipped off my shoulder, revealing the tops of my breasts.

"I don't care," Van clips, the muscle in his jaw flexing as he takes in my embarrassing state of knee-high socks and a heaving chest. Thankfully, he isn't privy to the heat gathering between my legs as I flat-out freaking ogle his bare chest, dripping with water as they follow the hard lines of his pecs, down to the deep ridges of his abs covered in tattoos—the most prominent one… a sunflower, surrounded by fire.

"Your client talks, or he spends the rest of his life watching his back. The choice is his."

"And yours," I whisper right before he ends the call, silencing the naked man before me. "You could show him mercy."

I don't know why I said it. Maybe I just wanted to piss off Van early in the morning to settle the score. Likely, though, I blurted out the plea because I, too, need his mercy.

I don't know what to think about this new man who punishes legally and not with a flame.

Van's jaw ticks, and I know my declaration doesn't make him feel better. He wants me to suffer, and as I've said before, I will. But I won't do it alone.

"On your knees," he repeats. "Tell me you're sorry like a good wife should."

I think a normal wife would junk-punch him, but I suppose that's not the wife I'm pretending to be. After all, I promised to pretend to love Van as a real wife would, and while I'm acting, I should also pretend that I'm not curious to see what he's packing. I've felt his stiff cock press against me numerous times and noticed the bulge from his tight-fitting boxer briefs. But I've never seen my husband bare, and I must admit that *my husband* holds an appeal that settles deep into my stomach. It's weird because marriage is just a useless contract and a pretty term that people use to show clout.

"Flower." Van's fingers interlace with mine, surprisingly gently.

There's no way I'm allowing him to make me do anything. This man has far too much power already. Ignoring the tingles and heat that rush down my body, I lift my eyes slowly.

"All right, husband. I'll apologize correctly." Without dropping my gaze, I lower to the plush rug of the bathroom, bring my hands up slowly to hips, and linger for just a moment, enjoying how his eyes flick with tension. His body is taut as he fights a war within himself. Van Gogh can tell me all day long that this is all about punishment. But it isn't. What we had that summer was real, and I knew he would come for me one day.

At my hesitation, Van throws his head back and makes this sound like he's either annoyed or fighting back a groan.

"Don't tell me," he says. "You've never done this before."

Oh, I have done this before. But not to him. Not to the man who lit a fire deep in my heart and soul. The man who stood up against everyone and fought for what he believed in. He fought for justice. He was just eighteen back then. But standing here, his body rigid, tattoos covering his forearms, this is no teenager. This is a man.

"Do you really want an answer to that question?" I ask, hoping to get a rise out of him and break that strong devil-may-care attitude.

"It depends," he says with his head still back. "Do you want him to live? Or would you prefer he burn, and you suck his ashes off my cock?"

It's a crazy thing to be charmed by the violence of a man and the promise of destruction.

Van would like me to think he's the devil incarnate. But I've always seen past his flames and angry glares. This man is a protector. He hates that he's weak. And he hates that he can't save everyone. Even the worst criminals sometimes escape, and he can't do anything about it. I think that's why Van became a criminal. I mean, he took that old saying, *if you can't beat them, join them*, a little too far. But that still doesn't change who he is. He may promise violence and destruction, and he may actually do some of it, but only to right the wrongs that the world couldn't.

"Actually," I say, familiarizing myself with the smooth skin I've never been able to touch.

"I'm not quite ready to suck the ashes of your enemies off your cock, but I do want to see the flames on your stomach flicker as I bring you to your knees." His head droops forward, and his heavy-lidded eyes open and hold my stare.

"As your husband, my body is yours, and yours"—his voice takes on a dangerous lilt—"is mine."

My throat dries, but it has nothing to do with fear and everything to do with the wetness pooling at my center. This man has been the only man who has ever turned me on and burned me from the inside out. It makes me want to believe that our vows are true and his promises mean something.

But I know that's just wishful thinking.

A girl like me has been abandoned far too many times. I've never been a prized treasure, only a possession. One that has been blackmailed and manipulated into doing a man's bidding.

But the man in front of me doesn't look like any of those men. At least his eyes have always looked at me differently. Not like they wanted to use me, but like they wanted to devour me and leave me broken in many wonderful and blissful pieces.

If Van's body is mine, then I'll show him what I can make his body do because if I'm Van's possession, then he's certainly mine.

Cupping his heavy balls in my hand, I put pressure on the center with my index finger, working him. I kiss over his cock as it swells and, begging for release.

"Stop," he moans. "Kiss the tip."

I swirl my tongue around the head.

"I'm not stopping," I tell him. "As you said, your body is mine, and I want to see you come, Husband."

A violent groan reverberates through his chest as his fingers tighten around the strands of my hair. "You will regret this," he warns.

I smile, kissing everywhere but the tip of his cock.

"Oh, I won't regret it nearly as much as you. You have one last chance," I warn, finally licking the line of his head. "I want you to look me in the eyes as you come down my throat, with your chest heaving and the flames dancing on your stomach. I want you to remember your sunflower will never be burned by your flames."

I don't know what set him off more, my dirty talk or my threats.

"Watch me, Van Gogh," I demand. "Watch me bring the fallen king of Eden to his knees."

Van says nothing, he simply snaps his mouth closed, and the muscle in his jaw ticks.

"Forgive me, Husband, for you have sinned." And then I close my lips over the head of his cock, wrapping my hands around the base, and I suck, licking and lavishing over his girthy length, pulling moans and noises from him that he struggles to mute.

I don't give him the space or time to catch his breath. I suck my husband off at a punishing pace, draining him of every threat he's ever made.

My gaze steadily hold his, and I watch the arrogance bleed from behind his eyes as he struggles to maintain his throne in my presence. And when he tries pushing me away, I simply massage his balls and put pressure on that one special spot before I wrap my hands around his ass and shove his cock down my throat so hard that he has no way to prevent the shout that leaves him as he comes down my throat. I swallow every drop of Van Gogh, not because I like it or even enjoy the taste of bitterness. I do it because I'm making a point.

I might be his sunflower, and he might be the flames of the East and the darkness of the West, but I can survive and thrive in either territory.

CHAPTER FOURTEEN

Van

"ARE YOU GOING TO ACT WEIRD ALL DAY?"

It's the first time I've been able to look at Reese since earlier this morning when she had my cock in her hands and my cum on her lips.

"Am I acting weird?" I arch my brows, finding her body relaxed in the passenger seat and her eyes all too playful. We certainly can't have that. "Don't get cocky, love. Your mediocre blow job didn't buy you any leeway. You're still my prisoner."

The tiniest flinch pinches her cheeks. If I didn't hate her so much, I'd be proud that she didn't drop her smile.

"Well, I didn't ask if having your cock in my mouth changed anything, now did I? I thought someone of your caliber—being the assistant district attorney and all—could understand a simple question."

It's been a long time since somebody pushed back at me. Honestly, I don't hate it.

"You asked me if I was going to act weird all day," I repeat. "And my answer is that I am *not* acting weird."

"All you had to say was it was your first time. I would've gone easy on you."

I slam on the brakes, halting the car, likely making us late to Enoch's.

"Be careful, love. While you may have distracted me this morning, you didn't do enough to put me in a better mood."

She holds my eyes defiantly, making my thickening cock strain against my suit pants. "The world burning wouldn't put you in a better mood."

"You would be correct there, Mrs. Cain."

I don't know why I am being such an asshole. Well, that's not true. I'm being an asshole because I *am* an asshole, but more so when I'm pissed off. I couldn't control myself this morning. Even now, when I should be thinking about my court case, all I can think about is her delicate hand squeezing tightly as she worked my cock and my head to a state of oblivion.

No matter how hard I try to hate her, I can't. Reese Carmichael is my weakness.

I want to hate the way her golden hair falls along her shoulders, teasing the tops of her breasts, and the way her shorts squeeze the innermost delicate parts of her thighs. And the way her toes fit into her sandals, and the chipped paint on her fingernails showing how much she types and doesn't give a damn about her appearance.

Several seconds tick by as we sit there staring at one another, waiting for the other to break. She used to be more talkative. I knew what she was thinking because she overshared all the time, but now she's locked me out of her thoughts, and I'd be lying if I said it didn't bother me.

While I'd love to say that I don't want to know what she's thinking or even her opinions about the weather, that would be a lie. Reese Carmichael wanted to share her life with me once upon a time, but now, with my ring on her finger, the last thing she wants to do is share more than my last name.

After a moment, she blinks.

"Do you always have breakfast with your family?"

I roll my eyes. "Do you always ask a million questions in the morning?"

"Do you always avoid questions in the morning?" she counters.

I can see that this is going nowhere. One of us must be the adult in the conversation. "No," I answer her original question. "I don't always eat breakfast with my family."

"Why not? Seems like you all are close."

"Seems like you're trying to get on my nerves."

Her eyes go wide, and she clutches her chest. "I am just trying to make conversation with my husband. Can I not talk to you?"

"No."

"Are you saying that you never plan to tell me about your family?"

"Yes." There's no need to elaborate on my decision. The last time I confided in her, she betrayed me. I won't make that mistake again.

"So, you still don't trust me?"

She sighs, like I'm being absolutely ridiculous, and I did not spend six years in prison because of her tattling.

"But you obviously trust me enough to sleep in the same bed."

I blurt out a laugh. "You sleep like the dead. I'm more likely to be stabbed by an intruder than you waking up to kill me."

She was out in about 2.7 seconds last night and snored the entire night. I'm lucky I caught a few power naps in between her hogging the covers and rambling in her sleep.

"I do not sleep like the dead. Thanks to you and your midnight groping, I didn't sleep at all."

I can feel my hairline rise as I pull back onto the winding drive, heading toward Enoch's. "Groping? That's a stretch. My hand brushed your hip one time, and that's only because you were on *my* side of the bed."

"You gripped me like I was trying to run away."

"No, I was asleep."

This is the most ridiculous conversation I've had in years, yet despite myself, I am enjoying the lightheartedness of it all. The fact is, she's right. I did grip her hip during the night. It wasn't because she was trying to run, though; it was because the heat of her body so close to mine had my cock so hard that whenever she brushed against me, thoughts of not treating her like a wife overcame me. She's lucky all I did was grip her hip and not bury my cock in her ass.

"Are you going to answer my question or not?"

It takes me a minute to remember what question she asked me in the first place. Oh, right. "No. I still don't trust you."

"You should."

I look at her like she's crazy.

"I am your wife." She shrugs. "And husbands should trust their wives."

She's been smoking Biscuit's catnip if she believes that. "You realize this is a punishment and not a real marriage, don't you?"

"And you realize that everyone—including your family—thinks that it is? If you want me to sell this marriage over pancakes this morning, you better sell it to me first. I can't act like your wife if you don't act like my husband in front of your family."

I don't have the heart to tell her my family already knows. They know she was the reason we moved to Georgia, and they definitely know I didn't ask for her hand nicely. Unlike her, my family saw what her betrayal did to me.

But she doesn't need to know all that.

"Fine." I sigh. "What do you want to know?"

She jerks back momentarily as if shocked that I'm agreeing with her. "How did you find Magda and the guys?"

The house of Enoch comes into view as I think back to many years ago.

"I didn't find them."

A VICIOUS PROPOSAL

I put the car in park and turn it off. For a moment, all we do is sit in the driveway. But then the front door opens, and Enoch steps out.

Reese's eyes flick to the door.

"I didn't find Magda and the guys," I repeat. "Enoch found me first."

Several seconds go by before she speaks, but I can hear the betrayal in her voice when she does. "You tricked me."

"No, I didn't. I gave you an option, and you married me rather than go to jail."

She shakes her head as Enoch stands at the door, looking confused. I hold my hand up, signaling for him to wait.

"Enoch married us," she says, still staring at the man I call Father.

"He did."

"He's a judge," she notes.

"He is," I agree, "but here, we call him *teacher*—the Father of Eden."

CHAPTER FIFTEEN

Reese

Y<small>OU WOULD'VE THOUGHT I WAS AN OLYMPIAN, WITH THE</small> way I sprinted past Enoch, barricading myself in the first room I came to. Clearly, I didn't think my escape through. If I had, I would've ripped out of Van's grip and ran through the fields instead of the house.

At the time, though, the only thing going through my head was Van had betrayed me again. Not that he's usually a saint, but I guess… I don't know. Maybe I just thought, somewhere deep inside him, he really did come back for me, but you know, in his blackmailing way.

I thought him forcing me to marry him was his way of admitting he wanted to be with me, but now I realize I was wrong. Love doesn't come freely. It always costs you something. "Flower." A deep voice filters through the office door, where I'm currently hiding with my back in a corner.

"You have nowhere to go." The asshole, my husband, is right. There are no windows in this room, and the only door is the one he's currently at. At any moment, he could stop playing this game with me, unlock the door, and yank me out into the lion's den, which he said was full of killers and men worse than him.

"I hate you." My voice trembles, and it pisses me off. "I don't know why I thought you could change."

I can feel the deep rumble of his laughter vibrate the door. "Your naïveté has always amused me. For someone who has been abandoned more times than I can count, you still risk placing your faith in others."

The blood in my veins rush with heat and rage. Before I realize it, I'm standing at the door, banging my fist against it. "Fuck you!"

"Tsk-tsk. Teacher doesn't like us to use four-letter words on Sunday morning."

"Does he like you forcing a girl out of her life and blackmailing her to marry you while threatening to burn her cat at home?"

I can feel the smile he wears in his voice when he answers. "He frowns upon it, yes."

He frowns upon it?

That statement is so blasé. So *I don't give a fuck*. So like Van Gogh.

Suddenly, the light that has been shining through the crack of the door is smothered out. It's like I could feel his hand resting there, darkening my life once again.

"Everyone answers for their crimes, darling," he coos, almost sensually, as if he can't wait to atone for the things he's done.

It's a weird feeling, but then again, Van Gogh has never been traditional.

"As you know, I answered for some of those crimes for years, behind bars, in a cement prison."

I roll my eyes—no, he can't see them—and scoff. "Oh, you think you're the only one who's ever had a rough life? You think you're the only one who suffered unnecessarily?" My voice rises as I struggle to contain the anger. "You think you're the only one who lost their family due to someone else's greed?"

I don't exactly know what I'm doing, but I know that it's not going to be what Van Gogh says. "Go away."

"You know I can't do that."

"Sure, you can." It's called turning around and walking away. "You're all too familiar with how it's done, remember?"

His voice is playful when he says, "Do you mean when you had me arrested and I couldn't meet you?"

I sigh. "This narrative is getting old, Van."

"So is this door, Flower. Should I do us both a favor and kick it down?"

My breath hitches, and there's a naughty part of me that is turned on by the thought of the tattooed arsonist kicking down the door, yanking me into a vicious kiss, and apologizing for all the hateful and manipulative behavior he's shown me.

That's clearly a fantasy.

Van Gogh never apologizes, nor does he want to kiss me. He's made me one of his enemies, but unlike those who crossed him, I didn't just lose my home to a fire. I lost my life to the arsonist.

"You know what, Van?" I call through the door, exasperated by this whole venture. "Do it. Kick the door in and show everyone here what kind of man you really are."

The eerie silence is a warning.

I take several steps back from the door. If there's one thing I know, it's that Van Gogh doesn't like to be challenged. To him, every crime has a consequence, and the only gray area is his own actions.

"Are you still there?" I ask as the silence becomes too much for me. "Or did you walk away like you always do, coward?"

I expect my last word to send the door flying through the back wall, but I am met with nothing, not even a growl or the flick of a match against the wood.

"Van, are you out there?"

A knot grows in my stomach as the fear of the unknown, of this fallen kingdom, grows into panic. They say it's better to deal with the devil you know than the one you don't. I know Van Gogh, but I don't know the others. And I definitely don't know what's on the other side of the door.

"My, my, Tennyson, what do we have here?"

The new voices at the door send shivers down my spine. I've seen enough scary movies to know that behind those deep tones lie chaos and unrestrained violence.

"I don't know, Shakespeare, but it seems our brother has left his pet all defenseless."

I could scream. Surely, Van Gogh would hear me, but the question is would he come for me? This morning in the bathroom wasn't love; it was survival and maybe even a little bit of a power play, but it definitely wasn't bonding.

Allowing two of his brothers to hunt me will not only teach me a lesson to watch my mouth when addressing my husband, but it will also show me what it felt like when no one came to his rescue or even visited him in prison. It's not that I don't understand his anger; it's just that I can't understand why he thinks it was me who put him there.

"Here, kitty, kitty, kitty." The voice I can't place calls to me as a silver blade appears from under the door. "Come out and play. We won't hurt you… yet."

"Where is my husband?" I finally call, kicking the blade out the door.

"Your husband?" Someone snickers like I've just told the most hilarious joke.

"Your husband served you up in a gilded cage. Didn't he tell you who we are?"

"I'm not scared of you."

It's one of the biggest lies I've ever told. I'm terrified of what lies behind the old oak door, but I will be damned if I go down begging these men. They don't know who they're messing with. I, too, am a killer, just not like them.

"If you're not scared, then face us."

They're taunting me, and if I were smart, I would threaten them by pulling out my phone and live-streaming the whole event. I might not know who these guys are, but the Internet will, and the second they come through the door and show their faces, they'll be exposed.

Unfortunately, I don't do any of that. I simply scan the big office until I find what I'm looking for and drop down in front of the door, holding my escape in my hand.

"Tell Van Gogh that he has thirty seconds to get his ass here before I burn this house down and we all die together."

I flip the lighter and hold it to one of the documents I found on the desk. "I don't know whose office this is, but in a moment, it won't exist."

Several seconds go by before someone speaks—if you can even call it speaking; it's more like laughing. "I can see why he is obsessed with her."

Their words stop me. Van Gogh is only obsessed with me because of what he thinks I did to him. He's always been adamant that we weren't friends, even though at one time, he agreed to take me on the run with him.

"All right, love," one of them calls sarcastically, "you win this round. We'll bring you your husband."

The air seems to calm as I stumble to my feet. I imagine they left and took their chaos with them, but it's short-lived since I take no more than a breath before the door to the office swings open, missing me by an inch.

"What the fuck?" My words trail off as my eyes focus on the dark, imposing man standing in the doorway, his eyes hooded and angry as they flip from the lighter to the flame in my hand.

"Flower," he says seductively, pushing through the empty space, "you should know that issuing threats here is a dangerous game."

His eyes rake down my body like he's never seen it before. "But using my own MO against me…"

He moves closer, stalking like the predator he is, and stands with a breath between us, holding my gaze as he plucks the lighter from my fingers. "That, my wife, will get you fucked."

CHAPTER SIXTEEN

Reese

MY WIFE.
Will get you fucked.
I think we can all agree that Van is romantic as fuck, but then again, my views on romance are a little tarnished and a whole lot twisted.

"I'm sorry," I clip like the delightful smell of bergamot and ash wafting off him isn't sending a rush of wetness to my center. "Did you think I was trying to turn you on?"

Hopefully, my voice sounds more annoyed than weak when Van surprises me with a grin.

"Not in the slightest," he agrees. "But that doesn't change the fact that you did."

Maybe it's the adrenaline from earlier, but I can't sift through the fog in my brain to understand the look in Van's eyes.

"Well, rest assured, dear husband, the only thing I want to make hard for you is your life—your dick can go fuck itself."

I'm choosing to ignore this morning's episode. That was an attempt to play nice, but Van shot that bonding experience to hell when he let his killer brothers taunt me.

"My dick," Van repeats, his hands going to my hips and resting there like a firm security blanket, "won't fuck anything but that pretty mouth of yours." Leaning in, his breath ghosts over the top of my ear. "I suggest you learn to control it before I do."

Holy freaking, wow.

I'm a sick woman.

This man with a power trip is threatening me, and all I say is, "I wouldn't be so confident. I'm a slow learner."

I might as well have given him a trophy and declared him the winner. I would have happily given him my virginity that summer we met, but he refused and broke my heart. What bad boy does that? Not a good one.

Van Gogh has always been more than he seems, but not even our friendship made him open up. He's always been a walking contradiction, full of hate and kindness. And my dumbass marries him, knowing nothing about who he really is.

"You know, Mrs. Cain, if I didn't know better, I'd say you issued me another challenge."

I smack one of his hands on my hips, but it doesn't move.

"Think what you want, Mr. Cain, but you do nothing for me sexually that I haven't already had." I shrug just to be an ass. "And better. I can't imagine you learned much while in prison."

It was a low blow. I know that, but I said it anyway. Van Gogh doesn't always get to be the bad guy in this relationship. He doesn't get to be overly confident and prey on my insecurities. I didn't send him to prison. This punishment isn't fair, and if he insists on exacting it, he can be uncomfortable, too. I'm done being his play toy when he's in the mood.

"My little flower has become a fighter." Sliding his hands along my hips, he grips my waistband and yanks me hard into his chest. "Let's see how brave you really are."

"So, Reese, I'm sure you have some questions." Enoch's eyes find mine as his head lifts from the bowed position it was in. Even the supposed killers rounding the kitchen table recited the prayer that Enoch led.

Since returning from the office where I acted like a complete fool, threatening to burn this family's home down, I've yet to say anything but *thank you* to Magda when she set a giant plate of food in front of me. Honestly, I'm too embarrassed to face anyone, let alone the man at the head of the table.

"Despite Alistair's creative tales, you are safe here."

I flash a wide-eyed look at Van Gogh—I can't bring myself to call him Alistair—that I hope he interprets as *what the fuck?* Did he tell Enoch that he called them all killers and scared me? Or was it all a lie, and Van Gogh is pulling out his trademarked behavior and using fear to control me?

"Our family has been through a lot," Enoch adds confidently, smiling proudly at my husband. "Our family is part of many pasts, but those mistakes are not who we are. The men around this table are just as noble as those who never make headlines."

"Aww, Teach. You're giving me a semi." The man they call Tennyson flashes me a wicked smile and shovels a mound of eggs into his mouth.

"Tennyson, now is not the time." Enoch turns his attention back to me. "What has Alistair told you about us?"

I'm suddenly taken back to a movie I once saw where the girl was human and fell in love with a vampire. When he finally took her to his home to have dinner with his family, he found it hard to control himself and nearly killed her.

Is this what this breakfast is? Did Van Gogh break some rule by marrying me and bringing me here? Is that why Enoch made such a big deal about *until death do us part*?

Oh, shit. What in the hell have I gotten myself into?

Van Gogh nudges me in the side. "Would you rather I answer?"

I can't tell if he's being friendly or sarcastic, but it doesn't matter. I don't need these people thinking I'm scared of them. I am, but the less they know, the better.

"He just said you found him and have been his family ever since." Surely, they know Van is a man of few words. He shares about as well as a stray cat.

Enoch smiles, and it seems genuine.

"He told you correctly. Alistair was my first son." Someone coughs, but it doesn't mask the distinct "Pussy" that is said with it.

Ignoring the juvenile outburst, Enoch continues. "As you're already aware, Alistair comes from a troubled past." I can feel Van tense beside me. His past has always been a no-go zone—not that he shares often. In fact, he's only spoken of his past with me once—the day he promised to take me with him when he left South Carolina.

I nod, hoping to ease the tension in the man I call my husband. "I know. His past doesn't bother me."

It sounds ridiculous. I'm now a serial arsonist's wife. If Enoch wants to share some of his past, I should jump at the chance and gather any information I can. I might be able to use some of it to get out of this mess.

But Van would know I was up to something. He knows that I have never cared about his past, but it has always intrigued me. He had no money, power, or wealth, but it didn't stop him from getting justice. He blazed his path and did what he needed to do to sleep at night.

Could he have been more legal about it? Maybe. But does that make him evil? No. He never burned or hurt anyone that didn't hurt someone else worse. At least, not that I know of. He could have been lying, and I could have been in love. I may never know.

"I was the assistant district attorney on Alistair's case." Enoch's calm timbre breaks through my irrational thoughts. "I was the one who offered him a plea deal."

My head snaps up to Van's, but his gaze is far away.

"I didn't know that piece of the story," I admit, trying not to seem eager to learn more.

Nothing good can come out of knowing who Van is. This isn't a real marriage, and it won't last long. Once I figure out who turned in Van, I'm leaving. Apart from what Van thinks, I did have a life, and I'm eager to get back to it.

"After Alistair served his sentence, I offered him a room with me. He was only twenty-four at the time and had the worst attitude."

I fight off a laugh and smile. "*Had?* He still has the worst attitude."

Van's head slowly turns in my direction, and like the best wife ever, I lay my hand atop his on the table for everyone to see. "I think it's cute, though."

Total bullshit. Van's personality could make a nun stabby. He's worse than Biscuit after a bath.

"You're right there," Enoch agrees with a chuckle, "but we love him anyway."

The muscles in Van's hand tense, making me wonder if the L word is another topic that makes him uncomfortable.

"I was so proud when he obtained his law degree in prison."

If there has ever been a time that I wanted a father in my life, it's now. The way Enoch looks at Van and then around the table at the rest of the guys with such pride is rare.

"I never thought he'd want to become part of the system that failed and then punished him," Enoch adds. "But I should have known my son would not only forgive but recognize his worth and take matters into his own hands. The road to purpose is never an easy one. Obstacles hide the turns, and failure to consult a map always results in a detour. But despite getting lost and missing a turn here and there, you will always find your way."

There are so many things in his speech that intrigue me. The first is that Van forgives. Do we know the same person here? The Van Gogh I know doesn't forgive. He gets even.

"All of my sons are gifted and will change the world someday."

I don't know what comes over me. Maybe Magda spiked the food, but the words come out of my mouth before I can stop them. "How can you be so sure they've changed?"

I don't need to clarify. There's a three-strike law that was implemented for a reason. Sometimes, living on the edge and defying authority is too exciting to give up. Van Gogh was a serial arsonist. How does Enoch know that he won't do it again? After all, he blackmailed me into being his wife by threatening to burn down my apartment. It wouldn't be hard for him to slip back into old habits.

"Are you saying you don't think people can change?" Enoch's brow rises as several eyes focus on me like lasers.

"No. I believe people can change, but I wonder how you sound so sure."

I likely already have a hit out on me for asking such a question, but at least I can die knowing his answer.

"I can be sure, Mrs. Cain, because they told me. Like you, these men aren't perfect. They will continue to make mistakes in their lives. If they recognize their mistakes and learn from them, they will not disappoint me."

That still doesn't answer my question. "Are you saying if they break the law again, as long as they say they're sorry, that's okay?"

Now would be a good time for Van to stick that dick into my mouth and teach me to control it. Clearly, I have a need.

Enoch smiles. "I'm saying that if they break our covenant after promising me their lives, they will suffer with no end."

The room grows silent, and if I weren't terrified of getting caught by one of Van's brothers, I would run until I collapsed.

"A promise to me is not like a promise to others. To be my son, I require only one thing, and that one thing is something my children fear losing."

They have got to be vampires.

"I think that's enough history for today," Enoch says after a tension-filled silence. "We are thrilled to have you as part of our family and wish you and Alistair a long and happy marriage."

CHAPTER SEVENTEEN

Van

"YOU'RE A VAMPIRE, AREN'T YOU? IT'S FINE IF YOU ARE. JUST don't drain me of blood in the middle of the night. I'm O-negative—the most universal blood type in the world. People count on my donations. You would be depriving millions of—"

I can't take it anymore. "Even if I were a vampire—which I'm not—the last thing I'd want to do is risk spending an eternity where you never die."

Instead of getting mad and lashing out at me, she grins.

"Welcome back, my friend. I thought you would ignore me the rest of the day."

I was planning on it, but admitting it would only make her happy, and that's not the relationship I want with my wife.

"Where are we going, anyway?" It annoys me that she didn't ask this question fifteen minutes ago when I opened the car door and sent her a threatening glare.

"Does it matter? Seems to me that if you'll get in the car with a potential vampire, you're up for anything." However, driving her out of town and off a bridge did cross my mind a time or two.

"True," she agrees, opening the glove box and digging through my shit like I won't stop this car and set it on fire just to prove that what's mine is mine and what's hers is mine. Just because I married her does not mean I plan to share my life or anything else with her. I clearly remember that not being in the vows.

"Holy shit." Her shocked gasps send a zing of electricity straight to my cock. "You are such a fucking liar."

She holds up a slip of paper she found in the glove box.

"This is not a stolen car."

I roll my eyes. "Of course, it isn't. I'm not a thief. That's Tennyson's wheelhouse."

"Tennyson is a thief?"

I shrug as if this is a typical conversation between a couple. "And a murderer."

Her eyes widen. "He's really a murderer? You weren't lying?"

"Believe it or not, you bring out the worst in me." I'm no Boy Scout by any means, but I'm generally an honest man when I do speak.

"Oh, so I made you lie; is that what you're saying?"

"Exactly." No need to continue to lie to her. "You're the only one who's ever made me break the rules."

"That is a crock of horse shit, and you know it."

I mouth *horse shit* and smile. "How so?"

Tossing the car registration onto the floorboard, she turns in the seat and folds her arms against her chest. "Setting a town on fire is breaking the rules, Van, or did you not know that rules and laws are basically the same thing?"

They aren't, but I'd like for her to hold this position a while longer since all she's managing to do is flash an extraordinary amount of cleavage that has my cock begging for me to pull over and plunge between them until I coat them in my cum.

"You broke so many laws when we were eighteen that I bet you don't even know what it feels like to abide by them."

"I know what it feels like," I interject. "I might not enjoy the label of being a law-abiding citizen, but I do it." I'm the assistant district attorney, for fuck's sake. I'm the poster boy for law-abiding.

Her delicate laugh causes me to swerve. "You sound like it's torture."

I cut her a bored look. "It's not far off."

It's not in my nature to follow anyone, let alone greedy officials, but I do it because someone has to advocate for those who are ignored.

"So why become an assistant district attorney?" she asks seriously. "Why not become a politician?"

I arch a brow, amused that she threw that career choice out there. "Because if I were a politician, I could consider myself above the law and do as I please?"

She nods.

"Where would the fun be in that?"

She throws her hands up like having this conversation is enough to make her throw herself into moving traffic. "You wouldn't have to suffer by following the rules."

"I also wouldn't be able to punish those who deserve it," I argue. "You should know I will sell my soul to serve justice." At one time, I did.

"You're suffering for her—for people like her so they can have justice."

I don't confirm her assumption. She's always known how I've felt. I'm here because of my mother's bleeding heart.

"Did you ever find him?" She asks the question so quietly I almost miss it.

"No." I pull into the shopping mall just as her mouth opens to ask another question.

"Your oversized rat needs a bed," I clip, holding up one finger to silence any sound she may be inclined to make. "If it sleeps on me again, I will toss it out the front door."

I expect rage, maybe even the finger, when she finally looks at me. But that's not what I find. "Is this my wedding gift?" Tears gather in her eyes as one escapes down her cheek. "A cat bed for Biscuit?"

Why did she have to name the damn thing after food?

Finding some of my old self, I flash her the meanest look I can muster. "Allowing Biscuit to breathe the same air as me is your wedding gift. Her sleeping on my chest again will be a housewarming gift for Simeon's new doghouse."

I fucking hate animals more than I do people. She's lucky I let her even put that shedding rodent in my car in the first place.

"Aww. I see what's going on here." She opens her car door, and I follow, catching her gaze over the top of the car. "You love my cat."

"Playing house with Blake has made you delusional." Slamming the door, I walk off, leaving my new wife doubled over in laughter.

"Wait!" She's still laughing when she grabs my arm. "Don't be such a baby. It's okay if you love my cat. Unlike you, I can share."

Maybe someone will kidnap her while we're here and save me the trouble of paying someone to do it for me. Pulling to a stop, I snatch her lithe body to my chest, causing her breath to hitch and halt that awful laughter.

"Provoking my anger," I warn, holding her gaze sternly, "will only end up pleasing me." Lowering my face, I press my cheek against hers. "Are you ready to please me, Wife?"

Like I anticipated, she jerks away with an aggravated huff. "One day"—she points at my chest like a heart resides there—"you'll stop pushing me away."

That's where she's delusional, but I humor her anyway. Call it another wedding gift. "You better hope not, love. As you know, when I enjoy something, I consume it until it becomes ash at my feet."

Until death do us part.

The vows hit me like a thunderous storm. No matter how much I want revenge, I must honor my vows to this woman. Unlike years ago, my word is my truth. I'm not Van Gogh anymore. Alistair Cain is an honest man, a dutiful husband, and a servant of justice—even if he still struggles with it occasionally.

I glance down at the pissed-off woman in front of me, who is anything but fearful. "Are you done? Or would you like to add a few more cryptic threats you won't back up?"

I cock a brow, enjoying this defiant side of her. "What makes you so sure I won't follow through?"

She nods to my chest. "Your tattoo."

"You'll have to be more specific. I have many tattoos."

She grins. "Yes, but only one that stands unscorched by the flames around it."

The sunflower.

"No matter how much you hate me, Husband, I will always be the one thing you can't destroy."

I don't miss the fact she said *can't*, not *won't*.

But seeing as I'm a giant asshole, I remind her of one simple fact. "Don't make the same mistake as others. I will destroy myself if it punishes my enemies."

She might be my wife, but she is still my enemy. I vowed to stay with her until death; I never said I wouldn't be the one who caused it.

"Yeah, yeah. Another day, another empty threat. I can help you come up with new material later. At least then I won't spend these six years bored to tears."

She at least got the tears part right.

"Come on, Mr. Cain." She waves off my glare. "Let's buy your pussycat a bed."

CHAPTER EIGHTEEN

Reese

THREE HUNDRED DOLLARS AND A TRUNK FULL OF CAT supplies later, we pull into Eden, winding down the long drive to The House of Cain. We haven't spoken since all the threats in the parking lot, but it wasn't for my lack of trying.

I tried to weigh in that Biscuit would prefer a pink bed, but one scathing look told me he was no longer in the playing mood. And while I love to piss him off, I was hesitant to do so in a public setting where innocent people could get caught up in his anger.

Alistair Cain might be an assistant district attorney, but Van Gogh still lives deep inside his cold, dark heart. I wouldn't put it past him to set the entire store on fire just to prove that he's still capable if pushed. So, I stayed quiet and let him spend a ridiculous amount of money on a cat he supposedly hates. Until now.

"Since I never signed a prenup," I start, watching his brows creep higher, "I'd like to know how we can afford such an enormous mansion. Do all ADAs make millions of dollars like you?"

"Billions," he corrects, "and no, my ADA salary does not bring in billions."

I try not to seem shocked that the homeless boy I once knew is now a billionaire.

"What does, then?" I prompt. "Please tell me you aren't a drug dealer, too."

I can only handle so much criminal activity. My husband might be hotter than a Dior model, but I must draw the line somewhere, and apparently, street corner dealing is it.

Those hypnotic green eyes pin me with dark secrets I'm shamelessly excited to uncover.

Maybe I wouldn't mind if he's a drug dealer after all. Let's be honest. Even before I knew Van Gogh was *the Van Gogh*, I couldn't stay away. I knew he was no saint, lurking around the cigar lounge I worked at, yet I didn't care. The dark and dangerous aura he exuded pulled me in with no effort on his part. I wanted him to rob the lounge and take me hostage. Hell, I wore the cutest, most uncomfortable outfits I owned just to be prepared for the day when he'd strike. Then he turned out to be an arsonist, killing my dreams of a bit of hostage role-play.

"Why are you looking at me like that?" Van's forehead pinches as if he's... No way. He can't be.

"Are you nervous, Mr. Cain?"

A scoff-like noise escapes his lips. "Don't flatter yourself, love. In no lifetime will you ever make me nervous."

He's a big, fat, arson-loving liar. "Then why are your hands twitching as you stare at me?"

I dip my head, nodding as if he needs to look for himself to believe me.

He doesn't.

Instead, he slips his hands into his pockets out of spite, kicking the car door open with his shoes. "Our vows require that I protect you." His mouth turns up into a smile. "I understand that to mean even from my own hands that yearn to surround your neck." He chuckles. "In a lovingly tight grip, of course."

This adorable asshole. "Of course. I'd expect nothing less from my charming husband."

"You've always brought out the best in me," he agrees sarcastically. "But to answer your other question, I'm not a drug dealer. The billions I have, I did not earn."

My brows pinch, and I find myself even more confused. "But I thought—"

Van rolls his eyes. "To get through these next six years, maybe it's best if you let me do all the thinking."

I'm going to poison his aftershave and patent it. I, too, can become a billionaire. Imagine the demand for such a product. Women everywhere would want a free sample.

"Are you even listening?"

I sigh at the use of his authoritative attorney voice. "I'm sorry, lover. It's just that your voice seems to be hypnotic… hypnotically annoying." Batting my eyelashes, I fold my hands like an obsessed little girl under my chin. "But please, continue wasting my time and avoiding my questions with petty insults."

Let him do all the thinking. Pft. Please. Asshole.

"I almost forgot," he muses, unbothered.

Oh, I can't wait to hear this. "You forgot what?"

"That you get mean when you're tired."

"I do not—" My traitorous mouth uses the opportunity to widen into the biggest yawn.

"You were saying?" The bastard has the nerve to laugh.

"You know what?" I say defensively. "I don't even care—"

"Oil," he interrupts. "Enoch's family left him an oil empire that he shares with us." Emotionless eyes blink several times as he pulls in a shuddering breath. "That's where our billions come from."

I don't miss his usage of the word *our*. But that little nugget of information is a thought for another day. I have a more urgent question I need answered first.

"Why is Enoch a judge, then? Who runs the oil empire?"

I'm not saying Enoch shouldn't follow his passion, but why work? Enoch looks well past the age of retirement.

Van hesitates for a moment—likely deciding how much information he can trust me with. "Enoch believes money is not the same thing as wealth. He works because wealth is earned, not given."

"Yet he gave you all that same wealth?" I'm so confused. "None of you wanted to dabble in the oil business?"

"No."

I rear back. Van Gogh would have shocked me less if he had set a billion dollars of cash on fire before me. "No?" Blinking, I try to wake up from this crazy dream. "You mean you rather work for shitty money with the government who failed you?"

His jaw ticks, and I can tell I hit a nerve. "You should nap," he says. "I insist."

"You mean, you demand?" Let's label this as what it is. We have enough bullshit between us already.

He tips his chin as he leads me with his hand on my lower back into the mansion. "Do you need my assistance finding the bedroom?"

"Depends," I say, in the same dick-head voice he's using. "Do you need my assistance pulling that giant stick out of your ass?"

I don't wait for him to answer. We all know a wench and 4X4 truck couldn't dislodge that stick. Turning from his touch, I find the hall I hope leads to the stairs where I slept last night—I refuse to call it our bedroom—hold up my middle finger, and wave goodbye.

Fucker. I hope Biscuit coughs up the biggest hairball ever on his expensive furniture.

I wake up cold—way too cold, considering I got lost and ended up in the basement. My pride wouldn't let me turn back and walk past Van Gogh. I didn't need his assistance finding the bedroom in his castle of a home. I would figure it out eventually—or draw myself a map later. Either way, I didn't need him or his fantastic memory of my grumpy moods when I missed my afternoon power naps.

"Stop picking at your nails."

The low voice stops my hands cold. I won't even bother admitting that I was, in fact, mindlessly chipping away at the black paint on my thumbnail. That would mean the devil thinks he knows me, and he doesn't.

"We're back to stalking, I see." I kick off the heavy blanket responsible for the beads of sweat on the back of my neck and sit up.

The basement is darker than I remember when I wandered down here earlier. It was also empty and Van Gogh-less. Clearly, things have changed. My gaze finds the man of nightmares sitting at an antique dining table that looks as if it seats twenty people or more.

Standing, I notice my shoes are off, and my hair is no longer in a loose braid like when I fell asleep on the—"You gave me Biscuit's bed to use as a pillow!"

The bastard snorts. "You were right. She preferred the blue one."

Where is the fire exit to this shitshow? I want out.

"*She preferred the blue one*," I repeat, still not believing my husband let me sleep on a pet bed. "And so, you thought, why waste the pink one when Reese could use it as a pillow?"

Am I the only one who thinks he's trying to get me to murder him?

"Actually," he says, turning his chair to face me, "we thought a water buffalo had found its way inside the house."

His head tilts towards the middle of the table, revealing the other half of 'we,' who is none other than my rescued fur baby, Biscuit. Her betraying butt gazes up at the demon who has more money than sense before burrowing back down in the overstuffed blue cat bed, twice the size of the pink one he'd purchased earlier.

"Since we had just returned from the store, I wasn't sure what you let in to kill me," Van continues. "I grabbed the first thing I saw."

"A plush cat bed?" Who the hell does he think he's lying to?

"I'm confident in my defensive skills." Van shrugs nonchalantly. "Not to worry, though. The only danger here was you choking yourself awake from sleep apnea."

Though his words are dry and lack emotion, the delight in his eyes gives him away. The jerk is enjoying this immensely.

"You should be evaluated by a professional," he continues. "It would be awful if you accidentally smothered yourself while I was away. I prefer you save that kind of gift for an anniversary."

"There's not a word horrific enough for what you are," I note, realizing that this man slipped a cat bed under my head instead of over it. Is this how he shows affection? By propping my head up off the floor and opening my airway?

Nah. Van isn't *that* sweet. It's more likely that he didn't want me drooling on his rug and interrupting whatever he was working on at the ridiculously large dining table…

The rest of the words die in my throat as I finally notice the wall before me. "Van?" My voice breaks in fear, and apparently, that disgusts my husband since he turns away and awakens the laptop in front of him.

"Van?"

I'm not going away if that's what he's hoping.

"Van!"

"What?" he finally bites back. "What do you want now?"

"I—" Hesitating, I search for the strength I'll need to get out of this mess. "I want to know how many women you watch on those hidden cameras?"

CHAPTER NINETEEN

Reese

I'VE NEVER BEEN A GREAT JUDGE OF CHARACTER. FOR SOME reason, my gut isn't like everyone else's. I swear it's a genetic predisposition—a gift from my mother, God rest her soul. The Carmichael women have always gravitated toward toxic men. Maybe it's because toxic men create unhealthy relationships—which are fun, if we're being honest here.

Don't roll your eyes. Not until you've tried one. Not that I'm suggesting you leave a good relationship for a toxic one—they're not that fun. But the truth is there's something exciting about a mysterious man. The fear of danger likely releases an extra shot of dopamine when they're around, which makes the vajayjay vibrate. You know what I mean. The feeling is addictive.

The point is, I've always known Van Gogh wasn't a picture-perfect citizen, but I *never* thought he would be a peeping Tom.

"Are you jealous, love?" His low voice carries an undercurrent of amusement in his words. "Did you think you were the only one I stalked?"

I slide back, my gaze volleying between the dozen or more screens. "Who are these women?" I can tell that none of the cameras are in weird places, like the bathroom or bedroom, which I guess is a little better.

The screens go dark, and before I realize what's happening, my husband's imposing body steps into my space and backs me toward the stairs.

"These women," he pauses, casting me a warning look, "are none of your business."

I beg to differ, but his palm claps over my mouth before I can tell him that.

"The next time you decide to defy my orders and sleep somewhere other than my bed, you will be punished."

Heaven help me, I laugh as his hand falls. "Your orders?" I arch a brow. "I don't recall the basement being off-limits."

That wicked smile of his flashes for only a second before it's gone.

"It isn't." he clarifies. "Sleeping anywhere but my bed, however, is."

I'm pretty sure he never vocalized this rule, but you know what? Other than the tingling in my lower body, I have more important things to discuss. "Whatever," I snap. "I really don't care. What I care about are those women and their privacy. It's not right!"

My chest is heaving by the time I'm finished. "Well, then. I suppose apologies are in order. I wasn't aware that stalking was so offensive." His cheek twitches as he struggles to maintain his smile. "You see, the last woman I stalked failed to tell me that when she caught me watching her through the lounge window, the way she slipped her fingers under her waistband wasn't because my behavior turned her on, but that she was soothing her fear and subsequent violation of privacy."

I hate him—mainly because he's right. I did pleasure myself and let him watch once upon a time after the lounge had closed. I told you. I don't make great decisions. My gut is a thrill-seeking whore.

"Why are you watching those girls, Van?" I don't expect him to answer, considering this is my third time asking. He won't disclose all of his nefarious things—especially not to the person he thinks betrayed him.

Again, those deep green eyes flash for a moment. And I imagine my husband is thinking precisely the same thing as me.

There's no level of trust between us. I don't know if there ever really was. Maybe we had respect for one another since I was doing something shady, and he was, too. We respected each other's criminal activities—as toxic as that may sound—but we all have things we do that are less than admirable.

I'm not one to say that I'm a saint. I've stolen money from men who sometimes worked hard for it for many years. Crime is crime, no matter what it's for. But there comes a time in everyone's life when they're so desperate they blur the lines between right and wrong. We should have a justice system that is not tainted by money and greed. It should be fair. But then again, people really shouldn't be so terrible, either.

When I was young, I honestly thought everyone should love one another. And I still, to this day, believe it would solve all our problems, but that's just me.

Van lifts my chin and holds my gaze. His eyes change from amused and standoffish to threatening. "If you come back into the basement, you will never leave. This room and my viewing preferences are off-limits."

I don't know why I get so pissed off by that statement. Regardless, I fail to keep my mouth shut. Instead, I push him hard in the chest. "So, I'm supposed to just fucking trust you?"

He smiles. "Absolutely not."

"Oh, well. That clears up everything."

"As my wife," he snaps back, "you're to do as I say."

Oh, no, that is so not happening.

"Listen, Alistair." I say his name all dramatic and uppity. "We're not back in the 1920s. It is not okay to be a condescending prick. I will not do as you say unless you do as I fucking say."

I'm picking a huge fight, and honestly, after that blissful nap, I'm ready for it.

Van grabs my wrist and yanks me to him. "Shall I remind you this is not a real marriage? I am your warden, and you are my keep. You will do as *I fucking say*, or I will lock you in solitary, and you will never see your precious sunrise again."

"Let me go before I slit your throat with Biscuit's claws." I wrench my arm from his hands, and he has sense enough to step back.

We don't say anything else. I simply walk up the stairs, lift my middle finger, hold it there until I reach the top, and slam the door, finding my way to the kitchen for something to eat.

I don't know what Van does all night down in the basement, but it's sure not ordering groceries. The cabinets are bare, with just a few essentials. And the only thing in the refrigerator is a few fruits and vegetables that I'd rather starve than eat. Not saying I'm a junk food addict. I'm just saying squash isn't my thing. Neither is eggplant.

I find it gross and don't want to eat it. Therefore, I'm DoorDashing. I'm not the greatest cook, anyway. I tend to live off Flamin' Hot Cheetos and dill-pickled cashews. Not together, obviously. That would be weird. But one is breakfast, and one is lunch. Dinner is typically ordered. Being a teacher's assistant, I don't always get off on time to cook.

I pull up the app for food delivery, finding something with some healthy food and some not-so-healthy food. I settle on a sub sandwich and a bag of chips. I call that a win. I also call it stupid to have to order when you could just keep sandwich stuff at home for half the cost, but whatever.

Every prisoner gets a meal. So, if Van Gogh won't provide, I will provide for myself.

I order my food, setting the destination to my pinpointed location. Then I proceed to wander the halls until I come to an office. I find a bar inside the room and decide I need a drink, like yesterday.

Van Gogh always had a taste for the finer liquors, so let's see what real money gets him now. I pour way more than two fingers' worth just to be an asshole and flop down in a leather chair behind the desk.

I don't know how long I stay in Van's chair drinking his finest spirits, but it's long enough for my phone to ring with a number I don't recognize. That's not all that uncommon for me, considering all the people I've scammed over the years, but unlike a wise person, I answer it, my voice only a little slurred.

"This is Mrs. Cain," I say. "How may I help you?"

The deep cackle on the other end surprises me. "Well," the vaguely familiar voice starts, "it's not so much me that needs your help. Unlike your husband, in my courtroom, trespassing is a crime, punishable by far worse than a fine, Mrs. Cain." He says my new last name with a chuckle. It takes me a second. And then I hear a dog growl, and the man on the phone says, "Watch him."

"Who is this?"

"You don't recognize my voice? Have you forgotten me already?"

A voice that leaves a taste of fear in my mouth has me sitting up at attention.

"Tennyson?" I ask.

"Good job, Reese." The way he says my name is haunting, but I don't have time to figure out why.

"Who needs my help?"

The dog barks again, and the man screams that he's from food service delivery and has my sandwich.

"Oh, shit." I jump up, and the alcohol hits me. I stumble into the desk, knocking over what's left of the cognac.

"I am so sorry!" I scream, hoping Tennyson has me on speaker.

"You didn't give him the gate code to deliver this, did you?"

"Well, if I knew the gate code, I would have. My dear husband forgot that little tidbit of information."

Tennyson laughs, but it doesn't sound like he's amused. "Did your husband also forget to tell you that we strictly forbid delivery service?"

My mind is fuzzy from the alcohol, and I find it difficult to think of a sane reason why they wouldn't allow food delivery.

"No, he forgot to mention that, too," I say, exasperated. "He's currently down in the basement, ignoring me, and I'm hungry. So, either I go down there and stab him and eat his heart—Wait," I chuckle, "he doesn't have one of those. Maybe his liver. Or, I suggest you permit this one exception and allow this poor delivery guy entry."

At this, Tennyson laughs harder, and I imagine the boisterous sound is from him throwing his head back as his German Shepherd keeps the delivery man frozen in place.

"I'll tell you what, princess, since you're new here, I'll let you have this one exception. It'll be our little secret."

"Thank you," I say genuinely. "I'm glad someone here is kind."

"And just to show you how generous of a brother-in-law I am, I'll even give him a head start."

Fear grips me by the throat, paralyzing me in the basement hall that I finally reached. "What?"

"Ten seconds ought to do it. If your delivery guy can make it over the fence and back without the dog getting him, he lives. If he doesn't, let this be a warning to you: Do not violate the rules of Eden unless you're prepared to suffer the consequences."

Suddenly, it hits me. The guys that rounded Enoch's table with me this morning are master manipulators that use their skills for inciting terror in the innocent. They aren't redeemable. They aren't good deep down.

"Ten," Tennyson counts down, and the poor delivery driver whimpers.

"Stop!" I run downstairs and bang on the basement door that's latched from the inside, just as Tennyson reaches eight.

"Don't be so pessimistic, Reese. This guy looks to be in shape. He might actually have a chance."

I'm frantic, shuffling around, trying to help a guy who was just trying to get me food.

"Please. Don't do this. He's completely innocent."

"None of us are innocent. Not even you."

CHAPTER TWENTY

Van

SHE WANTS TO DIE.

That's the only explanation as to why she's banging on the door.

"Reese!" I shout. "I will burn this bitch down with us inside it. Do not test me tonight."

A sob comes through the door. "I need your help. I fucked up."

Something like indigestion stirs in my chest, bubbling to the surface.

Are those fucking feelings?

Not possible. Alistair Cain does not have feelings—especially for Reese Carmichael.

"I'm serious, Van," she calls again. "I messed up. I didn't know visitors weren't allowed. It was just… I was hungry." The way she whimpers the word *hungry* gnaws at the wounds deep inside, creating a pain I had numbed long ago.

Was I supposed to feed her? Is that part of caring for my wife? Or is that part of independence?

"I had food delivered." Another sob racks over her words as she mumbles more. "But Tennyson..." I need no other explanation from her. Tennyson, like the rest of us, has his demons. He trusts no one. Even we are on a short leash with him.

"He's going to kill him, Van, and I can't be responsible for a man's death just because he was trying to deliver some chips."

I roll my eyes at her dramatics and yell back, "Tennyson won't kill him."

He may scare him, but he won't kill him. Tennyson might be a murderer, but killing a delivery driver is out of his wheelhouse. Tennyson isn't like the rest of us in that regard. His story is different.

"Please, Van. I need help."

That she does, but from a professional.

"What did you order?" I call, standing and easing my way to the basement door but not opening it.

"What?" She sounds shocked, which is slightly amusing. "What do you mean, *what did I order?*" I smile and trace a sunflower on the door with my finger. "I mean, did you order something that's worth my time in saving this poor man's life?"

Shock coats her next words. "Are you serious right now?"

"Deadly," I clip sternly. "I'm not in the business of saving innocent lives, if you recall."

I round out the leaves on the sunflower, envisioning the bright golds and yellows beaming from the petals.

"You know what? Fuck it. I'll save him myself. I just need you to unlock the front door."

Now, that really makes me happy.

"Oh, is my prisoner upset that she can't come and go as she

pleases?" It's like I can feel her anger pulsing through the door, which only thickens my cock.

"I swear, Van, I will bust every single window in this fucking prison if you do not get your ass up." I wrench the basement door open before she can threaten me further, and come in my pants.

"You were saying?"

Her eyes flutter as she takes in my bare chest. "What are you doing in there?"

Rolling my eyes, I push her to the side. "Again, none of your damn business."

Unlocking the front door, I throw it open, letting in the night air.

"Wait. I don't have shoes on."

I don't care. What's a few thorns to her? It can't be as bad as the knives she's stuck in my back.

She calls me a bastard under her breath, which is basically an *I love you* in my love language.

"Be sure and close the door behind you," I snap. "I don't want Biscuit getting out."

"Oh, Biscuit. Is she a prisoner, too?"

"Cute," I note, "but no. Unlike you, she is loyal."

"You do remember Biscuit is my cat. Before you came along, she was 'loyal' to me." A victorious grin emerges on Reese's face. "If you want to get technical, Biscuit is just as much a traitor as you think I am. Except, unlike me, she abandoned her partner to chase dick."

"Be careful, Wife." I'm in her face instantly. "Throwing around terms of endearment will occupy your mouth far longer than your delivery driver has."

Her pupils widen as the realization sinks in.

"I am a man of tradition," I add. "Being my prisoner does not exclude you from partaking in your wifely duties." My cock strains against my trousers at the thought of a nice hate-fuck later. "I am giving you time to adjust to your new cell." I grin viciously. "But know that you will consummate our marriage with my cock until I release you."

Fuck her sarcasm. "The only pussy that will chase my dick will be yours, Mrs. Cain."

I almost expect her to punch me, but she doesn't. Instead, Mrs. Cain pats me on the shoulder and shakes her head with a chuckle.

"Get your coat, stud. You may need it to keep in the hot air you're blowing. I'd hate for you to burn with your ego."

Not because she told me to but because I'm enjoying her eyes glazing me over as I become the man she remembers me to be, I slip my black hoodie over my head like I did all those years ago. In this world, I am known as Alistair Cain, and Van Gogh is only known as the original and famous artist. But for Reese, I will always be Van Gogh, the vigilante arsonist.

"Wow," she notes, finally closing the door behind her." Who knew the ADA wore bargain brands?"

Who knew she was this lippy?

"Should we save your delivery driver?" I ask, "Or would you like to keep chatting about my thrifty attire?" Honestly, I hope she picks the latter so that I can remember not to be charmed by her mouth. With her middle finger, she motions for me to proceed, and I find it rather charming. But not enough to leave the door unlocked. Flipping the keys out of my pocket, I pull out the lighter with it.

"You still carry it," she notes.

"It hasn't run out of fuel yet," I lie.

Actually, there are four containers of lighter fluid in the basement that prevent the lighter from ever running dry. I'm traditional and sentimental.

"Whew. Let's get out of here before the smell of bullshit is unbearable."

I made her walk the whole way to the gate. I wanted to remind her of the shadows that hide behind the rolling hills and expansive oak trees.

During the day, Eden is a picture of innocence—an infinite space of lush gardens. But like everywhere else, those gardens have thorns and decay and dying roots underneath that must be nurtured.

At least, that's the metaphor Enoch uses for us.

It took a long time for me to understand the metaphor. In my eyes, I will always have the roots of my past. But Enoch once said, *"Even young sunflowers can bear the burns of the sun, for they cannot control where they are planted. But they can adapt and bloom just as if they were sowed in nutrient-rich soil."*

Eden is our revival—our fresh soil, rich with nutrients and opportunities to start over and grow to our full potential. It's also the place I feel the most insecure. Living in Eden comes with expectations. It's not that I don't appreciate everything Enoch has done for me. It's just sometimes Eden and its expectations are overwhelming.

I want to be the man Enoch thinks I am. I don't want him to regret taking me in, but every day is a fight. A struggle to keep the vindictive thoughts away and replace them with forgiveness and understanding. The justice system failed me. It failed my mother, and while I can't change it overnight, I can make sure that one less family suffers at its hand.

"For a place that's so beautiful," Reese says, closer than I expected, breaking into my thoughts, "it sure feels spooky at night."

Thankfully, she can't see the grin that emerges. "What did you expect? Eden is full of criminals who come out at night to play."

Her breath hitches, and it only makes my sick smile widen.

"What did you think we'd have? Lights hanging from the trees, cute patio furniture, and a fire pit as we relax with our tumbler of brandy, gazing up at the stars?" I shake my head, knowing that's exactly what she thought. "Don't let this place fool you. Its beauty comes with flaws."

We try to be better men, but that doesn't mean we always make the right decisions.

Simeon is barking as we approach the gate.

"Please tell me he hasn't killed him," Reese worries.

"How am I supposed to promise that? You're the one who invited him here."

"I didn't know."

Tennyson's flashlight is aimed in our direction as we approach, and for a brief second, I can see a smile of amusement on his face before he masks it.

"Just in time," he clips, shining the flashlight on the man who is on his knees, whimpering.

There's a part of me that almost tells Tennyson to cut it out. But then there's that other part of me that remembers riding in the back of a cop car on my way to jail. I think Reese could use a little reminder of what happens when you play games you can't win.

"Tennyson," Reese cries, taking a step forward, but halting when Simeon stops her with a vicious growl. "Please don't do this. I didn't know the rules. I'm so sorry."

A pregnant beat of silence hangs in the moist evening air as Tennyson stares intently at my wife. None of us are trusting individuals, but Tennyson, even less so. He's been betrayed in a way that I'm surprised he hasn't burned the world down and taken everyone with him.

Tennyson scrubs the light stubble on his chin. "Tell you what, if you answer this question correctly, I will spare your driver and Simeon will kindly escort him off the property."

Reese turns back, and I shrug.

"Let's say I didn't offer you this deal, and let Simeon have him for dessert? Would you report me like you did my brother?"

I swallow, noticing the tension along Reese's shoulders.

"You are a part of our family now. And what happens in Eden stays between the brotherhood. So, I ask you, Mrs. Cain, will you betray us if we do not spare this man?"

Even the crickets go quiet in anticipation of her answer. This is a test that we've all taken, and at times, we have all failed.

Reese hesitates, her eyes dropping to the man on his knees and back up to Tennyson.

Just like me, she feels the weight of Eden and its presence. She knows what Tennyson wants to hear, and knows what she should say. But that's not who she is. She's fighting her base nature, just like we all do.

Several beats of silence go by before she finally sighs, and the tension releases in her body as her shoulders slump. "Yes, I would report you. This man is innocent. He has nothing to do with my past or my future in this brotherhood."

Tennyson doesn't react, and neither do I. In all honesty, I'm not shocked by her answer.

"So, you would betray your husband again?" Tennyson prods, finally. "For a man you don't know?"

Reese steps up, and Simeon growls, but this time, she doesn't let his growl stop her from approaching the man.

"My husband is a good man," she claims. "He doesn't kill innocent people, but if he does, I would have no problem abandoning my loyalty as his wife to spare a human life. My husband wants justice. He would never take it from someone who doesn't deserve it."

A strange feeling comes over me as I notice chills break out along her arms.

Tennyson smiles. "It seems she knows you rather well, brother. Dare I say, she might even have real feelings for you."

Reese's eyes flare wide.

I know what she's thinking. I told her to make my family believe we are in love. But Tennyson's words speak otherwise.

"You're right," he says, his focus back on Reese. "Van is no murderer, but that doesn't mean the rest of us aren't." A wicked grin pulls onto his face. "Let's see how sacrificial you are when negotiating with a *real* murderer."

Something like pride hits me straight in the chest when she stands taller, never looking back at me for support. She meets my brother's gaze head-on. My fearless little obsession, standing tall, growing stronger in the darkness of the West.

"We'll call it a lesson learned and let your delivery driver go without a scratch on him if you agree to one thing."

Reese tips her chin for him to continue.

"If my brother is the saintly man you claim, then you'll have no trouble agreeing to be his wife for another six years."

CHAPTER TWENTY-ONE

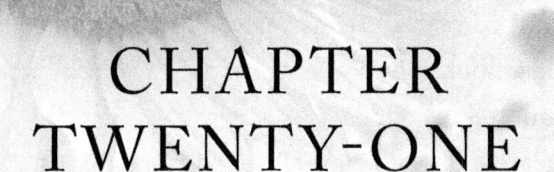

Van

FEW PEOPLE IMPRESS ME. MY BROTHER ISN'T ONE OF THEM.

"Can I ask you a question?"

The walk home was far less amusing than earlier. Reese didn't speak a word the whole way. At any other time, I would have enjoyed every delightful second. But her silence and droopy shoulders are carried with a brokenness I've never seen from her before.

"Depends." I grit my teeth and fight the urge to grab her.

"On what?"

Every muscle in my body hurts as I stand behind her, keeping my hands at my sides.

"On if you can turn around and face me like you have some balls."

I barely hear the tiny snort she lets out. "I hate to be the one to tell you this, lover, but I don't have balls."

"Bullshit." I flip her around faster than either of us expected.

"You have bigger balls than most men I know." She tries to smile, but it only results in a rogue tear streaking down her cheek.

"As my wife, I expect your honesty."

She doesn't move to wipe her face, and I don't either. I'm too concerned that Tennyson took more than her freedom with his deal.

"Whatever you ask of me, I will give you the truth." Even if it fucks with my head all night.

With a slight nod, she pulls in a ragged breath. "Tennyson was never going to kill him, was he?"

"The power of fear is evil's greatest weapon. Fear can take down armies and control our greatest adversaries."

"But no," I continue, "Tennyson wouldn't have killed him."

She nods robotically, dropping my gaze. "Why didn't you step in when he proposed the trade?"

I shrug lazily. "It wasn't my delivery driver's life at stake."

"Six more years as your wife isn't fair."

"You, of all people, know life isn't fair, Flower."

She shakes her head in exasperation. "Our deal was for six years."

"Yes, and your deal with Tennyson added six more. I'm not understanding the problem."

Finally, emotion flows through her. "I. Hate. You."

She says the words slowly, like I couldn't understand them in a normal rhythm. "You think I betrayed you, and you're punishing me for six years as your wife."

I nod. "I'm not confused about our arrangement. Are you?"

Something like shock passes over her face. "Why would you let your brother add six more years when you knew he would never kill that guy? Why punish yourself?"

That's a good question, but not one I'm ready to answer.

I want to punish her, sure, but I also want to tie her to the bedpost and fuck her so hard that her screams border on agony.

"You knew your brother wouldn't kill the delivery driver, yet you let me make that deal."

I did, and I enjoyed every second of it, but that's not for her to know or me to understand right now. So I'll offer her the truth about something else, instead.

"Are you still hungry?"

She throws her head back and blows out a frustrated breath. "Same old Van, avoiding questions."

I grip her chin, forcing her head up, meeting her eyes under the porch light. "Same old sunflower, always fighting a battle she can't win."

She rolls her eyes, and a rush of heat and anger flows through me. My patience snaps as my other hand goes into her hair, gripping the back of her head so hard the only thing she can move is her eyes.

"I'll ask you one more time, love." Leaning in, my breath fans over her lips. "Before I go back into the house and forget all about your rumbling stomach, are you hungry?"

Knowing this conversation is over, Reese admits defeat, but not without adding attitude to her words. "Duh, that's why I ordered food."

Her sarcasm puts a smile on my face. Tennyson didn't break her. No one can wilt my sunflower; she only grows stronger in the dark.

"You have three minutes to change," I clip, dropping my hands and opening the front door. "I suggest you be out in the car in two and a half."

With that, I leave her standing in the doorway with her mouth agape. I literally don't care if I take her in the pajamas she insisted she wear for an hour's nap. There's not much that embarrasses me.

I head to my office, where I keep the keys to the place we're going to eat. But instead of finding it neatly organized and pristine, I find the entire space a mess, with my brand-new cognac open.

Someone's been snooping.

Not that it matters. I'm not stupid enough to leave anything around that my wife could use against me, but interestingly, she spent her time looking.

My girl is resourceful.

She always has been. She can adapt to any situation and find a way out. She's an escape artist. You could say, a common criminal that no one has ever caught, except me. I know her betrayal was an escape plan.

I had drawn attention to the lounge—to the men she had been stealing from. We had common marks, but whereas she just wanted to siphon money from their accounts, I wanted to burn everything they had until there was nothing left.

I used to sit behind bars, wondering if our roles were reversed would I have turned her in to save myself? The criminal in me says yes, I would have done anything to stay out of jail and continue my mission for justice. But there's another part of me that knows I could have sought that justice within a matter of days and not months.

The truth is, I enjoyed my evenings watching my sunflower with her cunning smile and witty personality as she poured drink after drink and closed out tabs after running her client's card through the scanner, allowing herself access to their account numbers.

She was Robin Hood, stealing from the rich and giving to the poor.

I tried to tell myself I needed more time. I needed to be sure I wouldn't get caught—that I the mayor had the information I needed. I had a plan, but I got greedy, and wanted the girl, too.

Hearing the out-of-breath woman at my door, I look up. Reese is dressed in sweats and a tank top and looks like she could settle on the couch for the next few hours.

At least it isn't pajamas.

"I'm impressed," I deadpan, flipping the keys in my pocket, kicking away the pieces of glass on the floor, and walk through them. Her eyes track it carefully.

"I was going to tell you about that," she offers.

A throaty chuckle escapes me. "I bet. Likely, right after you told me you were rooting through my desk."

"I was looking for a pen." There's no apology in her tone, and I couldn't enjoy it more.

"I was going to write you a note and needed a pen."

A VICIOUS PROPOSAL

"How sweet of you,"

"I thought so." A smile graces her face as she shrugs. The memories of earlier with Tennyson seem to lift off her shoulders as each we joke.

"That's why you married me, right? Because of my thoughtfulness."

I cast her a wicked look. "Amongst other things."

Taking her hand, I lace my fingers through hers, not totally hating the feeling.

"Come on," I instruct. "My girls await."

CHAPTER TWENTY-TWO

Reese

I'D BE LYING IF I SAID I WASN'T WORRIED ABOUT WHERE MY husband was taking us.

By the country roads leading away from the city of Atlanta, I know we're not headed to a McDonald's. Like most car rides I've taken with my husband, he stays quiet, seeming to enjoy the midnight drive under the stars and the bright moon. In this light, he doesn't look like an assistant district attorney. He's not wearing a suit; instead, he's wearing casual clothes made up of athletic joggers and a black T-shirt that hugs his muscular torso. He's always favored black attire. I used to think it helped him stay hidden in the shadows, where he could stalk his prey. But now, seeing him in the all-black ensemble only makes him stand out under the moonlight.

"Just so you know," Van says dryly, "there's nothing in this car that you could use to slit my throat." I can feel my brows rising as he continues staring at me.

"That will only get you face down and ass up in my back seat." I don't know if he means anything sexually by that. I don't have time to ask as he turns on his blinker, pulling into an almost hidden driveway. Like Eden, it winds through the orchard trees. Peaches, I think.

"What is this place?" I ask, noting the beautiful grounds under the glistening moonlight, complete with a tennis court, playground, and swimming pool.

"Freedom," he says, offering no further explanation as he parks out in front.

A woman appears at the door with a smile brighter than the overhead lamp as we exit the car.

"Alistair!" she exclaims, opening her arms wide like she expects my husband to run into them like a five-year-old.

Which, he doesn't.

Instead, he leaves me in shock as he strolls up the entry stairs, takes the woman's face in his hands, and kisses her on the forehead. It's the most intimate thing I've ever seen him do with a stranger.

"We've missed you, my love." She wraps her arms around him, not giving a damn that he didn't return her embrace the appropriate way.

"I'm sorry, I've been a little busy. I wanted to get out here sooner."

The woman, who seems to have captivated my husband's heart, pats him on the shoulder. "Oh, honey, we know you're a busy man. We don't expect you to come visit us as much as you do." It's almost like he's embarrassed by her praise. But that can't be right because Van Gogh hates people.

Granted, I've never seen him truly hate a woman, but this seems out of character for him.

"Would you like to introduce us to your guest?" the woman prompts when Van just stands there. His body goes rigid as he stills, and then he stands up straight, gathering himself before he turns, allowing me to see the woman's face as she steps into the light.

The woman looks familiar. Her eyes are a little wider, her cheeks fuller, and her hair's the color of wheat in the fall. She's stunning. She takes Van's hand as he leads her down the staircase towards me.

"Miss Wynn," he says. "I'd like to introduce you to my wife, Mrs. Reese Cain."

Miss Wynn smiles at me, extending her hand as she says my name like it means more to her than a typical stranger. "It's nice to finally meet you." *Finally?* Does that mean she's been anticipating my arrival before I knew where I was going?

"It's nice to meet you, too." Her hand is warm and comforting as I take it, allowing her to pull me into a hug. This is when I realize Miss Wynn is no ordinary woman. She's extraordinary, and it's evident as she leads Van and me through the doors of the grand castle.

I look at Van as she opens the door to the brightly lit dining room, but he won't meet my eyes.

"This is one of the many common areas," Miss Wynn explains. "Every Sunday, we have dinner here, but each apartment has its own kitchen and dining area." She looks back at me when she says, "Mr. Cain insists that each family have dinner together." I nod and offer her a smile. She continues and points to the big TV in the corner of the room.

"When Mr. Cain can't join us physically on Sundays, he makes it a point to be here virtually, no matter the time of day. Mr. Cain always makes sure he's available for us, along with the staff he's hired."

It was then that I noticed all the cameras throughout the common areas. Alistair wasn't being a peeping Tom. He was being a family.

Mrs. Wynn insisted I call her Carol before offering to give me a tour of the grounds, including her own apartment, which consists of two bedrooms, one for her and one for her teenage son, who was too busy gaming to offer more than a hello.

We didn't end up eating in the community dining room, opting for a quick sandwich instead, though Carol assured us that it was no problem to fire up the industrial stove this late at night. Van claimed he wasn't hungry, and seeing how this wasn't a restaurant, I didn't want to put Carol out.

"Thank you for the sandwich and Cheetos.

"I thought, Alistair…" I use his real name instead of Van because I don't know if these people know who he was in the past. If they're anything like me, they wouldn't care anyway. But Van doesn't air his dirty laundry. My guess is they have no idea who he really is.

I shake my head and give her an apologetic smile. "I thought Alistair was taking me to a restaurant or something."

Carol wraps an arm around me. It feels motherly—something I've never experienced before.

"How long have you known Alistair?" A toothy smile graces her face, like it's her favorite question.

"I've known Alistair for nine years, not nearly as long as you have." I nod, but a nagging sense of guilt overtakes me. "But you'd be surprised how little I know about him," I admit. "We had a whirlwind romance."

"Those are the best kind."

If she only knew.

"I suppose, but sometimes I wish we would have gotten to know one another better before getting married." Carol gives me a slight squeeze as we walk down the corridor decorated with wall art, the most prominent being a finger-painted sunflower. Actually, they're *all* sunflowers. I still, taking in each one as Carol stands next to me.

"Alistair's mother loved sunflowers."

"I didn't know that." Carol pulls one of the frames off the wall and holds it in front of us.

"She was like us, you know." I nod, but I had no idea.

"She raised Alistair in a place similar to this one." My stomach knots as I think of the story Van once told me of how a fire raged in the group home his mother lived in, killing many, including her.

"Van's mother had Down syndrome?" I asked for some reason. When Van mentioned a group home, my mind immediately thought of a psychiatric home or a substance abuse group home. Never did I think it was Down syndrome.

She nods, gazing at the picture of Alistair's mother.

"How? How can that be?"

Carol smiles at me sweetly, knowing that my questions are coming from a place of complete education.

"Women with Down syndrome can have children. It's rare, but they can, and while the condition is a genetic mutation, most of the time, it's not hereditary."

Van has always been rare. His rage. His hate. His love. Everything that makes up Van Gogh is rare.

Carol puts the frame back on the wall and smooths her fingers over the glass.

"After the fire, my mother used to wake up at night screaming."

"Your mother was there?"

Carol nods. "Alistair was working that night, helping bus tables at the café next door. I think he was only fifteen at the time. When he saw the flames, he ran over and came through the back door, where he found my mother trapped in the community kitchen. He was able to rescue her and a few others before the smoke overtook the building."

My heart sank at the thought of a teenage Alistair, watching in horror as flames engulfed the only home he knew.

"The fire department came, but by then, the roof had started caving in. The firemen found Alistair on the fire escape, trying to find a way back inside." She blinks back tears. "Rebecca was standing at the window, a look of pride on her face. I think she knew that was the last time she would see her son, and I think in that moment, she was proud of the man he would become." Carol swallows as if it pains her to keep going. "It took three firefighters to pull him to safety. That poor boy kicked and screamed, fighting with everything he had to free himself, but they held firm, and that sweet boy watched as the smoke took everything he'd ever known." I didn't realize I was crying until several tears streaked down my cheeks.

"I didn't know this part of the story."

"He tried to save her. My mother said it was horrifying as they watched, hearing the poor boy's screams as he called for his mother over the sound of the roaring flames."

Carol pauses for a moment, not bothering to say what happened in the time between. We all know Alistair didn't find his mother that day.

Like coming out of a trance, Carol shakes her head and offers me a sad smile. "My mother never saw Alistair again. Not until he found me five years ago and told me of his plans to open this place."

"Is your mother still alive?"

Carol shakes her head. "She died a few years ago."

"I'm sorry."

"It's okay," she says, patting me on the shoulder and walking. "She lived a good life. We all have. Thanks to Alistair."

CHAPTER TWENTY-THREE

Reese

U NLIKE VAN, CAROL WAS A DELIGHT THE ENTIRE EVENING. I hated to leave. Freedom House was warm and welcoming—a distinct difference from the castle-like mansion where we've returned.

"I thought I might find you down here." His dark gaze lifts over the top of the computer screen.

"And I thought I promised consequences if you returned to this room."

How cute. He's pretending to be the villain after showing me his secret lair of women and children with special needs that he funds with all those billions of dollars he inherited.

"You know, Alistair"—I use his real name for the simple fact that he showed me the real man behind the flames—"I'm starting to think your threats are merely harmless flirtations."

Even in the dim light, I see his jaw flex, but I'm not like everyone else who retreats at his punishing stare. I move toward it, enchanted by the haunted boy buried beneath.

"I think you want me to break this burden of a façade you carry."

My steps are calculated as I stalk toward my violent husband—the man who rests only when justice is served.

"I think Van Gogh is tired of being merciful while Alistair Cain barters his justice away."

He chuckles darkly. "You have it all wrong, sweetheart. Alistair Cain has always been the warden of Van Gogh's dark cell. After all, he is the reckoning you pleaded for when you left Van Gogh to burn." He's lying.

"Shall we make a wager on it, then?" Using the tip of my index finger, I tilt his chin so he looks into my eyes.

"What did you have in mind?"

I don't miss the way his eyes light up. Dropping his chin, I move my hands to his knees. "If you admit you're a good man," I offer, parting his legs and easing my body between them, "then I'll allow you to add two years to my sentence." My knees touch the cool floor.

"And if I don't?" he challenges.

I offer him a polite shrug. "Then…"

His eyes flare with a punishing desire as my hands slide up his thighs. "You'll shave two years off my sentence."

A vigilante arsonist who is known for his extreme reactions looks at me like I've lost my mind. Maybe I have, but if that's the case, I'd argue I lost my mind the second I locked eyes with him many years ago. I knew there was so much more to this man—okay, fine. I didn't think that initially. At the time, all I knew was that he was hotter than indigestion after a fireball. But after that thought, I knew he was much more, even if that more was a common criminal.

Either way, I had to know who I was falling for.

"No." Van's deeply annoyed baritone pulls my attention back to the unsettled deal between us.

"The only way you will leave this marriage early is by God's will. So, unless you're praying for your heart to stop, it will beat at my side until I shatter it between my cold, dead hands."

Now he's just showing off.

"You could have just said you loved me. You didn't have to woo me with those sweet promises."

I was a sure thing after seeing the community he built and protected. But this hateful *I love you* is more romantic than that time he was too embarrassed to propose and chose to blackmail me instead.

Van's mouth twitches at the corner, seeming to consider smiling before he locks it down into one of his trademark looks of boredom.

"Do you need time to regroup and reconsider another plea deal?"

He thinks he's freaking cute with these negotiation tactics, but the thing is, I'm not like the defense attorneys he's used to dealing with. Like him, I'm a criminal—and we've never played by the rules.

"No, counselor. I wish to proceed with the trial." Those dark eyebrows rise in shock.

"I'm not scared to go against the famous ADA Cain," I offer. "I've faced him many times before." I flash him a wicked smile right before he lifts his hips, helping me jerk down the waistband of his pants, revealing snug black boxer briefs underneath. "And I still don't understand the hype that surrounds him."

His cock strains against the soft fabric as I inch closer, my lips parted in pure need. It's one thing to know a man wants you, but it's another to know that you can take down a man with nothing but your body. I don't need Van to tell me that he cares for me or even finds me attractive. Van has never been good with words. His passions have always been revealed through his hands. Unlike when we first met, a match isn't clutched between his fingers.

Instead, his hands are clenched into fists as the black titanium wedding band gleams against his whitening fingers. I can tell it's taking every ounce of restraint for him not to reach out and touch me.

"Whether you admit it or not, under that blazing hatred is a good man who hides his love behind his flames and protects it with the very thing that's destroyed him: fire."

Before I realize it, his fist is in my hair, and my head is yanked backward.

"Don't talk like you know me," he threatens viciously, hiding behind his truth.

I can feel the edge of my mouth curl into a smile. "I may not know you as intimately as a wife should, but that's about to change." He leans back against the leather chair, pulling me with him.

"Are you saying you intend to know me as a wife should?" A layer of caution coats his question, and tingles swirl in my belly.

"It depends," I answer, relishing the feel of his punishing grip. "Will you have me as your wife or as your prisoner?" It's a fucked-up question to ask your husband, but then again, Van and I have never been like everyone else. Our marriage is more than a sentence. We aren't the people who ask for permission—we take it by any means necessary. Don't think I'm oblivious to the fact that Van could have punished me in several ways. If he hated me as much as he claimed and knew where my sister was, he could have turned me in to the police.

I assure you, after what I did, their punishment would be much worse than marrying the man I wanted to run away with years ago.

Van's fingers comb absently through my hair, his eyes far away on something I'll likely never know.

"Alistair," I whisper, making his eyes dart back to mine. "I asked you a question." Leaning into his touch, I hold his gaze in challenge. "Will you claim my body as my husband and mark me as yours?" And then I do something completely stupid.

I chuckle and say, "At least for the next ten years?"

Let my mistake be a reminder to every woman that men—especially temperamental men—have a breaking point. Once you find it, proceed carefully, but never, ever plow through it without a pain reliever in your purse. You. Will. Be. Sore. Tomorrow.

Suddenly, I'm yanked forward, chest to chest, against a man who people fear. Yet, it's not fear I'm feeling as his heart pounds against mine.

"Let me assure you, *Wife*, you will bear the scars of our marriage. No one will ever look at you and not know who you belong to. Even after twelve years." He flashes me a wicked smirk. "Like any artist, I sign my work. Even if I have to burn my name into your flesh, everyone will know you are mine long after I'm gone. You will forever be my beautifully flawed sunflower."

He slides his hand out of my hair and puts it at my waist. Before I realize it, we're standing at the fireplace. It's not on—not yet. But like anything with Van Gogh, the fire is coming.

"You know what to do," he whispers in my ear, his hands tightening around my ass cheeks, and God help me, I do know what to do.

I reach into his pocket and find the matches he carries at all times and drag it against the box, watching the flame rise. "Are you sure you want to do this?" I ask, just as he flips the switch to the gas.

For a moment, all we do is just stare.

Van Gogh is a man of few words. I don't believe he's going to suddenly admit his love for me. But I also know that he isn't threatening me. He isn't giving me more time as his prisoner; he is simply staring at me with more emotion coming from his eyes than I have ever seen. That, ladies and gentlemen, is all it takes for me to know that this man still loves me just as much as I love him. He may hate me, and he may not trust me. But somewhere deep down inside of him, he must know that I didn't betray him.

Without any words. I toss the match into the fireplace, and the flames jump in celebration as the man who set fire to my town lowers us to the ground with me still straddling his hips.

"You don't want to do this in the bed?" I ask him.

"Do I look like a bedroom type of guy to you?"

"No." He looks like a *fuck by the fireplace* guy to me.

"But still, how comfortable can it be?" I ask.

He chuckles. "The better question is, how comfortable is it going to be for you?"

His sweatpants are still down, hanging low on his hips. But it's his words that creep up inside my heart.

"Do you think I'm a good man?"

"Yes."

"I'm not. I'm your husband, and before I claim you as such, you will ride my fucking face. You will fuck my mouth until I tell you to stop."

I was a second away from objecting and telling the infamous Van Gogh where he can shove his arrogance, but then the realization hit me. I get to shut Van up with my pussy. This man deserves a smothering like no other. And what better way to give it to him than by pleasuring myself?

"All right, Husband." I rip off my T-shirt and toss it to the floor. I'm not wearing a bra or panties because it's after nine. Who wears bras or underwear after nine? Instead, I straddle him, wearing nothing but my bravery.

"Are you scared of me, Flower?" That's the same question he asked me when we reunited in the woods. And just like then, I'm not scared.

"Are you scared of *me*?" I tease, my voice light and playful. There's something thrilling about having control of a man. Especially one as infamous as Van Gogh. So, when his back touches the floor, and his eyes lock on mine, nothing but sheer pleasure courses through my body.

"We won't stop," he reminds me. "Not until I say."

And I won't stop. Not until he says. I know he's a good man. He's more than just a vigilante seeking justice that he didn't get for himself. He's done more for this world, for his mother and himself, and for that, he can be proud.

I delight in the way his throat works as he gazes upon my bare body. It's the first time he's ever seen it.

"You like this dark side of me, don't you?" I memorize the way his eyes pierce me with conflicted hate. He can deny it, but the truth always comes out. Van feels something for me, something that never left even after all these years, and that knowledge is enough for me. I move up his body, hovering my bare pussy an inch over his face. "Are you scared to touch me, Husband?" His hands move like lightning as they flash beside me and grab on to my ass. I'm thrown forward onto all fours. And then there is no more taunting. I'm consumed with the heat and fire of Van's mouth as he pulls my lower body to his face, smothering himself in my wetness and my desire. There's no talking, just a thrill and the heat, as Van says everything with his mouth. He works me to a fever pitch. His tongue pierces my center and stretches me to the point of sheer bliss.

His tongue laps and worships, consuming me as if I'm a forbidden treat.

Van and I have always burned bright around one another.

We are combustible materials. We are tortured souls. But in the heat of one another, we become one.

And the moment that I feel him bite my clit, sucking fantastically hard, he stops. His breath falls in uneven pants, as his mouth glistens with my need, but it's his eyes asking for permission that sobers me. Van Gogh doesn't ask, he takes. "Ride my cock," he finally growls, seeming to find the dark side of himself again.

"No," I pant. "Not until you say it." He knows what I need. And from the way his hard cock presses against my ass, begging for entry, I know exactly what he needs, too.

He wants to claim his wife, and he wants to do it his way. But not today.

I recite the sentiment I swore I'd never honor. "From the vows we've taken, my body is yours, and yours is mine. You will sacrifice your desires and compromise for mine."

Van's hands dig into my side seconds before letting out a vicious roar that sends my heart straight into my throat.

"I'm not a good man!" he growls. "But I can be… with you."

He doesn't give me time to digest his words. Instead, he steals my breath as he slams my hips over his cock. He doesn't allow me to ride him and claim him as my husband. Instead, he fucks me from below, grinding himself deep and hard and angry. It's everything that's inside of him boiling to the surface. He is a good man but would never want anyone else to know.

"Say it," he growls. I guess I'll say it right now.

"I am not your prisoner." I can see the strain in his neck as the veins protrude. "Say it right now," I pant with seriousness.

"What am I to you?" Another silent second passes by, and his hands come up to palm my breasts.

And then he roars, "You. Are. My. Wife."

We come together, collapsing onto one another's sweat-slicked chests.

CHAPTER TWENTY-FOUR

Reese

"**S**AY IT ONE MORE TIME."

This man and his ridiculous threats.

I let out a big sigh and roll my eyes dramatically.

"If I reveal who you are, my sister will burn, blah, blah, blah." I cast him a grin and hold up two fingers. "If I attempt to run or ask for help, I'll burn with the poor soul who was stupid enough to help me." My eyelid quivers as the mascara brush drags along my bottom lash, coating my annoyance with Van's signature color.

No matter how Van Gogh paints himself, I know the real person behind the art. "Good," he clips, ignoring my theatrics and blah-blah-blah insertions. "I do not care to repeat myself."

Thank goodness. I drop the mascara wand into the sink, not even bothering to cap it in its reservoir. It was old and empty anyway, and my cheap ass was trying to salvage the last little bit of color from the outside walls. It leaves a mark in Van Gogh's sink, and I see his gaze narrow at it.

"Would you like me to clean it, sir?" I offer with a teasing lilt to my voice. His eyes flash up to mine.

"No," he clarifies. "I'll clean it, and you can suck me off while I do it." There's the man who struggles with feelings.

"Whatever you want, lover." I shrug my shoulders and brush past him. "Hurry. I don't want to be late." Van doesn't know I've been habitually late to Professor Arden's class. I might be the teacher's assistant, but I am not an example to the students about punctuality.

Van Gogh continues to stand still and unemotional, like a wannabe sociopath.

"Hello…" I prompt. "Did you hear me?"

Van's head doesn't turn in my direction, but his voice is loud and clear when he says, "Don't fuck with me."

"Why?"

"I have very little patience for people. Much less for people plotting against me." It's like ice freezes inside me, and my muscles lock up from the cold of his threat.

"I'm not plotting against you," I counter. "I didn't before, and I'm not now."

Some people may be stupid enough to go against Van Gogh, but I'm not one of them. Not to say I don't do stupid shit. I do, but I don't do anything that betrays the only man I've ever loved.

There's a stillness in the bathroom that wasn't there before. All the joking, teasing, and bullshit rules that were threats seem to be locked in the stagnant air as Van Gogh gazes at the empty spot where I was standing.

"Run, my love," he threatens, his voice calm and collected. "Run as fast as you can. Hide behind the women's shelters you feed with the money you steal from hacking wealthy men. Pull out every weapon you have against me, my darling, and run. But know that every whisper you feel on the back of your neck is me inching closer. Every ounce of sweat dripping down your forehead is my heat behind you—coming for what's mine."

The moment is so eerie that I can't even find it in myself to make a snarky comeback about what is *his*.

"I will find you, my love," he continues, unaware of the chills breaking out along my skin. "You will pay for every second you are away."

I could crack a joke about how hardcore criminals are treated better than me. But Van doesn't seem to be in the mood. It already took a blow job and excessive begging to convince him that I wouldn't run if he allowed me to go back to work. Don't get me wrong, I thought about it. But the thing is, I could have run many years ago, and we both would have enjoyed the chase.

I've never needed a companion, and neither did Van Gogh. I had no friends, only a sister I hadn't seen in years. And Van had no one. We have both been isolated from everyone we had ever known by circumstances beyond our control. We didn't ask for a lonely life but were handed one, nonetheless. Running is our specialty. But not this time. Not anymore.

"Are you done?" I pitch my voice a little lighter, hoping he doesn't notice the fear he instilled deep in the bottom of my soul, where it belongs.

"Yes," he says slowly, carefully, like he isn't so sure.

"Okay, then. Let's go to work."

Like a traditional suburban couple, Van and I drive in silence, taking sips of our coffee, which he actually brewed.

"Don't ruin someone's life today," Van clips as soon as he pulls into the college and parks.

"Ditto, my love." I get out of the car without another word and slam the door a little extra hard before flipping off Van Gogh or Alistair, whatever the hell his name is today, and head into Dr. Adler's accounting class.

My eyes scan for Blake, who's riding the back row like the slacker he is. His eyes rise from his computer and find mine, as if he feels my gaze.

I wiggle my fingers and give him a little wave and smile, mouthing silently for him to meet me after class.

Fifty-two minutes later, Professor Adler dismisses class early, having a secret agenda of banging the girl in the front row.

"What do you want?"

I laugh, a hearty chuckle at the audacity this fucker has. "What do I want? Well, that's a new one for you."

I could feel eyes drift in our direction from the lingering students. So, like the criminal I am, I loop my arm around Blake's, ignoring the way he jumps, and pull him towards the door.

"Can't I just have a conversation with my boyfriend?" I pretend as if the camping incident never happened as we walk down the hallway.

Blake's eyes flip from side to side frantically.

"If you scream for help," I threaten, just as Van Gogh did me earlier, "then the next time, it will be more than your tent that catches fire."

Blake's arms stiffen, and he flashes me a hateful glare. "I knew you were angry. I knew you tried to kill us."

Let's be real here. He knows about as much as a mosquito knows about pest control.

"Well, darling"—I smile as the crowd parts around us as we walk through the busy hall—"let that be a lesson to you: If my jealousy results in a campfire, what in the world am I capable of when I'm angry?"

Blake's mouth drops into a frown. And honestly, I don't know why I didn't try this tactic before. Van was right. Fear is a great motivator—the best that ever existed.

We walk out into the open air, and immediately I feel the warmth of the sun.

But she grows stronger in the dark.

I can hear Van's poem of his sunflower repeat in my head. That makes me smile. The romantic fucker.

"Okay, Carmichael, tell me what you want."

Without further hesitation, I yank Blake to my chest and put my arms around his neck so it looks like we're the happiest couple on the whole fucking planet. Leaning in, my lips to his ear, I whisper, "Your uncle. I want a meeting with your uncle. The chief of police for Orange Grove, South Carolina."

CHAPTER TWENTY-FIVE

Van

FUCKING BLAKE.

Just seeing her with him burns me from the inside out.

I lift the flask from inside of my pocket, pry open the gas tank with my key, and pour cognac into this fucker's gas tank before getting back into the fucking car.

Fuck my wife and her disgusting habit of betraying me over and over again.

Let me remember that she is my prisoner, not the woman I love.

The only vow I mean to take seriously is *till death do us part*. And hopefully, hers will be painfully slower than mine.

After a rather enjoyable plotting session of Blake's death, Reese finally appears through the passenger window, flashing me a smile I don't return.

"Unlock the door," she hollers through the window.

This time, I smile and flip her off like she did me this morning. "Walk," I instruct, tapping the gas hard enough that the car lunges forward. I watch her situate herself on the sidewalk from the rearview with a grin that she'd hate.

"Are you shitting me right now?" Her eyebrows shoot up her forehead as she hurries to my side, where she belongs.

"I assure you," I clip, "I am not *shitting* you. It's prisoner work detail. Your job is to pick up trash on the side of the road as you walk home."

Lest she not forget, she is a prisoner, not a real wife.

She lets out a deep sigh and bangs her fist on the window before she composes herself and her anger. "Okay," she chides. "You had a bad day. What's it going to take to make it better? An ice cream? A nice little blow job?"

She says the last bit, like all this time she's been fucking me just to get on my good side, and it meant nothing. That alone sends me into a rage as I rev the engine and pull out of the parking space with fervor.

I crack the window. "You have two seconds to start walking—in front of the car."

She gasps. "In front of the car so you can run me over when the mood strikes?"

Look at my wife, coming up with all the fun ideas.

Flashing her a spiteful grin, I take a deep drag off my revenge cigarette and release the smoke in one blow. "You walk, or I put this cigarette out in Blake's gas tank, and we can both enjoy the flicker in his eyes."

Reese's eyes lock on mine in fear.

Yeah. I fucking saw you.

"It's not what you think," she starts, but I've had enough. I'm done with her lies and her excuses.

"Walk," I repeat. "I won't ask you again."

Did I not warn her this morning? Did I not tell her what would happen if she asked for help?

"It's not what you think."

It's never what I fucking think and always what I *know*—the smell of betrayal.

"I hate you."

"And yet your hardened nipples suggest otherwise."

Reese may fool Blake with her fake persona, but I know the woman she is to her core. She loves the hate in me. My vengeful words are her personal lullaby.

"People will stop you. They won't let you chase me with your car."

My brow rises. "Your expectation of others has improved. Tell me, love, has Blake filled your black heart with promises of a better life?" I cluck my tongue. "You should know better. People like us never get happy endings."

"You don't know that," she argues pitifully.

"You're right. I have been wrong before. I'll amend my statement and say you might have gotten your happily ever after before you betrayed me."

She rolls her eyes defiantly but doesn't offer to feed me more lies. "The police will pull you over. They will ask why I'm walking in front of your car."

This again. "All right, love. Since you seem to take exception to my punishment, I'll offer you another." I nod to the car next to us. "Lie face down over the hood of that car."

"That's Blake's car." She gasps.

"It is, and after he sees my hand ripen your ass cheeks to a beautiful pink, he'll never forget that you belong to me."

Her eyes widen. "That's archaic. I'm not a possession."

"You're correct. You're a prisoner."

"No! Last night, you admitted I was your wife, not your prisoner."

It takes all my strength not to fly into a rage and burn this entire college down. "That was before you left my bed and ran into another man's arms."

"For fuck's sake, Van. I didn't run into his arms. We were having a conversation."

"That ended with a kiss."

My words stop her cold. "Oh, my." A wide smile plumps her cheeks. "Tell me it isn't so. Is the infamous Van Gogh jealous of a commoner?"

I scoff. "That would delight your simple mind, I'm sure, but no. I'm not jealous of your college boy toy. I merely like to remind my prisoners that they are never free."

"Bullshit." She lets out this very unladylike snort and doubles over, dragging breaths between fits of laughter. "You are jealous. Big, bad Van Gogh is jealous over a business major."

That's it. Fuck it. I've had enough of her mouth for today.

Throwing the car into park, I barrel out of the vehicle, grab her by the upper arm, and haul her over the hood of fuck boy's car.

"Go ahead," she wheezes, as tears of laughter streak down her cheeks. "Show Blake how not jealous you are. Show him how deeply you care about your prisoner."

My mind is clouded with fury that this woman can work me into such a frenzy to the point I behave like a psycho.

"Here"—she tugs one side of her leggings down her legs—"I'll help you."

She manages to work her leggings and underwear down to her thigh, baring the smooth, creamy skin of her tight, rounded ass. "How's this, my lo—"

I slam my hands onto the hood, caging her in by pressing the weight of my body against the back of hers. "Stop taunting me before I fuck you and mark your lover's car with your orgasm."

Her laughter seems to die with my anger, morphing into something far more dangerous.

"Go ahead," she whispers. "Spank me. Punish me for speaking to another man."

Our breathing quickens as I press my hard cock against her ass. "You weren't just talking to him. You were asking for help."

She shrugs from under me. "It doesn't matter what I was doing. You wouldn't believe me, anyway."

She's right, but I don't think she wants verbal confirmation.

"You're a man of proof, not my word. So, until I can prove my loyalty, you can think I was whispering sweet nothings into Blake's ear and dreaming that it's his cock pressed against me."

And... she went too far.

Before I realize that I've moved, my palm stings against her warm skin, shutting her up with a loud smack.

"Say you love me," I roar, unhinged. I couldn't give more fucks if I had them. This woman makes me crazy enough not to care that I'm an assistant district attorney in the middle of a parking lot of a mediocre college, spanking my wife against a frat boy's car, demanding she admit she loves me.

Maybe Shakespeare is right in believing love makes us killers because right now, all I want to do is kill Blake for giving my wife the upper hand by exposing my need for her.

"Say it, Reese!" My hand stings her ass again just as she moans.

"I love... Biscuit."

Fuck her.

My palm comes down again. "Stop toying with me, dammit."

She chuckles, twisting her head to look me in the eyes. "I'll admit it if you do."

I hate her. I absolutely fucking hate her.

"Say it, Van. Say it so the whole world understands what happens when Van Gogh loves."

I could leave her here—let Blake deal with her annoying ass. Punishing her is too much like punishment for me.

"Tell me, Van. Tell me why I'm on Blake's car with my ass feeling as if it's on fire. Tell me—"

Fuck!

"Because I fucking love you!"

CHAPTER TWENTY-SIX

Reese

HE LOVES ME.
It's not that I didn't already know that, because please, what man stalks you, makes up some bullshit that you betrayed him, and punishes you by forcing you to be his wife?

A crazy man in love, that's who.

But hearing him say the words feels different. It feels... real.

And yes, I understand I had to taunt him into admitting his feelings, but Van Gogh has the patience of a lion. He can sit for hours, watching his prey before he attacks. He stays calm and in control and doesn't get flustered or deviate from the plan when his prey toys with him.

But he didn't with me because that hard-headed man with his eight-pack of glorious abs *loves* me.

And as crazy as it is, I love him too—every mean and snarky inch.

I don't care what anyone says, that's true love.

Our love might be twisted, but it is a love that supersedes mistakes and misunderstandings.

My phone buzzes next to me where I lie naked in Van's bed, covered with only a sheet that survived Van's wrathful pounding. The man needed an outlet after admitting his love, and my vagina was happy to provide.

Blake: He's agreed to meet with you. We leave early Thursday morning.

Eww.

Reese: That's not going to work for me.

Van will kill us both.

Blake: It's the only way it works, sweetheart. You either make it happen, or you don't speak with my uncle. The choice is yours.

I hope someone bites his dick off one day.

Reese: Fine. I'll be there.

Someway, somehow, I'll make it work—I have to.

After deleting the messages—just in case Van gets nosy—I pull the sheet around my naked body and pad into the kitchen to look for Van.

"Anyone here?" I call out into the open space, hearing my voice echo in the vaulted ceilings. "Hello, warden?" I giggle at the term. I should have known behind all the threats, Van was a gooey, wannabe warden with an ass that looked as if it were sculpted from steel. He's as much a threat to me as Biscuit is.

Shaking my head, I chuckle. I knew I loved this man for a reason. He's—

A buzzing noise interrupts my train of thought. I can't quite grasp what it is, but it sounds familiar as I amble towards the back of the house to check it out.

Knowing Van, he probably paid someone to put bars on the door so he never has to worry about me talking to Blake again. That's if he agrees even to let me go back to school again.

As we lay in bed last night, Van issued about two billion threats if I didn't tell him what Blake and I spoke about. Of course, I didn't tell him shit except that he could take those threats and shove them between his tight white butt cheeks. My business with Blake is not his concern. When I'm ready for Van to know, I will tell him. Until then, he'll just have to continue to pound out his frustrations into my pussy like a good husband who... oh, my gosh.

My breath catches in my throat at the sight before me.

My husband is...

I blink several times, as if that will change what I see through the French doors: my husband, the vigilante, shirtless and on his hands and knees, pulling weeds out of the garden bed as he hums along to the radio. He looks like a true Southern gentleman ripped right out of a magazine.

What arsonist do you know cultivates a garden—a billionaire arsonist, at that? Van could easily pay a gardener to tend to his plants, but he doesn't. He protects what's his—that which enriches this world with a purpose.

He values life.

My heart feels too big for my chest. This man—this enigma of a man—is extraordinary.

He might be a hard-ass, scary motherfucker on the outside, but on the inside, he is protective and kind. I bet his mother smiles down from heaven every morning as she watches her beautiful boy-turned man, care for the most vulnerable. Heck, I'm proud of the bastard. He's so much more than he lets anyone know.

"You know," his voice pulls me out of my revere, "you could get a better look if you came closer."

My eyes snap from the beaded sweat on the back of his neck to the half smirk on his lips as he turns to face me. "Most wives," he continues, like the ass he is, "would offer to help."

I snort, that comment finally breaking through the haze of

admiration. "No, they wouldn't. Most wives would offer to bring you something to drink."

"I'm not thirsty." The playful expression on his face falls.

Well, well. Look at that. My husband can be more than a threatening criminal. He can be a shy and caring guy.

A grin tugs at my mouth. "Breakfast, then?"

"No." His bottom lip seems to become fuller.

Is he?

No way. It can't be.

The infamous Van Gogh is pouting. Pouting!

"Are you sure? I was thinking I—"

His growl of annoyance interrupts me. "I said no."

He said no.

Look at him, being cute this morning, thinking I give two shits about what he says. "Well, that's too bad, lover." I step out onto the back patio, my bare feet connecting with the cool concrete. "Because most wives would ensure their husbands are well fed while working in the yard."

I ignore the sarcastic scoff coming from his direction and continue across the covered patio until my feet step onto the dewy grass. "Go back inside," he orders, not bothering to turn around and face me, "before something out here bites you."

Two of us can play this game. "You promise?"

He whips around, his eyes narrowed and jaw clenched as he notices how close I am. "I suggest you find something else to do this morning. Pissing me off isn't one of your options."

"That's unfortunate." I flash him a wicked smile that promises much more than aggravation. "And here I was, hoping we turned a corner last night."

His hardened gaze finds mine. "Not unless you want to tell me what you were conspiring with Blake about."

Oh, yeah. I forgot he was still hung up on that little nugget of information. "I'll tell if you do." I flash him a pointed look. "Where's my sister?"

Immediately, he stiffens.

"Is she dead, and you're trying to keep it from me?" He knows he'll have no leverage to keep me here if Julia is dead. Without her, I have no reason to care if I'm arrested and convicted. I only ran from the crime scene because she made me. I knew. I freaking knew she would tell the police it was her and serve out my time, or worse, Robert's druggie friends would find her first and kill her.

I have no idea what happened to my older sister, and that mystery keeps Van's ring on my finger. Well, that, and I love him. But just because I love him doesn't mean I am ready to live cooped up in his fancy dungeon forever.

Van turns back to his garden as if I didn't ask him if my sister was dead. "So, you're just going to ignore me?"

"Yes."

There's no hesitation.

"You don't think I deserve to know what happened to my sister?"

"I think you deserve to pay for your crimes for what you did to her boyfriend."

I try. I *really* try to stay calm, but I can't. I lose my shit on this man.

"He was abusing her! What was I supposed to do? Let him kill her?"

Van yanks what looks like grass away from a flower. "You were supposed to call the police and report him."

Fuuccck him. "Is that what you would have done?"

"No." He tilts his head so he can see me. "But you aren't like me."

"Of course, I am! That's the whole reason I wanted to run away with you."

"You wanted to run because you felt guilty." His eyes hold mine. "You've dedicated your entire life to making up for your sins. But your sins can't be atoned by good deeds, my love."

Well, at least we're back to *my love*.

"They can only be forgiven. There is no going back. What's done can never be undone."

Give me a break. Who let Mother Teresa in here?

"I know that, *Van Gogh*." I say his name like a curse. "I'm not trying to make up for what I've done. I'm simply trying to help other women like my sister."

Van's lips purse as if he's holding back a smile. "By helping other women get away with murder?"

"My sister didn't murder Robert. I did!"

I gasp and clap my hand over my mouth. It's the first time I've ever admitted what I did aloud. It's sickening.

"I didn't mean to hit him that hard," I say after a moment. "I just wanted him to stop hitting her."

Van chuckles. "From the photos I saw, I say you managed to do that and then some."

"It's not funny, Van."

I should have known my husband would find humor in the mistreatment of an abuser. That's absolutely his kind of justice.

"Actually, Reese"—he says my name in the same exasperated tone I said his in—"neither of you killed him."

I swear the earth stops mid-rotation until I can catch my breath.

"What?" Did he just say Julia and I did not kill Robert all those years ago?

"No. You're wrong. He wasn't breathing when Julia pushed me out of the house and told me to run."

Van, always politically correct, rolls his eyes. "Oh, well I stand corrected, then. Tell me, which one of you is a doctor again? I could have sworn you were both teenagers at the time. I highly doubt either of you knew where to even check for a pulse."

Apart from wanting to punch him in the face, he does have a point. Did I check for a pulse? Did Julia? Or did we freak out and think he wasn't breathing?

"How do you know this?"

This time, the bastard does smile. "You think I'd let an actual murderer join me on my quest for vengeance?"

This man. "You had me investigated!"

He scoffs like I'm an idiot for even thinking such a thing. "I remember you calling it stalking."

"You mean, you didn't have someone from law enforcement check into it for you?"

"Yeah," he quips sarcastically, "because I wasn't going from town to town, burning down the homes of dirty cops and mayors."

Oh, right. "Well, still. You could have told me back then!"

"And what would you have done differently if you knew you didn't kill Robert?"

I know what he's doing. He's setting me up to say that I would have run back and found my sister—that I would have never started hacking and funding various women's shelters.

"I don't help battered women because I feel guilty."

He shrugs. "I guess we'll see."

We'll see if I don't smother his smug ass in his sleep.

"I don't get your deal. Why tell me now? You think I'm going to run back to my sister now that I know I'm not wanted by the authorities?"

"Why stay away when you don't have to?"

He's trying to push me away. I taunted him to admit his feelings for me, and now he regrets it. Well, that's too fucking bad.

"Why not tell me where she is and see for yourself?" Because he doesn't trust that I actually love him. He thinks I'll run, and it'll take him years to find me again. But unlike before, the only leverage he'll have is this bullshit fire Detective Lee thinks I started. I'm positive I can get Blake to drop those charges.

"Unless… you're scared—"

I don't see him jump to his feet. I only see the door slam in my face after he shoves me inside.

CHAPTER TWENTY-SEVEN

Reese

I DIDN'T HAVE IT IN ME TO GET MAD.

Okay, well, I was mad for a while and sat at the door, glaring at my secretive, emotionally fragile husband until I grew hungry. It wasn't like Van looked back to see if I was sitting there, plotting his demise. Nope. He just kept on working like nothing was freaking wrong.

Am I relieved to know I didn't kill Robert? Sure. But I still want proof. I've never known Van to be a liar, but why keep my sister's whereabouts a secret if I didn't kill Robert? Julia said she would take the blame and tell the cops it was her that hit him with the cast iron pan.

We didn't have long to think our plan through. We were both runaways who had rented a room with Robert and his friends. It was only a matter of time before someone came home and found him lying in a pool of blood.

So, I took the pan and ran, holding Julia's promise that she would call me when she was safe. It's why I always send money to women's shelters. As runaway teens, they were the only places we trusted not to send us back to foster care after our parents died. Not that we gave them a chance to do it. We moved quickly before people could get suspicious. It wasn't until I met Van in South Carolina that I started to relax. If Van could get away with burning down a cigar lounge the mayor owned, then I was perfectly fine living in Orange Grove and lusting over a hot-as-sin arsonist.

We were a match made in bad decision heaven.

I shove another handful of chips into my mouth, not bothering to be ladylike by using a bowl. I've never seen Van eat anything but vegetables, so I figure he won't mind if I eat from the bag since he likely gags at the sight of processed food. After all, the refrigerator and pantry I found stocked full of food had to be for me—or the safety of delivery drivers in the area.

You know, that's probably the source of Van's attitude. He eats nothing but homegrown food that someone probably grows on this property somewhere. The man needs some sugar and carbs! When I'm angry, I can usually stop it with a handful of gummy bears and Hot Cheetos, but seeing how Van didn't buy any, I'll have to improvise and bake him some cookies. I'll call them Asshole Reducers. The cure for the common cunt.

We've been arguing for an hour. The cookies are cold and still wrapped in a napkin on Van's bedside table. Not that their being cold is all Van's fault. After I finished baking the tastiest cookies in Georgia, I ran into our room—see how I used *our* and not *Van's*? Van should take note. Anyway, I found my naked husband freshly showered, asleep on the bed with my traitor of a cat curled into his side.

Something came over me, and it felt a lot like jealousy. I'm not ashamed to admit that I moved that damn cat, stripped off my clothes, and took her place next to my husband. Immediately, his eyes opened, and I did what any loving wife would do. I threatened his ass. No one needed him to make a big deal about my jealousy or that I was snuggling with the bastard. I simply told him to close his eyes and go back to sleep before I set his precious cat on fire.

He did, and we both slept in peace for several hours.

Now, it's a whole different vibe.

"For fuck's sake. Can you not be a paranoid criminal right now? I swear, I'm not going to kill you. Just close your eyes and open your mouth."

Those dark brows arch sarcastically. "Your pussy might cloud my judgment on most of your requests, but not enough to close my eyes and expose my throat to the enemy."

And we're back to that again. "I'm naked." I sweep a hand over my body to punctuate a fact he already knows. "You can see I'm not armed."

"Therein lies your problem, Mrs. Cain. You never learn."

After several ridiculous seconds of dramatic pause, he slips his hand under the sheet and reveals a book of matches.

Have mercy on my soul—this freaking man.

Snatching the matches from his hand, I level him with a scolding look. "Therein lies your problem, Mr. Cain. Even when you know the truth, you still can't manage to trust."

"I don't know the truth. I know your version of the story."

"Aka—the truth," I interject.

"The only truth to a story is that there is none. Truth only exists in the eyes of the beholder—the rest is merely a perception of events."

"That's bullshit, and you know it." I strike the match against the strip, and the flame flickers between us.

"Don't lie to me, Flower. I can see it in your eyes. You're hiding something."

I hate that I care what he thinks of me. If he wants to paint me as the villain in his story, I should let him. Amongst other things, a little humility could do Van some good.

"You're wrong."

My eyes never leave the flickering flame.

"Is this what it feels like," I ask solemnly, "to be behind one of your flames? Where fear becomes resignation?"

"That depends." His words are shrouded by his low tone that's made the strongest of men plead.

"Depends on what?"

As much as I've grown comfortable around this man, he still can incite fear with two words.

"Only if you're resigned."

I don't see him move until his fingers break my gaze on the flames.

"I have a video of you walking into the police station that night…" His fingers dance over the flame, soaking up the blistering heat as if they are starved for its pain. "Are you ready to tell me why you chose that day, of all days, to betray me?"

"I didn't betray you."

He sneers and plucks the match from my grasp. "You sat there, wearing a deputy's jacket, while they descended from their cars and took me to the ground." He chuckles, but there's no humor in it. "You waited until I was stripped and behind bars before you left the station… arm in arm with the detective."

Reaching up, I tangle my hand with his, the heat a brutal reminder that Van Gogh and I only burn brighter together. His silly beliefs be damned. "I had a flat tire and no spare. He stopped to help."

I expect him to swat my hand away, but he doesn't. He grips my palm against his, the calloused skin underneath a rough reminder of the damage they've done. Except, it doesn't scare me; it calms me, just like his flame and promise of destruction in the name of justice. It's my own personal lullaby.

"This accusation has grown tiresome, husband," I coo, spinning the wedding band around his finger. "The brick that's built my prison is more entertaining."

An intrigued hum sounds in the back of his throat. "Careful, Flower, the brick that lines the federal penitentiary also loves to listen to the lies of the guilty."

Our hands dance over the flame right before Van brings the heat to my lips. His eyes find mine, watching me intently with a smile that only means one thing—mischief.

"Put it out."

He's got to be kidding.

"And if I don't?" I offer, cocking my head to the side, studying his hazy gaze. "If I let it burn my prison to the ground, preferably with you in it?"

His laugh vibrates his chest. "Let's not play with fire, Flower. It has a way of scarring those who misuse it."

So I've been told. But if there's one thing Van Gogh loves, it's my scars—especially the ones of his doing.

"Scared?" Heat burns my bottom lip, searing the skin, but I keep my hands tangled in the sheets. If anything, my suffering would only humor him, and that's something I can't have.

My lips part on instinct, letting the cool air brush past the pain. It helps for a moment, but Van doesn't wait long before bringing it closer, the pain reaching my tongue.

The burn feels intimate in our twisted way—painful but intimate. It was a test of sorts—one I've failed in the past.

But before I can close my lips around the blaze, Van invades my space and settles his tongue over mine, soothing the ache. The flame diminishes on our tongues, its bright light dying with its maker.

An arrogant grin pulls at Van's lips as he drops the match onto my pillowcase—a silent reminder that I'm just as capable of controlling the flame as him.

Something I never thought Van would ever share.

And for some reason, my stomach flutters at the sentiment that it's me.

But he can't know that.

"Your tongue only intrigues me for one reason, and your little party trick isn't it," I bark, pushing up and away from his sculpted body. That is, until he pulls me back down.

"Don't pretend, Flower." Amusement dances in his eyes as the sheet falls, leaving me bare and exposed to the enemy. "You enjoyed the pain just as much as I did."

The urge to slap him weighs heavily inside me.

I made a mistake thinking things would be different now.

No number of angry confessions or sex-filled nights will change the fact that Van Gogh and I are not real lovers.

Part of me, the delusional part, just thought it may have been enough.

But I was wrong.

Van Gogh still thinks of me as a traitor, and if my words can't convince him that I'm innocent, my stained soul certainly won't.

"And if I did?" The question lingers between us. "Would that excite you?"

"Not in the least," he muses, smoothing his fingers down my thighs like he's mesmerized by the sight. But I know the only thing that mesmerizes my husband is the glow of his enemies burning.

"Good, because I despised every minute of it." My fingers fall to his chest—tracing the tattooed sunflower that lingers there.

"The way your tongue molded to mine spoke otherwise."

He's insufferable.

"I came here for a reason, and I'm not leaving this bed until I get it." Puffing my chest, my boobs bounce slightly, enough to catch his attention. His eyes never stray from my chest as I'm reminded of the internal question of what happens to the sunflower that favors the darkness of the West.

Will he torch it and turn it into nothing but a beautiful memory?

Or will he mourn it as he paints the others in ash?

At this point, I'm not so sure.

"You'll leave my bed when I command it."

There he is, my husband, the asshole.

"Well, command it after you indulge me," I say, lifting his chin so our eyes meet. "Please. Trust me and open your mouth—taste something for me."

His eyebrow arches, creasing the smooth lines of his forehead. "Trust? Don't be foolish."

Before I realize what's happening, his arms snake around my thighs, and he thrusts me forward, my center hovering over his full lips. "But taste, I can do."

I press my hand against his chest. "You can taste me after you taste what I made for you."

It's like I flipped his bitch switch. He sits up, shoving me off his face, and grabs one of the cookies, taking a huge bite. "Done. Now sit on my fucking face."

CHAPTER TWENTY-EIGHT

Reese

HE'S CHOKING.

I'm talking, throat grabbing, turning blue-style choking.

"Van!" My scream falls on deaf ears as I spring from the bed and rush to his side on the floor. "What's happening?" Tucking my hands under his head, I study his face for some kind of answer.

"Bathroom," he manages to garble out. "I need Epi."

I don't know what the hell Epi is, but I rush to the bathroom, throwing open every drawer to search for it. With no luck, I pop my head back into our room.

"What does it look like?"

The sound of his wheezing fills the room, but he manages two whispered words, "Yellow, injector."

"What? A yellow injector?"

A VICIOUS PROPOSAL

His breathing is shallow as he melts to the floor.

Crap.

A yellow injector... I have to find a yellow injector before he dies in front of me.

Darting back into the bathroom, I toss everything that isn't yellow or an injector onto the floor. "It's not here!"

He tries crawling toward me but collapses, his hand reaching out to me. "H-help me up," he stutters.

Dashing to his side, I try lifting his shoulders, but it's useless. "We need to call 9-1-1."

"No."

"Now is not the time for you to be stubborn. You're going to die if we don't."

His voice is merely a whisper. "Then I'll die."

The hell he will. "You have two seconds to tell me where the injector is, or I'm calling an ambulance. I don't care what you say or do to me."

Even on the brink of death, he manages to flash me a glare that promises retribution. "Top drawer. Taped to the underside."

What in the utter fuck?

I sprint back into the bathroom, but not without yelling, "Why is it taped to the underside of the drawer, Van?"

Who does that?

Van, apparently—someone who would rather die than let anyone know he has a severe allergy.

Reaching my hand under the drawer, I find the auto-injector under a slab of tape, exactly where Van said it was. Rushing back to his side, I hold the pen up like some grand prize.

"I've got it."

But I don't revel in my accomplishment for long because his skin is red and splotchy, and his lips have turned blue.

"Van." His body is stricken with sweat as I shake him and place the injector in his hand. "I have the medicine."

177

His eyes barely open as he struggles to bring in air. "You have to do it," he murmurs breathlessly. "Stab it into my leg."

His eyes close again, and I think he's passed out, but I'm not sure.

Crap, crap, crap.

The device looks bulky and scary, like I'm about to stab him with a knife.

The directions say that I should swing my arm and press it into his thigh until it clicks. Inhaling, I pull in a deep breath, read the directions one more time, and then swing my arm down and press the pen into Van's leg. He barely jerks, and I hold it there for ten seconds like I'm supposed to before removing it.

I don't know what's supposed to happen, but when Van sucks in a deep breath and exhales, I know it worked.

"Are you okay?" I'm back at his side, smoothing his hair and watching his lips regain color. "Can you talk to me?"

"You tried to kill me."

Out of all the things he could have said, he chooses to say something stupid.

"Yeah, yeah. I know you love me," I retort. "And you're welcome."

He chuckles, but it sounds more like gurgling. "You want me to thank you for trying to kill me?"

"I didn't know you had food allergies! That's what you get for keeping secrets from your wife. Who even does that?"

"Me," he mumbles. "My enemies would love to know how to kill me and make it look like an accident."

I roll my eyes. "Not everyone is trying to kill you, for goodness' sake."

His chest is rising steadily now, and his breathing is much better. "Sometimes, Van, you have to take a chance with people—especially your wife. I could have killed you. And Magda!" I throw my hands in the air. "Does she know?"

"Yes," he clips, opening his eyes and finding my gaze.

"Ahh. So, it's just me, then?"

He tips his chin almost as if he's ashamed.

"Whatever. I'm glad you didn't die." I'm pissed as I stand up. "I'll go get you some water."

I just want to get out of this room and rid myself of the feeling that I'll never be able to get close to my husband. I'll always be in his outer circle.

"Wait. Don't leave." His hand clutches mine before I can stand up.

"I'm not leaving," I say. "I can't. Remember? I'm your prisoner."

His gaze drops to his chest. "I'm sorry. I should've told you."

Something in the way he says it convinces me his apology might be genuine this time.

"You have to know I would never try and kill you." My palm goes to his cheek, and he leans into my touch. "I love you. I've always loved you."

My words aren't taunting. They aren't meant to get a rise out of him. They are meant to simply state the truth. I have always been in love with Van Gogh. He needs to know that. He needs to know that I did not turn him in all those years ago, and I certainly would never try to kill him.

"I—I." He swallows thickly and squeezes his eyes shut. For a moment, I think he's trying to fake passing out, but then his hand squeezes mine tightly, and he says, "Ditto."

Ditto.

I don't know if he could possibly get more romantic, but maybe I'm just weird. I don't need my husband to repeat the words verbatim. I just need to know that he feels them, and if saying the word ditto is all he can manage, I'll take it with a smile.

"So, you believe me now?" I ask, a teasing lilt in my voice.

"Maybe. Let's not move too quickly."

This aggravating man.

I smile. "How do you feel? Can I call an ambulance now?"

"Not unless you *really* want to be chained up in the basement."

He's insane—absolutely insane.

"Someone needs to check you out," I argue. "What if this comes back?"

He pulls himself up into a seated position, still holding my hand. "It won't come back. I'll be fine. I promise."

There's one thing I know: When you become a wife, you become responsible for certain things. For instance, scheduling doctor appointments and haircuts—not that I've done that for Van yet, but I know it's coming. Why not start now?

"You're going to the doctor," I demand, "or I'll chain you up in the basement." I nudge his shoulder, and he goes back easily, proving that he wouldn't be able to stop me in his current state. "Now, tell me who to call."

"You did great," Enoch assures me. "You saved his life."

"And I almost took it, as well." I laugh, but there's no humor in it. "I had no idea he was allergic to cookies. I added milk to the recipe to add moisture. It was in the refrigerator, for goodness' sake!"

Enoch smiles. "He wanted you to have everything you needed."

"Well, I need him to live and tell me he's deathly allergic to milk products in the future."

"You won't have this problem again," he tells me, patting me on the back as we stand in the kitchen with a cup of coffee.

Van agreed to let me call Enoch, who called a doctor friend, who came to check him out. The last thing I needed was Van dying in the middle of the night and Biscuit eating his remains.

"It takes Alistair a while to trust," Enoch explains. "It doesn't seem like he trusts you, but he does. He would never let you live here if he didn't."

I don't know how Enoch can be so sure. "He threatens to chain me up in the basement all the time. I think that's pretty damning evidence that he doesn't trust me."

"Psh, that's how he communicates love. Don't let him scare you off."

If he didn't scare me off with the arson and stalking, he most definitely wouldn't scare me now. "I won't. I just wish he would open up to me more."

I don't know if Enoch is aware of the terms of our arrangement, so I don't elaborate. As far as he's aware, we are simply two people in love, trying to figure out how to navigate this marriage thing together.

"Oh, my dear. If you only knew how my son was before, then you'd know that he has opened up." The elder man faces me. "And we owe that all to you." He pats me on the shoulder and turns to leave.

"Where are you going?"

No way is my husband going to let me live after this. I need a witness or at least a referee.

Enoch flashes me a comforting smile. "You'll be fine."

I'm starting to think Enoch has no clue who my husband is. "Okay, if you say so."

"I say so. My son will not harm a hair on your head."

He sounds so sure of Van's nature that I don't argue, even though I am highly skeptical. "Will you stop by in the morning?"

At least so my sister has a body to bury, in case you're wrong.

"Sure. How's brunch sound?"

Like long enough for Biscuit to chew off my cold, dead finger. "Maybe a little earlier. Like in an hour?"

A deep chuckle goes through the old man. "I can see why he loves you so much."

Huh? "He loves me because I'm paranoid?"

"No," he corrects. "He loves you because you're never afraid to speak your mind. You'd be shocked to know how many people are scared to stand up for themselves—especially to my son."

Yeah, the man knows his son is freaking scary.

"I'm serious, though." I get back to the issue at hand. "Will you stop back by?"

Enoch turns, heading toward the front door with a chuckle. "Don't worry. The medicine the doctor gave him will knock him out until brunch. You're safe. Enjoy some freedom while the warden is down."

And the truth will set you free…

The teacher, aka Father Enoch, knows his son is a straight-up demon.

Yet, he loves and forgives him… just like me.

CHAPTER TWENTY-NINE

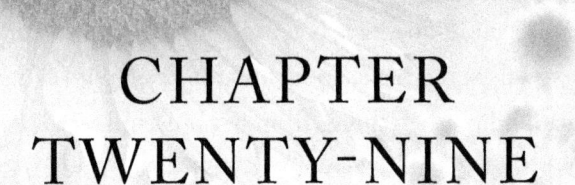

Van

MY HEART FEELS READY TO EXPLODE, AND IT'S NOT FROM fucking love.

"You tried to kill me!" I bark at my wife, sounding like a drunk frog from the antihistamine the doctor gave me. If I weren't so pissed, I'd scratch my skin off until I passed out for the rest of the day. It's been a long time since I've had a reaction this severe. I've forgotten how shitty it feels.

"I didn't know!" she screams, no longer treating me as delicately as she was earlier. "You're supposed to tell your wife that you have a severe milk allergy!"

"Dairy," I correct. "It's not just milk that you can kill me with; yogurt and sour cream work just as well."

She jams her finger into my chest. "It's not funny! You should have told me! You shouldn't have stocked it in the house!"

"I did it for the DoorDashers," I tease. "I didn't want more blood on my hands the next time you got hangry."

She belts out a laugh, her cheeks turning a slight shade of pink. "You are such a liar."

And fucked up the ass. When did I risk my life for love? Hell, when have I ever cared if someone was hungry or comfortable in my presence? Never. Never have I cared about someone like I do my aggravating wife.

"And you're a beautiful killer."

She sits up and pokes me in the chest. "For the last time, I wasn't trying to kill you."

"I know." I shouldn't have been so wrapped up in worrying about what she was talking to Blake about and the possibility of a pussy apology for withholding such things from her husband.

"So, why not tell me?" Her voice is soft—a gentle caress that stirs my dick through the fog of drowsiness. "Haven't I proven that I love you? That I care about you?"

What is proof, really? As an attorney, I can spin anything into proof if I need it to win a case. Did the camera catch you entering the store that was robbed twenty minutes later? Based on that information, I'd argue you were the thief, but your lawyer would argue you were buying a pack of smokes and using the restroom when the crime occurred. Everything is perception—even cold, hard facts.

Does my wife love me unconditionally as I do her? Did she try to hate me for punishing her? God knows I tried to hate her. I tried to make her into a monster who betrayed me, but I kept circling back to that summer when she begged to run away with me.

She was never scared. Never judgmental about who I was or what I'd done. She accepted me for everything I was and everything I wasn't. I wanted to be a better man for her. I wanted to take care of her and keep her from harm.

I saw redemption in Reese Carmichael—redemption I thought I would never have after I failed to save my mother.

But I could keep Reese safe.

I could find happiness again.

As long as we were together, we could heal from our pasts.

But then I was arrested, and the new beginning I dreamed of turned into a nightmare until Enoch came along.

Finding Reese's hand, I interlock our fingers and gaze into her eyes. "On my first birthday, my mother gave me whole milk as my pediatrician recommended."

Reese gasps. "Oh, no."

"Needless to say, I reacted the same back then as I did today. Except, my mother had given me a bottle in the playpen while she took a shower." I shake my head, remembering her tears as she told me this story when I was old enough to understand. "I wasn't breathing when she found me."

Letting go of my hand, Reese lies beside me, draping one arm over my chest. "I can't imagine how scared she was."

I nod. "The paramedics were able to revive me, but when they took me to the hospital, my mother was met by a social worker. They were concerned that a mother with Down syndrome couldn't care for a child with an allergy that severe. They asked about the whereabouts of my father, and that's where things apparently took a turn.

"The Hanson House had several births that year. The facility was suspicious that someone had been purposely impregnating these women or, worse, raping them, but no one was talking—especially not my mother."

"You think your mother was raped," Reese adds.

I yawn, feeling the medicine trying to take me under. "I don't know what I think. She was always adamant that she loved my father and that he was a good man, but she never told me his name. She didn't want him to get in any trouble."

"Why would he get into trouble?"

"Because he didn't have Down syndrome."

Reese scoffs. "And? What does that have to do with anything?"

"Well, you'd be surprised how many people will assume abuse before love. Granted, there's history of unspeakable things happening to women with disabilities, but still, my mother found love and didn't want anything jeopardizing that until he came home."

"Came home? Where was he?"

I shrug. "She wouldn't say."

"So, what ended up happening with the social worker at the hospital?" I can tell Reese is holding back a dozen more questions she'd love to ask, but she knows me well enough to tread lightly. I don't know why I'm telling her all this in the first place. Maybe it's because I'm tired and my defenses are down, or it's simply time to confide in someone other than Enoch.

"They allowed my mother to take me home on a conditional basis."

"Which entailed what?" She huffs, disgusted with people she doesn't know. "Someone periodically checking up on her?"

"Basically, but that's not what I remember sucking the most." I make this low noise in my chest, fighting back my anger whenever I think of them. "My mother's parents were never any help to us," I start. "To this day, I've never met them. They wanted nothing to do with me, even after she passed. They were positive I was the product of rape and disapproved of their daughter's choice to proceed with the pregnancy. I think losing them was the hardest on my mother, though she never admitted it."

Reese's head settles on my chest, her hair smelling of rosemary and mint. "Fuck them right in the armpit."

I chuckle. "Yeah. We never wasted any energy thinking of them, but they aren't what used to depress me." I find a smile, thinking of the first time I handed my mother a yogurt. "My mother loved yogurt more than anything. I would see her look longingly at it every time she saw anyone with it in the community dining room. We couldn't keep any dairy products in our apartment because of me. Even when I promised our social worker I wouldn't touch it, she still said no. It was a precaution."

The self-loathing I fight off every day blisters under my skin. "I heard the rumors. I knew some children there weren't conceived out of love. My mother had been through so much because of me. Her parents disowned her, social services and the police were always up her ass, and she couldn't even have a fucking yogurt. I was sick of being a burden."

"I'm sure she would disagree that you were ever any trouble."

I laugh, but it sounds half-asleep. "I was always a nightmare, but she was a saint and would never admit it."

"So, what did you do?"

Leaning my cheek to Reese's head, I sigh. "I got her killed."

"What?"

I push Reese's head back down to my chest. "Do you want me to tell you the story or not?"

"I do, but what the fuck, Van? You can't just drop that tidbit and expect me to sit still."

"That's exactly what you will do if you don't want me to stop."

Her body relaxes next to mine. "Fine. You're so sensitive."

And she's so brave to be talking to me like that.

"Anyway, before someone interrupted with theatrics, I was about to say that I started working at this café across the street, bussing tables and washing dishes. I wasn't old enough to be working, but the owner knew we were residents at the Hanson House and agreed to pay me off the books. With my first paycheck, I went to the grocery store and—"

"Oh my gosh! You bought her yogurt, didn't you?" She jumps up and plants a rough kiss on my lips. "You sweet, sweet, man. I knew I loved your ass."

Ignoring her ridiculous outburst, I shove her back to my chest. "Would you like to finish the story since you know so much about it?"

"I'm sorry, please continue, sweet boy."

I don't know if I'm more annoyed that she called me a boy or that I was sweet again. I'm neither of those things, and I'm about to cut her bedtime story short by shoving my cock down her throat until I pass out from the meds.

"This is the last time you interrupt me," I threaten, gripping her hair and giving it a slight tug. "Got it?"

She tries nodding, but I hold her head still. "My lips are sealed."

They better be.

"Anyway, I brought her yogurt—a lot of it. It was the first time I'd ever seen her cry. I knew then that I would spend the rest of my life making her happy. She'd done so much for me; it was the least I could do. So, I started with the person I believed made her cry the most—my father."

My stomach clenches. I've never shared this with anyone, not even with Enoch. "I started asking questions, meeting with the teens my age, seeing if their mothers had shared anything about their fathers. I was able to piece together enough information that led me to a contracted groundskeeper—"

"That's the guy you asked me to find, wasn't it?"

Did I not ask her to stop interrupting? "Yes. It was."

Neither of us commented that she could never provide his name since I was arrested the night she was supposed to give it to me.

"I broke into the administrative office the next night and couldn't find any records for groundskeeping."

She gasps. "Those administrative fuckers destroyed them!"

I nod. "I thought so, but I never got to ask since the very next day, the Hanson House was nothing but a pile of ash."

Reese sits up and holds my eyes. "You asking questions did not lead to your mother's death."

She's wrong. My mother kept my father a secret for a reason, and I opened the portal to hell and let the demon back in.

"You wanted to know why I didn't tell you about my dairy allergy." I place my palm on her cheek. "It's not that I don't trust you or question your devotion. I simply don't ever want you to be without because of me."

If she ever needed proof of how much I love her, this would be Exhibit A.

CHAPTER THIRTY

Reese

Thinking I had killed Robert doesn't feel as bad as sneaking out of Van's window. It's early Thursday morning, just as Blake requested, and I'm running across the grassy hills of Eden, toward the gate, where I will proceed to walk a mile, maybe two—just far enough so the Uber driver can pick me up without Tennyson or Simeon detecting my escape.

In all honesty, it's not like Eden is a true prison. But for some reason, Tennyson likes to comb the grounds at night. It's like he's watching for someone or is overly paranoid of burglars. I'm unsure, but I won't repeat my mistake. I know Tennyson is out here now, and I'm prepared.

The air is calm and cool in the wee hours of the morning as I approach the gate, seemingly undetected. I pause and look to the left and then the right, ensuring I wasn't followed. So far, so good.

I make it about a quarter mile down the street before a car approaches that I know is not my Uber driver. The blacked-out paint, rims, and low beams tell me the driver of this car wants to go undetected.

I slip off the shoulder of the road, heading toward the fields in case I need to run. I don't know where I would go because it's nothing but endless hills and open pastures. But it's better than being chased by a serial killer.

The car pulls to a stop beside me, and I'm readying my muscles to sprint for the race of my life when I hear a familiar voice. "Well, well, well. Look who we have here. Someone's going to be in trouble."

I whip around and see messy, dark hair and fathomless eyes that look void of anything peeking from the window.

Shakespeare.

My heart sinks to my toes. It's not just Tennyson that walks these hills at night. Shakespeare does, too.

"I couldn't sleep." I lie. "I was going for a walk."

A dark brow, illuminated by the car's interior lights, rises. "Outside of Eden?" he asks sarcastically.

At this point. I know I'm caught. There is no way Shakespeare won't tell Van I was out here. The best thing I can do is mitigate the damage. I need to meet Blake so I can talk to the chief. Van and I will never be able to move on if I can't prove that it wasn't me who turned him in that night. He may love me, but he doesn't trust me. And love and trust go hand in hand in a healthy marriage.

Casually, I smile at Shakespeare. "Is this not Eden? I thought you guys owned all of this land."

Shakespeare makes a tsking noise. "I highly doubt that. Why don't you get in the car? Let me take you back to your husband. Scary things lurk out on this road."

I am 1000 percent sure he's talking about himself. "No, no, that's okay. I would hate to interrupt your drive. I'll turn around and go back the way I came."

The door unlocks. "I insist. My brother would kill me if he knew I left his wife alone in the dark."

And he keeps sounding creepier.

"He won't mind. He knows I do this all the time."

"Oh," Shakespeare says, holding up his phone. "Well, then, he won't mind coming to get you. It's a long way back—at least a quarter of a mile. You might catch a cold, which would anger the Prince of Vengeance."

I might catch a knife to my throat if I keep playing these games with Van's brother. But I know better than to run from a predator. They love the chase. So, like the idiot I am, I let out a big sigh and walk toward Shakespeare's car.

"Fine," I tell him, yanking open the door and dropping onto the leather seat like a petulant child.

Fair is fair. He caught me. The question is, will he return me to Van, who will go crazy? Or will he take me somewhere worse?

The doors lock, and immediately, I turn to Shakespeare, finding a wicked gleam in his eye as the interior lights reflect in them.

"I know that look," he claims. "That look is trouble."

I swallow thickly. "I don't know what you're talking about."

Deny, deny, deny. He can't tell Van anything that he doesn't know.

"No judgment here, darling. I love trouble. So, tell me, where are you really headed?"

This is insane. I am about to be bound and gagged in the back of this man's trunk. I can feel his crazy vibe chilling the hair on my arms. But since Shakespeare loves trouble, maybe he'll love it more than tattling.

"Okay, fine," I admit. "I need to see a friend. He's not really a friend, but I need to meet him."

"What's his name?" Shakespeare doesn't bother with pleasantries.

"Blake?" I say it as a question. "Yeah, his name is Blake. He was blackmailing me not too long ago. Van's not his biggest fan. To be honest, neither am I. But he has something I need." It's like word vomit spills out of me, confessing exactly what I'm feeling to a man I don't know.

"And this Blake... he's a bad guy?"

I almost ask him to give me a range of comparisons, but I don't. That would be insulting, and I need Shakespeare to be on my side right now.

"I wouldn't say he's a bad guy. More like a shitty guy, but not bad. You know what I'm saying?"

A smile creeps along Shakespeare's face. "I got you. But how about, just in case, I give you a lift over there, for my brother's sake?"

Nothing in his tone backs up his words. Shakespeare is not doing this for Van. He's doing it for the thrill.

"Are you going to rat me out to my husband?"

"Do you want me to?" His eyebrows waggle playfully, pulling onto the road. "Sometimes, those result in the best makeup sessions."

I'm sure they do.

"No, that's okay. I'll tell him when we get back." That way, I can soften him with the truth of who turned him in that night.

"Whatever you want, sweetheart."

Chills break out along my skin when he says the word sweetheart. I don't know if it's the seductive tone in which he says it or how he fingers the chain around his neck.

"What's that?" I ask, referring to the small glass vial hanging from the silver chain. "Don't tell me you're a vampire, too."

His brows furrow. "You know more than one vampire?"

"No." I chuckle. "It's just an inside joke between your brother and me."

He still seems confused.

"When I first met him, he always came out at night and lurked in the shadows. Part of me thought he could be a vampire."

"And me? Why would I be a vampire?"

I point to the vial on his chest. "Your necklace. Does it contain the blood of your enemies?"

As if I just told him the funniest dad joke ever, he burst out in laughter for several seconds. "No, sweet girl. Not blood—poison."

Immediately, we both go silent as the air turns serious.

"Like your husband, I have my vices, too. My enemies don't escape flames; they accept their fate with the law, or"—he fingers the vial of poison—"they do the world a favor and spend eternity where they belong."

HOLY. SHIT.

Did he say—You know what? I don't even want to think about what he means. Some things are meant to stay a secret.

"So, what do you do for a living? Are you a lawyer, too?" I try changing the subject because damn. The guy scares the shit out of me.

He scoffs. "I look like a lawyer to you?"

No, not really, but admitting he looks like an assassin seems rude. "Van doesn't look like a lawyer, but he is." I shrug. "You guys are full of surprises."

"I'm no lawyer." He says lawyer like it disgusts him. "I'm a profiler."

"Oh, cool! Like the TV show?"

He rolls his eyes. "No wonder Van locked you away. You're far too innocent for this world."

What the heck? "I'll have you know, I'm a hacker. I've stolen thousands of dollars from wealthy men over the years."

Shakespeare chokes on his laugh. "That's called a gold digger, sweetheart. Hackers destroy the lives of their victims, not steal vacation money from them."

Could I punch him and run before he catches me?

"I'm not a gold digger," I argue.

"You're no hacker either."

"We'll agree to disagree."

He shrugs his shoulders like he doesn't give a fuck either way. He's made up his mind about me, and nothing I can say will change it.

"So, this Blake guy..." he finally says after several minutes of silence. "He won't hurt you?"

I can't tell if he's worried about me or eager to kill. "No, he won't hurt me. Now, the chief of police that we're going to see, I'm not so sure. But if I had to guess, I'd say he won't hurt me either—bad PR and all."

Shakespeare grunts like he'll believe it when he sees it. "And where, exactly, are we meeting these two upstanding men?"

"The university. Blake wants us to go together."

A deep rumbling that could be a growl or a laugh fills the car. "Blake better adjust his expectations. You go with no one but me."

Great. Just what I need—another territorial man with a hero complex.

CHAPTER THIRTY-ONE

Van

FOR THE FIRST TIME IN A LONG TIME, I SLEPT WELL.

I should've known that would be a problem.

Rolling over, I slide my hand over the cool sheets, finding only the fluffy cat beside me. "Where is your fucking owner?" I ask Biscuit, not expecting an answer. "She better not have done anything stupid."

Biscuit looks at me like *of course, Reese has done something stupid. What would a day be like if she wasn't going against my wishes just to piss me off?*

I let out a big sigh, hang my legs over the bed, and stretch. The medication still lingers, but I am not nearly as tired as yesterday. Standing, I lumber to the bathroom and quickly shower, checking my phone as soon as I finish. Several texts and emails from work await me that I'll deal with later, but the one that stands out to me is the text from Bach.

> **Bach: You're not going to like what I need to tell you. Get your mind right before you head over. I don't want to kick your ass this morning, no matter how much it puts me in a good mood.**

Somehow, I know this has to do with Reese. Call it intuition from stalking the girl for years. "Reese!" I call out. "Get the fuck in here."

She better not make me ask again. After all that *I love you* shit and a near-death experience, I'm in no mood to worry about her more than I already do.

"Reese!" I'm pulling on clothes, my voice becoming louder each time I call her name. "You won't like it if I come find you." I don't know who she thinks I am. Some forty-year-old dad who plays games for fun? Not hardly.

"Don't be stupid, Reese. You can't escape me."

Doom seems to settle around me as the only noise in the house is mine. My wife is on the run.

Quickly, I take out my phone and text Bach.

> **Me: Where the hell is she?**

I don't know what pisses me off more, the fact that she ran or that I trusted her again.

People are fickle. I know that firsthand. They will go to great lengths to get what they want. Reese is a very good actress. She's always been able to convince me she is not like the others, yet I still haven't learned my lesson.

No more. I am done with Reese Carmichael.

She'll no longer be my brutal sunflower, rather she'll be my wilting example. Anyone who crosses me will feel the heat of my vengeance and bear the scars from my retribution. And once I'm done marring her supple skin with my flame, no one will ever spare her a glance without knowing I was there.

Bach never answers.

He waits for me in the House of Enoch. He's lucky I've deemed it a part of my home or else I'd burn it down with him inside it.

Descending the stairs and reaching my car, I hightail it up the hill, where everything looks like it should, and march into my first and only home.

"Bach!" My yelling goes unanswered, but the music filling the upstairs hall gives him away. Bounding up the stairs, I find my brother perched on the bench, bent over the piano, his bloodied music sheets littering the floor.

Although, the one that sits upon the piano is crisp white—untainted by his vice. A new song plays on the keys as he presses each one with precision and focus. We've all seen Bach play before, but never before a piece was done.

"Do you like it?" His voice carries over the sound, his eyes still plastered on the moving keys. He's never asked for our opinions before—mostly because he doesn't give a shit whether we like his songs or not. They're not for us. I don't plan on changing our system today.

"It's fine," I clip. I came for Reese, not to ease his insecurity. "Where is my wife?"

He tsks, holding up a finger that isn't strumming a key. "I would tell you, but I'm not finished."

His gaze settles back on the grand piano he had Enoch buy when he was found and sworn into the brotherhood. It was his only request, and Enoch stupidly delivered. Now, we can never escape Bach's depressing lullabies.

I don't have the time or the patience for this.

Lunging forward, I grip the collar of his shirt and yank him forward so I'm in his face. The bastard smiles, much like I would have, but it still pisses me off. Letting go, I push him back, and he barely wobbles. He grins like he's discovered all my weaknesses and returns to his song.

"Do you think she'll like it?"

What the fuck does he care?

"My wife"—I enunciate the words in case he's forgotten whose prisoner she is—"prefers something more chaotic. Such as my flame biting her skin when I burn the lies from her."

A laugh bursts from his chest. "In that case, I'll up the tempo. After all, we all need to be laid to rest to a melody of our liking."

My eyebrows arch, and I'm immediately in his face again. When Enoch chose my brothers and the covenant was formed, he commanded we not cross each other. It was written that we were forbidden to harm anyone—our brothers included. But threatening my wife may be my breaking point.

"After all, I'm assuming once I tell you she ran off with Blake and one more favorite person of yours, you'll kill her for giving you a headache. I was preparing."

He's so full of shit.

He wasn't doing this for me. Or Reese.

He's twisted and likes watching me squirm under my weakness.

"If you don't tell me where she is, I'll kill *you* for inducing a headache."

His eyes roll at my empty threat before he takes the clean music sheet and scribbles something with a pen that he grabbed from his coat pocket. I can't make out what he's writing until he drops it to the floor over all the bloodied ones. Plucking it from the pile, I make out his cursive handwriting, a quote covering the notes.

"*Woe, destruction, ruin, and decay; the worst is death, and death will have his day.*"

Shakespeare.

She fucking left with Shakespeare. Blake is annoying but not a threat. However, Shakespeare…

Something like worry claws at my throat.

Bach stands and rounds my side, where I'm frozen in place, my blood simmering with rage. His hand finds my shoulder as he motions to the sheet in my hand.

"You keep it. You can set it ablaze next to her body. It's normally my signature, but in your case, it will be your freedom."

Bach steps in front of me, his eyes finding mine. "An end to all ends—where death finally parts you both."

Part of me wants to kill Reese for leaving my side, but the weak part wants to find her and protect her from the horrors that my brother can inflict. Maybe that's why I set the paper on fire right there, watching as the ashes fall around my feet. If I do kill her, sheet music won't fall on her grave. The petals of the eastern sunflower will be right next to where I burn beside her.

Bach snatches the paper from my hand, and I happily let him. "We both know you won't do that, though. Your newfound feelings for your wife have made you soft."

He'll burn, too.

Right after Tennyson, who's been eavesdropping, with Simeon sitting at his side as he drags his hand along his head.

I don't bother with niceties.

"My wife is my prisoner to punish as I please." But right now, the urge to punish her doesn't rage inside me. Only Blake and whatever lie he fed her that convinced her to run from me. Reese has always been easy to fool—promise her something pretty on the other end, and she'll do whatever you wish.

Freedom.

Her sister.

It's all too easy.

But I wasn't the only one Reese confided in. Fucking Blake knew her needs just as much as I did. For some reason, she believes he can provide them, but when I find her and torch Blake at her feet, she'll realize her only option is me.

1

"I'll ask one more time." I clip as Bach holds one of Blake's friends by his throat in his overpriced dorm, right next to a picture of him, Blake, and Reese at one of their many bonfires, where I watched from the shadows. "Where is Blake?"

The kid shakes his head slightly, paralyzed by Bach's grip. "I told you; I don't know! He didn't come home last night."

How convenient.

Tennyson had the bright idea of starting at the dorms, and I had the wonderful idea of smoking them out, but it was quickly vetoed.

Unfortunately, Blake and Reese never came here, but his roommate knows where they rendezvoused. Either he'll tell me, or he'll burn with his secret.

"What about his girlfriend?" The word stings as I force it out.

The no-name shakes his head rapidly. "Haven't seen her."

What a shame.

Bach glances back at me as I pace, weighing my options. If we kill him, it sends a message. If we don't, it sends a message. Decisions, decisions.

"Well, I suppose there's only one thing left to do," I coo, eyeing Simeon and Tennyson, who demanded they come and be part of the chaos. Simeon has sat quietly under Tennyson's palm, waiting for release. And Tennyson... well, he's lounging on the bed, enjoying the scene before him.

"If I can't convince you, maybe he will."

A wicked smile breaks out over Tennyson's face. He brushes a hand over Simeon before dropping it onto the covers. Like a soldier, the mutt charges forward, his teeth bared and threatening.

"Wait!" the boy yells, squirming under Bach's hands. "Wait! Blake did come by for a minute around midnight. Said he was meeting someone, but I was half-asleep, so I didn't ask questions."

It's amusing how information magically appears when people's lives are on the line.

Tennyson claps his hands, and Simeon stops, becoming completely compliant. If only it were that easy.

Tsking, I lazily march forward next to Bach, whose hand tightens around the dipshit's windpipe. "That's not good enough. Brothers, I'll let you decide his fate."

Clapping Bach's back with my palm, I turn to the door before dropping an unlit match onto the floor—a reminder for later.

"I have a wife to find."

CHAPTER THIRTY-TWO

Reese

BLAKE IS SUCH A PUSSY.

Orange Grove's police chief is his uncle—and even he fears him.

I look at Shakespeare to my left. His eyes dart all over the property as we descend the front stairs.

"If you're scared," I tease, "you can always stay in the car, like Blake."

Which I'd rather he do. The odds of Blake's uncle telling me what I need to know with a killer by my side are low. Not that I know for sure Shakespeare is a killer, but with the vial of poison around his neck and the vacant look in his eye, it's pretty believable.

"Didn't your husband tell you?" He clucks his tongue. "I love some good family drama."

I try to smother the laugh, but it's no use. Shakespeare has been quite the charmer. "Hopefully, there won't be any drama." I raise my hand to knock on the door. "As long as the chief gives me the information I need, this will be a peaceful conversation. "

An evil grin that seems proud emerges on Shakespeare's face.

"Spoken like a true Cain. After your stint in solitary, maybe your husband will agree."

His words are an unhappy reminder that Van will be pissed when he finds out where I've gone. Even though I'm doing it for him, he won't care. His rules are law. Unfortunately, like my husband, I only answer to the law of a higher power.

"He'll be fine," I lie before knocking on the door.

"Whatever you say, princess."

Before Shakespeare's cheery attitude about my doom can affect me, the door opens, revealing Chief Benton, clad in jeans and a flannel shirt.

"Can I help you?"

Shakespeare chuckles. "I sure hope so."

I swat at his side like I have known the man for years. "Stop it. Let me handle it."

Shakespeare throws his hands up in surrender, and I focus back on Chief Benton. "We're sorry to bother you, sir, especially on your day off, but your nephew, Blake"—I point to the pussy in the car behind us—"said you agreed to a meeting with me."

The chief's eyes narrow on Shakespeare. "Yes, with you, not your friend." It's probably pointless to mention that Shakespeare is not my friend.

"I understand that, sir. He was a last-minute addition—a stipulation from my husband." I offer him an innocent smile. "He's heard Orange Grove can be dangerous for a woman out on their own."

It's a small lie, but one I hope the chief will agree to.

"You have thirty minutes," he barks, turning and heading into the house. "Follow me."

I glance at Shakespeare, and he gives me a thumbs-up.

"You are so... unpredictable."

"That I am, love." He shoves me out of the way, grabs my hand, and pulls me behind him. "That. I. Am."

The chief sits in a room that looks like something out of a magazine. The entire back wall is full of windows overlooking the Atlantic Ocean's rocky shore. The white gossamer curtains blow into the open area with the breeze off the water.

"Have a seat," he says, pointing to the white overstuffed sofa.

With my hand still in Shakespeare's, I let him lead us to the sofa while the chief sits in a chair to our left.

"My nephew tells me you have questions about a fire years ago."

I nod, pulling in a deep breath. Here goes nothing.

"I do. A friend of mine's mother died in the fire. I was wondering if you ever caught the arsonist behind it. I've checked the local news outlets, and no one ever mentioned it."

The chief drags his pointer finger across the top of his lips.

"Hmm… do you remember where this fire occurred?"

"The Hanson House."

"I see. Well, Miss…"

"Carmichael, I mean, Mrs. Cain."

Neither name registers in the chief's eyes.

"Well, Mrs. Cain. The Hanson House has been gone for quite a while. I don't know that I remember all the details to answer your question."

I shift in my seat and unconsciously squeeze Shakespeare's hand.

"I can help with that. Rumor has it the arsonist was the father of many of the children there."

One of the chief's brows rises mockingly. "Are you saying the arsonist is a rapist, as well?"

"Yes."

After Van told me everything last night, I texted Carol and asked if she had heard the theory about the rapist. She had and gave me a couple of names of some women I could talk to. Obviously, I took her word for it.

"Let me get this straight." He sits up and puts his elbows on his knees.

"You think there was a rapist abusing women at the Hanson House and then set fire to it to cover his crimes?"

"Yes, that's exactly what I'm saying."

The chief scoffs. "Well, I'm sorry to say that's the first I've heard of that theory."

If there's one thing I know, it's when somebody's lying. I've seen it all too many times before, with my sister's boyfriend. He promised not to hit her again, promised he would change. The same lines on his forehead creased every time he said it, just like they are now in the chief's.

"I don't believe you." Shakespeare shifts at my side, his grip on my hand tightening. "I think not only did you know someone was raping those women, but I think you helped cover it up."

The chief is on his feet and in my face within seconds. Unfortunately for him, so is Shakespeare.

"Now, now, pig. Let's not get excited. I would hate to have to medicate myself later."

Medicate? What kind of medication does Shakespeare take?

"Listen, I didn't invite you here to make accusations. I had nothing to do with the fire at the Hanson House, nor was I aware of any rapes that occurred."

He's lying. I know he is. This man knows what really happened that night, and without his help, my husband will never be able to move on. Slipping my hand into my pocket, I do something I never thought I would. I pull out a box of matches.

"Chief," I say calmly. "We can do this the hard way or my way, but either way, you will tell me what you know."

Visions of that night, when I found the mayor tied up in the cigar lounge with my husband looming threateningly over him with the flame, come to the forefront of my mind. I knew then I loved that man. The fact that he did what he had to do for justice. Maybe it wasn't the proper or legal way, but it was the only way he knew. No one else had bothered pursuing the events at the Hanson House. So many children like Van were without parents—without closure. Someone has to fight for them—and that someone is us.

"You have two options." I strike the match and hold the flame in front of his face, watching as fear saturates his gaze.

"You can tell me what I want to know, or my friend will hold you down while I set everything in your home ablaze." In my peripheral, I see a big-ass grin emerge on Shakespeare's face as he begins to bounce on the balls of his feet.

"As you can see, my friend would love for you to take option two, but I think you're a smart man, Chief Benton. The truth is the only way to escape this without destruction."

Like most people, Chief Benton underestimates me.

"I'll call the police."

I shrug.

"Only if you can reach your phone before my friend catches you." I have no idea if Shakespeare is fast or deadly, but if my husband is the scariest motherfucker I've ever seen, Shakespeare is the runner-up. The simple fact that he carries a vial of poison around his neck is enough to convince me not to fuck with him.

"What's it going to be, Chief? The truth or a call to the fire department?" It takes a minute for him to answer, but after a long stare-off with Shakespeare, he finally agrees, so I snuff out the flame.

"I heard of an alleged rape at the Hanson house," he begins. I sit back on the sofa, motioning for him to continue as Shakespeare stands guard.

"We did investigate but found no evidence or anyone willing to make a statement."

"They were scared! Did you not think about that? They were scared you would take their children."

Van says they were always scared to have the life they loved ripped away from them.

"I don't know what to tell you, Mrs. Cain. I can't arrest somebody if no one will come forward."

This asshole.

"What about the arsonist? Did you have a suspect?"

He shifts uncomfortably. "We did."

"And?"

"He was arrested by a neighboring department and jailed. Last I heard, he died in prison before he could be convicted."

What?

My mouth drops open in shock. How did Van not know this?

"Did his arrest make the papers?"

The chief sits down in his chair, a smug look on his face, and shrugs. "You'll have to ask them."

I don't need to ask them because I've already checked.

"Why was his arrest kept a secret?"

"It wasn't."

None of this makes sense.

"Listen, I understand your disappointment, Mrs. Cain. I'm sorry your friend didn't get the closure he or she needed, but the case is closed."

How can it be closed? How can Van still be searching for this man and not know he's dead?

The chief takes a step back. "Now if you'll excuse me. I need to speak with my nephew."

I step in front of him, blocking his way to the door. "I have one more question."

He sighs. "What is it?"

"My husband, Assistant District Attorney Alistair Cain, was arrested here many years ago."

The chief chuckles. "I bet your parents are proud of you both."

Fuck him.

"They are, but that's beside the point. I want to know who called in the anonymous tip that led to his arrest." Because it certainly wasn't me.

"I'll have to check our records. Do I have your word that no harm will come to this person?" I can't speak for Van, but I can for myself.

"Blake has my number—and needs a ride home—but yes, you have my word. No harm will come to this person." I step back and drop my hand, still holding the chief's eyes.

"But don't let my mercy fool you. If I don't hear from you in two days, I'll drop in for a visit. You won't see me coming, but you will witness the wake of my destruction."

CHAPTER THIRTY-THREE

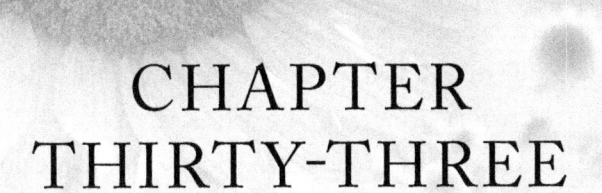

Van

I'M GOING TO KILL HER—RIGHT HERE ON THE CHIEF'S DOORSTEP.

"Van," she gasps. "What—oh, never mind, I know what you're doing here."

She sends me a glare that will get her spanked later and takes my hand, pulling me to the car like I'm obnoxious.

"Bach. Tennyson." She greets my brothers as she flops onto the passenger seat, already rolling her window down. "Thanks for the company, Shakespeare. I'll see you at home if your brother doesn't have a horrible case of PMS."

"What are you two? Fucking besties now?"

I can feel the jealousy creep up my neck, heating my skin with a delightful shade of red.

"Can I not have friends? Or is that another unspoken rule?"

I can't deal with her, not after the day I've had tracking her ass down. "Ride with Shakespeare," I bark out to my brothers. "Give us some privacy."

"Uh-oh," Bach teases. "Looks like someone's upset."

Someone is about to set fire to the entire state of South Carolina. "Get out!"

As soon as the door closes and we're alone, I turn to my wife. "What the fuck were you thinking, coming out here alone?"

"I wasn't alone. Shakespeare came with me."

"Because he found you sneaking out!"

She turns in her seat, pointing her finger in my face. "I wouldn't have had to sneak out if you trusted me."

Trust her... because she makes it so fucking easy.

"How can I trust you when you never do as I ask?" My brothers pulled onto the road, leaving us in the driveway.

"How can I do what you ask when you always tell me no?"

This conversation is going nowhere. "I'm just trying to keep you safe."

My stomach clinches at the declaration. Is that what I'm doing? Keeping her safe or holding her prisoner?

"Okay, Van. No bullshit this time. If you tell me the truth, I promise to obey." She shrugs her shoulders. "Within reason."

"Tell you the truth about what?"

She leans across the console, her hands going to my cheeks, pulling me closer. "Am I your wife or your prisoner?"

Did I get angry because my prisoner escaped, or did I get angry because I thought my wife's safety had been compromised?

Thoughts of her lying against me last night, checking every hour if I was still breathing, cross my mind. She was worried—something I haven't felt from a woman in a long time.

"You are my wife," I admit. "But you are also my prisoner until you're proven not guilty."

Even I'm tired of saying the same thing over and over. Enoch says that I should forgive and that everyone deserves a second chance. I understand that sentiment better than most, but that doesn't change the fact that it happened. The question is, will that person use their second chance to make amends? Or will they use it to repeat the behavior? At this point, I'm still not sure what my wife's intentions are. As long as I dangle her sister over her head, I'll never know if she doesn't run away because she needs information or wants to stay.

Reese's warm hands fall from my face as she leans back into her seat. "That's the problem, Van. We will never be more than warden and prisoner. My word isn't enough for you."

I want it to be, but I've been burned many times.

"I came here for you," she finally says, after a moment of us sitting in silence. "I came here for us. Chief Benton was the patrol officer back when your mother was killed."

I know that. I investigated him back then, and he was no help.

"Did he give you what you needed?"

The gesture of her coming out here for me does something to my chest. I don't have the heart to be rude.

"Sort of."

My eyebrows rise. "He was able to provide you with useful information?"

She nods. "Did you know they caught the arsonist who set the fire?"

Immediately, at the mention of the fire, rage boils under my skin. "I didn't tell you that information for you to endanger yourself. I don't need your help."

"Maybe not, but you're getting it anyway."

I don't know how there aren't more spousal murders. I can't even imagine making it to our first anniversary without stuffing her in a closet with my cock in her mouth to keep her quiet. "If they caught the arsonist," I challenge, ignoring her backtalk, "then why wasn't he tried?"

"He died in jail before they could bring charges against him."

Interesting. "Benton told you this?"

She nods. "He also told me that he would call me within the next couple of days to let me know who made the anonymous tip that led to my husband's arrest." She flashes me a wink. "Because it certainly wasn't me."

Seven hours later, we pull into the House of Cain.

"You have a two-minute head start."

Her head whips in my direction. "For what?"

"You seem to like running from me." And I seem to relish chasing her. "So, I'm going to let you run as far as you can before I catch you and redden your cheeks for every minute you worried me today."

She grins. "So, you were worried today, huh?"

I'm not dealing with her shit. "Time starts now. I suggest you hurry. I ran cross-country in high school."

She puts her hand on the door and stops. "Seriously? Were you any good?"

I tap my watch. "You won't know unless you run."

She's out of the car in a flash, darting behind the house and heading straight for the field of sunflowers—my favorite. Fuck her head start—I can't wait to get my hands on her defiant ass.

Slamming my door closed behind me, I leisurely walk through the sunflowers facing the east, not caring to chase after her yet. I'm enjoying watching her think she has a chance.

"I hate to tell you," she laughs as she runs, "but you aren't even a remotely good runner. Your team must have hated you."

That they did, but not for that reason.

I let her get a few feet further before sprinting the small distance between us. In one swoop, she's under me, pliant on the ground.

"I underestimated you," she admits, defeat coating her tone.

I press my palm against her head and bury the side of her face into the dirt. I know it's not gentle or romantic, but I can't find it in myself to care.

Did she care when she ran from me? No.

Did she care when she uprooted my life? No.

So, do I care if she's comfortable while I remind her whose wife she is? Not in the slightest.

Her legs scrape the ground as I snatch her hips up to meet my throbbing cock. I rub against her, hoping the friction will ease the pain, but it only makes it worse.

I don't give her long to adjust or get comfortable, mainly because I don't care if she is.

I only care that she learns.

That I love her.

And that if she ever leaves again, I won't be so forgiving.

Gripping the band of her shorts, I tug them off and toss them to the side, showcasing smooth skin and a thong that rounds her beautiful ass.

"Someone's needy," Reese muses, while I slide down her panties.

"Someone's mouth needs occupying," I taunt, pulling her legs apart.

"I've told you—"

She goes silent when my mouth finds her center, sucking violently until she's shaking against me. Moans fill the evening air, and I can tell she's on the cusp of coming on my face, but after all, this is a punishment.

Prying myself away from her wetness, I push up on my knees, watching as her body goes limp in frustration.

"Bastard," she croaks.

"Language," I muse, licking her taste off my lips. Running my finger down her spine, I revel in the chills that follow my path and the gasp that startles her once my hand connects with her ass cheeks. It barely leaves a mark, which disappoints me.

"Tell me to stop," I plead, part of me hoping she will because once I'm done with her, she'll never be able to leave again. "Now."

She scoffs before going silent.

Fine. I tried to be accommodating, and in return, she wants to stay quiet for the first time in history—her mistake.

"You drive me fucking crazy," I growl, slapping my hand against the smooth skin that's starting to turn red with my marks. If I wasn't possessive before, I sure am now.

"Likewise," she breathes, her body coming back to my hand as if it's searching for me.

"I was supposed to hate you." My hand tangles in her hair as I thrust my hand against her. "I want to hate you."

She laughs as my hand ripens her cheeks. "Hate me, then."

I can't.

That's always been my problem.

With one final slap, I press my tongue to the red skin, much like when putting out a match, and soothe the heat there.

Possessiveness takes over me as I pry her from the dirt, finally meeting her eyes.

"I'll only ask you this once."

Reese's eyebrow arches.

"How would you like me to fuck my wife?"

Her breath hitches at my words, but she recovers all the same.

"My husband should worship me as he wants. For my body is his."

Truer words have never been spoken.

"Take off your shirt." Her eyes widen, but she does as she's told for once, unclasping her bra, too.

"Give me your hands."

They shake as she holds them up while I wrap her shirt around her tiny wrists, bounding them together until she's immobile.

"Now, lie back and put them above your head."

She hesitates, and I almost fear I've scared her, but like the brave woman she is, she lowers to the ground, offering herself as a sacrificial lamb.

Her naked body is stunning as the dwindling sun hits her tanned skin, illuminating every freckle. I rid myself of my jeans and boxers, unable to wait any longer, and line up with her slick entrance.

She moans, her head tilting to the side as I rub up and down her sweet cunt. "I need you to speed this up," she teases, "before I finish on my own."

The hell she'll ever finish on her own. Her pussy belongs to me and only me. I thrust inside her, unceremoniously burying myself to the hilt.

My thrusts aren't slow or gentle.

They're punishing and angry, burying all the worry and rage I've felt over the years deep inside her.

"I thought you hated me," she breathes with tear-stained cheeks.

God knows I tried.

"I never hated you," I admit. "I've always loved you," I grunt. "Unfortunately."

A smile breaks out on her face. "Am I still your prisoner?"

Her body bounces rhythmically as I pound the thought out of her mind.

"No, you're my wife—my eternal sunflower—until death parts us both."

CHAPTER THIRTY-FOUR

Van

"I WANT A TATTOO."

I flash her a glare under the spray of water. "I want world peace. Looks like neither of those things are happening anytime soon."

"You can't tell me what to do with my body."

My gaze narrows on hers. "Was it not you who said that by holy decree, my body is yours to do as you please?"

There's a wicked sparkle in her eyes that matches her smirk. "Are you saying that isn't true, Mr. Until Death Do Us Part?"

I groan. "Must we delve into deep topics first thing in the morning?"

For fuck's sake, I haven't even had coffee yet.

"You're the one who started it with your caveman retort. All you had to do was say, 'Sure, sweetheart. Do you have a place in mind?'"

Yeah, that isn't happening.

"All you had to do was not bring it up."

And we're back in grade school, arguing about irrelevant topics on the playground.

"How would I know you wouldn't like the idea? You have what? Thirty percent of your body covered in ink?"

"Who the fuck counts tattoos by coverage area?" What is she, a fucking mathematician?

"I'm just saying you have a lot of tattoos. Why is it such a big deal if I get one?"

Because her body is untainted, she's pure—devoid of marks and scars. I plan to keep her that way. "Can't I just prefer you exactly how you are?"

"Aww. You are so sweet."

She's just trying to piss me off.

"Would it help if I told you I wanted a matching tattoo like yours?"

Ah, fuck. Now my dick is hard. "Which one?"

She turns me around, finding the sunflower engulfed in flames down my spine. "I want this one." Her finger traces the flames surrounding the flower, whose petals never singe from the fire or wilt in the darkness.

"This is me." Her lips graze my ear. "I am the flower who withstands your dark vengeance."

I swallow harshly. "You were always my muse."

She was a perfect masterpiece that I could never destroy—even when I tried.

"Let me bear your mark, love," she whispers reverently, "and together, we'll share its weight."

Her fingers grip my arms, and she turns me to face her.

"You don't want to bear the weight of my sins," I confess. "You're unworthy of such suffering."

"I thought we established you didn't get to tell me what to do anymore?" She grins and lowers to her knees, her palms trailing across my arms, over my chest, and down my abs until her knees rest on the tile.

I swallow thickly. "I don't recall ever hearing that rule."

The way her eyes sparkle under the shower light, loving and mischievous, she could get me to agree to anything, and by the way my body stands frozen under her touch, languid and pliant, she knows it, too.

"Shall I stop, husband, so we can debate?"

Fuck no. I'd rather gouge my eyes out with the shower sprayer than for her to stop now.

"Is that a no?" she teases me when I can't answer, and it makes her all too happy to know she has this control over me. I should be more shocked that she has this much authority over me, but I've always known that Reese Carmichael has held me a prisoner long before I held her.

Reese's tongue swipes out under the warm spray of water, licking the seam of my cock, where a bead of pre-cum awaits. "Mmm. You taste like mine, Mr. Cain."

Gripping the back of my thighs, she pulls me closer, opening her mouth wider and burying my cock down her throat. My knees buckle from the pleasure as I lean forward, my palm smacking the tile wall behind her.

"Oh, fuck," I groan.

I've fucked this woman's mouth before, but it feels different this time.

Sure, she angers me to the point of murder, but she pleasures me to the end of salvation. This is my wife. The woman who was created just for me. She's more passionate about justice and kindness than anyone I know. Above all, though, she's brave. She dared to love a man, despite his faults, for all eternity.

"Are you still with me, lover?" she taunts from below before cupping my balls in one hand and applying pressure while she works my cock with a steady rhythm.

"I am with you," I pant as the pressure increases with each of her pulls. "I—"

Her mouth seems to grip me from the inside, sending an explosion through my body as I come down her throat, watching as she drinks me dry.

Yeah, this woman is mine—forever.

"Stop," Reese clips, narrowing her eyes to slits. "You're scaring everyone with your bad attitude."

I think it was when I threatened to set this shitty parlor on fire when her tattoo artist lingered after asking Reese to remove her shirt, but if a bad attitude is what she wants to call it, fine by me.

"He has to see my back to put the tattoo there, Van."

I'm aware of the process; doesn't mean I have to allow another man to help her do it.

"No one helps remove your clothes but me."

I dare the bastard to offer again. Not only will I burn down his tattoo parlor, but I'll also incinerate the entire street just for allowing him to work here.

Can he help my wife remove her shit… Yeah, when I can help him see God.

Fucker.

"Fine. Do what you need to do to keep these people safe."

At least Reese understands the severity of this man's fuck-up.

"Lie down," I demand.

She knows she has to pay the price. Did I not warn her at the courthouse not to draw attention from other men? I believe I did.

"You are so ridiculous," she huffs and stretches out along the table on her stomach.

"That might be true, but you enjoy it."

She's just as twisted as I am.

Pulling a lighter from my pocket, I hover over her and flick the flame to life.

"Do not even think of burning down this room. He made a mistake. Humans do that sometimes."

I smile. "Really? I had no idea." Apparently, this particular human doing her tattoo isn't the brightest, either.

Bringing the flame to her shirt, I drag it slowly down the middle until it sears the fabric.

"Stay on your stomach." I drag my finger down the parted seam, exposing her smooth skin and unhooking her bra. My palm finds her spine, which will soon be like mine. "Let this be my last warning: If your sweet artist volunteers to touch you more than he must, your first tattoo experience will begin and end with his screams."

Like the pain in the ass she is, she turns to me and grins. "Always the romantic."

Always so fucking sarcastic.

Stepping away, I bang my fist on the inside of the door, signaling that she's ready, and sit in the chair closest to the table. I flick the lighter repeatedly, freeing the fire, then capping it. It's not much of a threat, but enough that when the tattoo artist walks in and sees her seared shirt, he gets it.

It's a long three hours of occasional groans and winces, but my girl handles getting a tattoo like a true champion.

"Help me up?" she asks after the artist leaves us with a bandage that I insisted on handling once he got the fuck out.

Reese rolls over and I take her hand and pull her into a seated position. "How does it look?"

Turning her, I brush my fingers along her shoulders, leaning in and pressing my lips lightly against her inflamed skin, kissing away any pain that still lingers. "It looks like my sunflower."

A bright smile reaches her cheeks. "I want to see."

Turning her, I watch as she lights up at all the hues of yellow and orange. Flames lick up the side of the flower but never mars it. The flower stands strong amidst the darkness—just like her.

"Do you like it?"

My fingers trace over the ink, familiarizing myself with this new part of her.

"My rock-solid dick says yes."

She shakes her head and grins, slipping her arms into my coat I hold out for her. "Next time, I'll bring you an extra shirt." I wince. What was I thinking, burning her shirt off her body? I wasn't. My cock was staking claim.

She smiles as she moves closer, looping her arms around my neck. "I don't know… I kind of want a repeat."

A repeat she will have, then.

"Though, I think it's time for you to admit that the sunflower of the east,"—her fingers trail up and down my spine as she molds herself to me—"survived the darkness of the west."

I laugh. "You haven't survived yet." A lifetime will afford many more opportunities to fail.

"Yeah, but—" Her phone rings in my coat pocket.

"Unknown number." She shows me the lit screen. "You think it's the chief?"

I shrug, my heart already pounding in my chest. "Only one way to find out."

"Hello," she answers, putting the phone on speaker.

"Mrs. Cain. This is Chief Benton. I have the name you requested."

"And?"

My throat tightens in the seconds that follow.

"The person who made the call was Assistant District Attorney, Enoch Gadot."

CHAPTER THIRTY-FIVE

Reese

"You're free."

It's as if he reached into my chest and shattered my heart with his bare hand. "What do mean, 'I'm free?'"

He takes a pen from his desk. "Give me your hand."

I do, dreading what comes next. "I never lied to you. Your sister is in Georgia. You can find her at this address." He jots the street address on my palm and looks up, finding my eyes blinking back tears. "It's a safe haven—an underground shelter I've funded for several years."

I suck in a sob. "Why didn't you tell me?"

He shakes his head and finishes writing out the address. "Even when I hated you, I loved you." Taking my hand, he closes my fingers into a fist, safeguarding the address he knows means the world to me. "I wanted to tell you," he starts. "I would have soon if this hadn't happened."

"Van." I press my other palm against his cheek. "I'm sure Enoch has an explanation."

His eyes close solemnly. "I'm sure he does, but that doesn't change the fact that he let me spend all these years blaming you for something you didn't do."

The snark in me flares to the surface. "I did try to tell you."

"You did," he agrees, "but I was too fucked-up to believe you. Out of everyone in my life, I never thought Enoch would have been the one to send me to prison."

I can't argue with that. "Maybe you should hear him out. See what he has to say first."

Enoch seems like a really good man. I can't imagine he wanted Van to suffer.

"If it makes you feel any better, I don't harbor any ill feelings that you thought it was me who turned you in." I shrug. "We all make mistakes. Next time, you'll believe me when I tell you I didn't do something."

He smiles, but it's sad. "There won't be a next time, Flower. I don't deserve any more chances with you."

Have mercy. "Please don't make decisions during shark week. I've learned that the hard way. Now, I always wait until my period is over to make major life decisions."

I went too far; I realize that now.

Removing my hand, Van stands up straight. "When you get to the address, ask for the widowmaker. He's a mean motherfucker, but he won't hurt you."

"The widowmaker? What is he, some Marvel villain?"

Van shakes his head. "His real name is Kane."

Well, I'll be damned. "Might he be related to you?" It seems like an awful lot of Cains are popping up lately.

"Fuck no. We aren't related. I only know him from tracking down your sister."

My heart starts beating erratically. "You have been sending money to my sister all these years?" I can't stop the tears as they leak from my eyes. "You funded the shelter that took her in."

He sighs. "Someone had to. You kept funding the wrong ones."

"They weren't the wrong shelters. I still helped the women there."

Van tips his chin arrogantly. "Just not the woman you wanted to help."

He's got me there. "That didn't mean *you* had to help her."

His full lips purse, almost as if he's embarrassed to admit, "We made a deal. You got the mayor to give up the name of the security guy at the Hanson House."

"Yeah, but I was never able to give you the information. You were arrested before I got there." And the name disappeared from my pocket, just like Van Gogh.

"It didn't matter. I told you I would help you find your sister, and I did." And the fucker kept it from me for years.

"You really are the sweetest, aren't you?"

My husband, the arsonist, chuckles, rolling his eyes in the process. "Clearly, my motives changed over time."

"Clearly."

He shoves me away. "Go, before I change my mind."

Doesn't he realize that's exactly what I want him to do? "Fine," I agree. "Push me away, but just know when you come to your senses and figure out your shit, I'll be with my sister, waiting for the most epic groveling session ever performed by an arsonist."

This man did not stalk me for years to leave me again. For fuck's sake, he moved to Georgia so he could stalk me at college after he was released from prison. I know him better than he knows himself, and when my husband wants something, he won't stop his pursuit until he gets it. He's a relentless man—something that I've always loved about him.

Exhaling a deep sigh, Van looks at me, his palm going to my cheek in a loving gesture. "This is goodbye, Flower, now and forever."

A VICIOUS PROPOSAL

Come to find out, the car Van used on our wedding day was mine. The liar bought it for me as a wedding gift so I could go back and forth to the university. Can you believe that shit? The man is a complete sweetheart—yet he'd rather you believe he was a soulless monster. I've always seen through his bullshit, though, and right now, while he's reeling from this revelation about Enoch, he probably believes it.

I don't know why Enoch would have been the one to turn him in, but I know that Enoch loves him more than anything. There has to be a logical explanation, and as soon as Van pulls his head out of his ass and talks to Enoch, he'll realize that, too.

And maybe… I'll also practice what I preach and stop being a chicken and get out the car. I've been parked outside the address Van gave me for fifteen minutes, too scared to go up to the door and ask for my sister. I mean, what if—

A man covered in tattoos taps on my window, nearly startling me into the backseat of the car. "Can I help you?"

"Depends," I shout through the closed window. "Are you the widowmaker?"

I didn't even see him approach—that's how deep in my head I am. The drive to Madison, Georgia, from Atlanta, didn't take very long. I was here in a little over an hour, driving the back roads through rolling hills and farmlands—much like the ones at Eden.

"Who wants to know?"

This man has a fucking attitude the size of Mount Rushmore. No wonder Van hates him. They're very similar. But I'm used to dealing with assholes.

"Your mom," I say just as sternly, narrowing my gaze at the man in the window.

His muscled cheek twitches. "Cute, but I won't ask you again. What do you want with the widowmaker?"

I almost say *a baby* just to be funny, but this man's stern glare changes my mind. "Fine. My husband, Alistair Cain, told me to ask for the widowmaker. He said he would know where I could find my sister, Julia."

This man, with his oversized chest, swollen arms, and multitude of tattoos, immediately tenses. "I don't know a Julia."

A wedding ring glimmers on his left hand. No way. No. Freaking. Way. My sister better not have gotten married without me. Well, I did get married without her, but still, she's the oldest. She should set a better example.

"Sure, you do, pal." Opening the door, I push the man back. "My husband is never wrong." He's also stupidly protective and would never send me to a place where someone could hurt me.

"Listen," I offer, coming to stand in front of him and only reaching his pecs. "I'm alone and wasn't followed." I hold up one finger, just in case he's thinking of finding a place to dispose of my body. "But if I don't call my husband in the next hour, he will destroy this entire planet with fire. You don't want me to miss placing that call, sir. So, why don't you go inside and ask my sister if she knows a Reese Carmichael. I'll wait out here for her hug."

I'm talking a whole lot of shit right now, considering Van hasn't picked up the phone when I've tried calling. But if there's one thing I know, it's that Van *knows* I'm here. I don't call him a stalker for nothing.

"All right, sweetheart. You've sparked my interest."

I bet I also remind him of someone he knows—like my sister.

"I'll see if I can find this Julia person." He steps back, a casual smirk planted on his face. "Wait out here. I don't want to shoot you if you rush my door."

That comment makes me nervous. "You a Marine?"

He scoffs. "Not hardly."

"Army, then?"

He laughs, turning around and heading back to the front door.

"Air Force!" I try one last time before he slips inside, shaking his head and flipping me off as he closes the door.

Navy. He's got to be Navy—or Coast Guard, but there's no way he would waste that attitude not getting to shoot people. He's definitely Navy.

And I'm definitely smiling.

It seems nice out here, with the sprawling acreage and hateful company. If this is Julia's house, I bet she loves it. She's always wanted farm animals and several kids. We were the opposite in that regard. I never desired children or wanted to get up early and feed a bunch of animals. I was just fine living a life of excitement.

I snort. Boy, did I fulfill that dream. Van is nothing but excitement, and while I don't have to call him in an hour, I will because that man has had long enough to stew. I've never listened to him before, and I'm certainly not going to start now. Enoch may have betrayed him, but I didn't.

We are not getting a divorce, and he is not running away from me again.

We have an agreement—twelve years of marriage and not a day less.

The front door bangs open, and I barely catch the streak of blonde hair that races down the porch and freaking sprints the remaining distance, right into my arms.

"Reese!" Her body hits me before her voice registers. "Reese. Reese. Reese."

Tears fall down my cheeks as I bury my face in her soft hair. It's been nearly a decade since I've felt a hug from my big sister. "Julia." A snort escapes me as my legs quiver, struggling to hold me up. For so many years, I've prayed that she was safe and healthy, and here she is, solid and firm, wrapped around me in a bear hug.

"I can't believe you're here!"

Finally, Julia lets me pull away, brushing my tear-soaked hair off my face. "Look at you!" Her smile has changed. It's brighter, much like our mother's used to be before she was killed in a car accident. "You're all grown up!"

I laugh. "I was always grown up." Hell, I was eighteen when I found Van.

"No." She shakes her head, tears welling in her eyes. "Not like this. You look…" She brings my hands to her face, leaning in as if she's going to kiss them, and stops. "You look *married*."

Ah. "I am." Holding the enormous garnet stone encased by diamonds in the sunlight, I smile. "I married my best friend this year."

"Oh my gosh! Come in. You have to tell me all about him!" With my hand still clutched in hers, she pulls us toward the front porch, where the giant man awaits with half a smile.

"Navy," I guess. "You're a Navy SEAL."

My sister's entire face lights up. "The best Navy SEAL."

"It's nice to meet you—" I hold my free hand for him to shake, even though it's my left one.

He stares at it for a moment, but as soon as my sister clears her throat, he moves, taking my hand. "Widowmaker," he offers, "but most people call me Kane."

CHAPTER THIRTY-SIX

Van

I RETALIATED THE ONLY WAY I KNEW HOW—I SET ENOCH'S CAR on fire.

"Did that make you feel better?" The only man I've known as a father comes to stand next to me, watching as his beloved Bronco turns to ash.

"Depends. Did it make you feel better when you reported me to the Orange Grove Sheriff's Office?"

"Ah." He sighs. "You know."

"Yeah, I know everything—except the reason why."

It's been three days since Reese left to find her sister. Three days since I heard from her. And three days that I've stewed in my fury.

"My reasoning was complicated."

I turn and face the only man I've ever trusted. "Let me guess, then. You were part of their cover-up?"

"Not at all." He pulls in a shuddering breath. "I was the prosecuting attorney then and had been assigned the Hanson House case."

I scoff. "You're not helping yourself, Teach." Not only did he rat me out, but he had unlimited access to cover up the assaults.

"Alistair." He sighs. "I'm your grandfather."

Everything south of my ears seems to disappear with his words. "I'm sorry, what?"

As if suddenly tired, he eases to the ground, keeping his eyes on the burning car before him. "I wasn't always a good man, son. I was cocky and had an ego that you wish yours could orbit."

I choke down a laugh. Nothing about this moment is funny.

"I was wealthy beyond my wildest dreams, yet I was still unfulfilled."

"Spare me the lecture. I've heard it before." The story I want to hear is the one he's never told.

Enoch motions for me to sit. "Settle, and I'll tell you everything you want to know."

The last thing I want to do is sit next to a traitor, but at this point, I'd do anything to get the closure I need.

Less gracefully than Enoch, I sit on the grass, bending my knee to prop up my arm, watching as the flames lick the ceiling of his car. "I'm sitting. Now talk."

On any other day, Enoch would have backhanded me into oblivion for speaking to him in such a way, but things have changed. Just like respect can be earned, it can be taken away.

"It took Magda and me years to conceive. I was thirty-five by the time your father was born."

I shake my head. "My father was a rapist at Hanson House." He had to be. Why else would he stay away and let my mother raise a child alone?

"Your father was no rapist. He was a good man—much better than me."

I can agree with that point.

"Paul, your father, met your mother when he was in basic training for the Army. I don't know the details of their relationship, since the first I'd heard of her was when Paul told me she was pregnant, and they would be getting married."

I chance a look at Enoch, hoping the heat warming my body is from the car fire and not the thought of having two parents who loved me.

"He told me your mother would join him once he received his station orders." A tear streaks down his face. "You must understand, I only wanted what was best for my son."

Immediately, I'm on my feet, rage pumping through my veins like pure adrenaline. "Are you saying my mother, who had Down syndrome, wasn't the best for him?"

Enoch doesn't move. He finds my gaze and holds it. "No. Her having Down syndrome did not factor into my wants for my son. My concern was that he wanted independence from me and his mother. He wanted to serve his country, and I was afraid I would lose my only son, who wanted to fight for people who didn't appreciate his sacrifice."

I can see that. "You wanted him to decide to stay based on the few ungrateful citizens and not the thankfulness of many?" I, for one, appreciate the sacrifice of the men and women in the military. Like with any servicemen, there's always a rotten few, but the many are good people.

Enoch grunts. "I did. I wanted my son close to help him and your mother." A sob wracks his body. "I wanted to know my grandson, but we had a fight, and then he was killed in a freak accident during training."

My chest spasms as I think of a father I never knew, fighting for a future with me and my mother.

"You have to understand, Alistair. All I wanted was my son back. It took me years to even be able to say his name."

The anger bubbles up again. "So, you figured, fuck me and my mother?"

Enoch's head droops to his chest. "I'm not proud of my behavior. I was grieving, but I did come for you and your mother."

What? "I would have remembered seeing you," I argue. "Why would you keep your existence a secret?"

"I didn't want to, but you were a teenager by then, and your mother had said you had been asking many questions about your father recently. As you were aware, alleged assaults were circulating through the Hanson House. Your mother's first concern was the safety of the women who helped raise you."

Emotion weighs heavy behind my eyes, threatening a migraine.

"She asked me to look into it."

"And did you?" Please say no so I can hate you—and hate my mother for always looking out for everyone but herself.

"I did. I helped arrange a task force through the police department that sent him on the run."

"Not on the run, Teacher," I correct. "You cornered him, and he burned his way out. He killed as many witnesses as he could that night." Let's not try to sugarcoat that night. That task force cost the lives of many.

"I'm sorry, Alistair. If I had been there, I would have saved your mother myself. She was a good woman. I had never been prouder of my son's decisions as I was the day I met your mother, and she pulled back the curtains, revealing the heir to our family, cutting grass for another family."

This is all too much to digest.

"Why did my mother never tell me this story?"

Enoch looks weary. "I don't know. Maybe she didn't want you to hurt the way she did when she learned of Paul's death. Maybe she thought you had already lost too much."

My mother was a fucking saint.

"I believe she was going to tell you, though. Once we dealt with the assaults, she was going to introduce us."

I can't take much more of this. I finally laugh. "So, you thought, *what better way to introduce myself than to put a call into the tip line and have my grandson arrested.*"

"It wasn't like that."

"Oh, yeah?" I clip. "How was it, then? Did I not look enough like Paul, or was it the fact that I was the last piece of your son's mistake?"

Now, I'm just saying stupid shit out of anger.

"You offered me a plea bargain!" I yell. "You pretended not to know me." I can barely breathe. I'm so livid. "You watched me cry. You watched them put me behind bars! How can you live with yourself?"

The older man pulls himself off the grass and faces me. "I saved you," he says calmly. "I promised myself I would do whatever it took to ensure you survived this world, as your mother and father would have wanted."

I shake my head like that eighteen-year-old boy again, but Enoch grabs my arm tightly. "I wasn't going to let you roam the streets, searching for vengeance instead of peace. Justice isn't always what we want it to be. The law can only do so much, but it is not for you to decide. Your mother wouldn't have wanted to know that her brilliant boy was sleeping alone in whatever abandoned building he found, stalking people he thought deserved justice. You cannot be the judge in this world, Alistair. You didn't create the rules; therefore, you cannot exact the punishment."

"He murdered my mother! My innocent mother!"

I'm on my knees, dragging Enoch to the ground with me as tears leak from my eyes.

"I needed you to know you were not alone in this world," Enoch continues. "I needed you to make something of yourself—find justice the right way. Your mother would be proud of the man you've become… your father, too."

"And you?" I scoff. "Are you proud that your only heir is a former convict?"

He guides my chin up and levels me with a stern look. "Yes. I am prouder of you than I was of your father. You have been through so much, Alistair, and still, you are a good man. I didn't want your vengeance to take that from you. I wanted to arm you with the tools that would give you the justice you craved but not get you killed in the process."

"You could have just told me," I argue. "You didn't need to have me arrested."

He looks apologetic when he says, "But I did. Every action has consequences. You were too far gone to have listened to anyone. You trusted no one but Reese."

I scoff. "Congratulations. You fixed that problem."

"I know you're angry, and this is a lot to understand, but sometimes the only way to reach people is through hardships. They must be stripped down to their very core to see what remains. You are not an arsonist, my son. You are a brilliant attorney with a passion for justice that I've never seen before. Just because you made a mistake and went down a longer path to get here doesn't mean you deserve it any less."

I still think he could have had a conversation with me.

Like he knew that's exactly what I was thinking, he adds, "Had you not spent those six years in prison, you wouldn't have felt hopeless. You wouldn't have realized that you were just as smart as Harvard grads and obtained your law degree in prison."

"I also wouldn't have been your captive audience when you visited me every day and insisted I try law."

Enoch grins. "I had motives, too, but that doesn't change the fact that I believed in you. I knew you were an amazing man, and when the time was right, I would tell you about the amazing man you got it from. I know this isn't easy to hear, and you feel betrayed, but know that I suffered with you every single day. I felt your pain and cried with you on those lonely nights. But I had to wait until you were ready to accept my role in your life."

Is that true? Would I have shut him down if he came to me with some bullshit grandfather story?

Yeah, I most definitely would have. I'm still paranoid about the people I allow in my life. After my mom's murder, I was even more so. I would have thought Enoch was part of the cover-up, no matter what he told me. And did my behavior need to be checked? Probably. I was out of control and had spent every night with a match in my hand and rage in my veins. Hell, I started getting justice for anyone I saw who needed it—down to small shit like purse snatching and alley fights.

"Why not tell me when we moved to Georgia? You had to know I was coming for Reese."

Enoch nods. "I knew what she meant to you, but I also believed you would know she didn't betray you deep in your heart. You wouldn't have married her, Alistair, if you had believed she did."

"But—"

He holds up a finger. "You swore on God's word that only death would separate you. I know what His law means to you just as you know what it means to me. You won't divorce her unless she breaks the covenant outlined in the Word, and you wouldn't promise the rest of your life on a punishment."

Fuck him. "You don't know me."

"That's one thing I do know, son. I know your heart. I was there when you picked up its pieces and rebuilt it stronger. You loved Reese, and I didn't care how much property I had to buy in Georgia. I wanted you to find her and show her the man behind the pain—the redeemed man worthy of love."

I scoff. "You're wrong. I'm not worthy. I let her go."

CHAPTER THIRTY-SEVEN

Van

"So, the reason you're throwing all her shit in a bag isn't because you're going to set it on fire?"

I cut Bach an annoyed look. "I asked you to come over and cat sit, not ask dumb questions."

Why can't he grab the cat and fucking leave?

"I thought you were just making excuses for me to come over."

I blink. "What am I? A vagina? I don't need a fucking girl chat. I save those for my therapist."

If I still saw my therapist.

"So, you don't want to talk about what happened with you and Teach?" He pushes off the wall, finding another perch on my dresser to annoy me.

"Nothing happened between Enoch and me," I lie.

Bach chuckles, knowing good and fucking well what happened. All of my brothers know what happened. They're all a bunch of fucking gossips. "You mean to tell me the Bronco simply combusted?"

"Stranger things have happened." I shrug.

"You are one cagey bastard, Al."

I hate when he fucking calls me Al.

"And you are one nosy bitch, Zo."

His eyes narrow at the nickname, but it doesn't stop his mouth from opening again. "We've all had to pay the price for Eden, not just you."

"I know that." I just wasn't aware what the cost of mine was until yesterday.

"And do you understand how painful that must have been for him?"

Unfortunately, I do. Bach is wasting his time with this chat full of life lessons and feelings. After speaking with Enoch yesterday, I understand why he reported me. Sometimes, the best things in life are born from pain. Not that I didn't already have a shit-ton of pain, but still, I understand I was dead inside when Enoch found me.

If I had run away with Reese back then, I would have only caused her pain. I couldn't love or sacrifice—all things required for a marriage. She and I would have used the pain from our past, and the world would have suffered because of our hate. Reese deserved better than that. I wasn't the man for her back then, and I'm likely still not, but I've waited long enough to have her.

My relationship with Enoch might be just as damaged as my marriage with Reese, but they aren't broken, per Enoch. Damage can be mended through love and forgiveness. I'm not Van Gogh anymore. I'm not a vigilante who doesn't know how to channel his rage into justice. I am Assistant District Attorney Alistair Cain. Justice has become my paint and the courtroom, my canvas.

I don't fight for others to chase out the demons in my head any longer; I fuck my wife for that. I fight for others because justice is my passion. I promised the people of Atlanta that I would clean up their city, and now, as I stand, shoving every item of clothing my wife owns into her suitcase, I know I can't do it without her.

Reese has always been my muse—my passion.

I've loved her more than I've hated her.

And for the first time in my life, I'm going to allow her to tell me what to do.

"What's that stupid look on your face for? You fart or something?"

For fuck's sake, is Bach still here? "Take the cat and fucking leave," I snap. "I'm fine. I don't plan on burning Eden or anyone living on its acreage for at least a few more months."

Enoch always said we shouldn't make promises we couldn't keep.

"Whatever." Bach slides off the dresser and casts me an annoyed look. "Have fun groveling to your wife. If you need any tips, call Tennyson. He's a bigger pussy than you are."

I don't understand why Enoch felt the need to "give me brothers" a year after I moved in with him. One asshole is more than enough in a community.

"Don't forget the fucking cat," I say, watching as Bach's back disappears into the hall. "And you better not kill her while we're gone!"

What was I thinking, asking this moron to watch Biscuit for a few months? He's the least paternal figure out of the four of us, but Tennyson would let Simeon eat her as a snack, and Shakespeare would likely forget he was even supposed to watch her. My options were limited. The fucker better not let me down.

My phone buzzes in my pocket again. It's the third time in the last half hour, and I smile before I unlock it.

Reese: I know you're ignoring me on purpose.

That I am. I don't want to reconcile with my wife over text. I want to see her shocked look when I tell her she is never leaving me again. Honestly, it's her fault for even giving me the opportunity. She should have used the chink in my madness and ran when I permitted her. But she's crazy and said she would wait until I pulled my head out of my ass. Not very smart on her part.

Reese: Fine. Don't say I didn't warn you.

Immediately, my phone starts dinging with text messages. Two are from my personal banks, stating that my account balance has dropped below $1,000; the others are from an offshore account where my portion of the oil business resides.

I couldn't be prouder. My wife has emptied and frozen all my accounts.

Reese: If you don't call me in the next five minutes, I will donate all this money to Blake's dorm.

Now, she's gone too far.

Me: Blake will be dead before the money hits the account.

Reese: Hello, Husband. So nice of you to check on me. I'm doing fine with my sister and her HUSBAND here in the country. Can you believe she's married?! The guy looks like he eats children for breakfast!

This is why I have ignored her calls and texts. Once she knows she has my attention, she will suffocate me with stories of her sister and questions about Enoch. I'm prepared for those conversations, but again, I don't want to have them on the phone.

Me: Do you have comfortable shoes on?

Reese: Define comfortable.

Have fucking mercy.

Me: Never mind. I'll deal with it. Be there in an hour.

Reese: You're coming here?

I refuse to answer her last question. She can spend her last hour with her sister worrying about it. Latching Reese's suitcase, I scoop Biscuit off the bed and rub her head a few times. "I'm going to go get your frustrating mother. Use Bach's expensive piano as a scratching post if the mood strikes you. He'll love it. I promise."

The cat in my arms purrs like she'll do just that. At least one woman in this house pretends she can be obedient.

Setting her down—Bach better come back to get her—I grab the suitcase and head downstairs. The house has been cleaned, and the refrigerator has been emptied. I don't plan on coming back here for a few months, so I've made sure my brothers know to come by and check on things in our absence. It's not like they have anything better to do with their time. They definitely don't have a wife to take back.

The drive to Madison, Georgia, was *almost* boring enough that I called Reese to pass the time. But I fought the urge and managed to keep my eyes open after passing the billionth dairy farm. After all, Reese will have plenty to say when she finds out what I'm really doing here.

Spoiler alert: It's not about my frozen accounts that she still hasn't released.

The red mailbox appears just as my GPS announces that I have arrived at my destination. I turn left onto the gravel drive and follow it down until my wife's car and Kane's dumb ass come into view.

"Alistair," he says as I get out and ascend the steps. "It's about time you came to get her. If I hear one more story about how amazing you are, I will feed her to the pigs."

I scoff. "She's scrappier than she looks. I doubt your slow ass could even catch her, much less lift her over the fence when she's kicking and screaming."

Kane chuckles. "Speaking from experience, huh?"

"No, I've always caught her." Lest he think I can't handle that ball of fire in his living room. "Now, where is she?"

I didn't come here to talk to him.

He flashes me a no-bullshit look that I ignore. "Remember, she's welcome here; you're not."

"I suppose if that's the case, I should take my money somewhere more welcome, too." Just because my wife's sister is here doesn't mean I have to support their cause. I can easily send resources to many other organizations that do the same thing. Kane's isn't the only one, though it is the most successful.

"Through here." Ignoring my comment, Kane opens the front door and leads me through a hall, stopping at the end. "She's in here."

I nod. "Thanks for looking after her."

"I owed you."

Yeah, he fucking did, but I don't waste breath acknowledging it. I rip open the door and find my sunflower in a chair, watching out the window.

"I have one question for you," she says, never turning away from the window. "Do you love me?"

I leave no room for hesitation. "Yes."

I can feel her grin warming the space around us.

"Is that all? Would you like to know my social security number, too?"

Finally, she faces me, and the grin she wears is much bigger than I expected. "No, thank you. I have that already. I want something else, though."

Anything. "It better not be another cat. I already don't like the one we have."

"Liar." She laughs, getting up and walking to me. "You love Biscuit more than you love me."

Maybe, but I'll take that tidbit to the grave. "You wanted something from me, Mrs. Cain. What is it?"

She taps my chest. "This, right here. The empty space in your chest."

"Where my heart should be?"

I know she doesn't mean my literal heart.

"Yes, that. I want to own that space forever. Not six years or twelve—forever." She grabs my chin, forcing me to hold her gaze. "Now, ask me to marry you."

A slow smile tugs onto my face as I remove her hand from my chin, holding it as I ease onto one knee. "Reese Cain, I will never stop coming for you. If you run, I won't be far behind. If you hurt me, I will punish you; if you hate me, I will love you. But I will always come for you. Will you spare me the hassle of always having to hunt you down and chain you in the basement by marrying me? I promise I can be the man you need for the rest of your life."

Like I gave the greatest proposal in history, she smashes her lips against mine, her tongue pushing through my lips and claiming every inch of my mouth as her.

"Yes," she pants. "Yes, I'll marry you for real this time!"

I stand, pulling her up with me. "Good because we're making up for lost time and leaving for Hawaii. I think society calls these trips a honeymoon."

EPILOGUE

Van

"**W**HERE'S YOUR WIFE?"

I look up from my desk, finding Enoch in my doorway, and sigh. "She texted. She's running late."

He glances at his watch. "I've never known her to be this late."

"Would you like me to slit her throat when she gets here as a punishment?" I suggest. "She has been a little unruly lately."

Enoch, not in the mood for my antics, taps the door frame. "Call me when she gets here."

I tip my chin and focus back to the brief on my desk, but it doesn't last long. Now, I'm worried since Enoch pointed out that she's never been this late before. Could something have happened to her? Surely, no one would be stupid enough to breathe in her vicinity. Everyone in this town knows she's my wife and off limits to anything with opposable thumbs.

Fuck it. I'm just going to be one of those pussy husbands who checks on their wives when they leave the house for longer than thirty minutes. The phone rings several times before she finally picks up, out of breath. "I'm in the building," she says in greeting. "Did you know the elevator is out?"

"No, but I will fire whoever failed to fix it in a timely manner."

She laughs. "You are so ridiculous. You aren't firing anyone. Besides, going up the stairs with a baby and a diaper bag is oddly refreshing."

Someone is so getting fired. "Where are you? I'm coming to help since you didn't call me when you got here like I asked you to."

Two years of marriage, and my wife still doesn't listen worth a shit.

"No, you won't. I'm already at the door."

I get up anyway, rounding my desk when I hear, "Cohen! You came to see us!"

Smiling, I follow the coos and squeals to the lobby, finding my soon-to-be-son grinning while showing off his new glasses.

"Da!" he hollers when he finally sees me, wiggling furiously in Reese's arms. "Da!"

I walk over, take the squirming three-year-old, and kiss his wet cheek. "Happy Gotcha Day, buddy!"

This day has been a long time in the making. Reese and I knew the minute we saw him in the arms of a social worker that he was our son. With his extra chromosome and my sparkling personality, he will be a heartbreaker—just like his mother.

"Do you want to see Great Grandpa before he makes us promise a bunch of legal nonsense to make you an official Cain?" I bounce the little boy on my hip. Like our marriage, Judge Enoch Gadot, my grandfather, is signing off on our new addition to the family at my request.

Like anything, time has helped heal the distance I put between us after finding out that Enoch betrayed me. While I know his actions were for my own good, they still sting. But if there's one thing I've learned from my grandfather, it's that everyone deserves second chances—even well-meaning judges.

"Pa!" Cohen screams. "Pa! Pa!"

Between my brothers, Enoch, and Magda, this boy's feet barely touch the floor. When they do, we all have our phones recording. Cohen has been a blessing to our family and has given me something I never thought I'd have: an heir.

Reese and I couldn't be happier. Not only has Cohen given me a future, but he's also provided Reese with a new career. Since she no longer needs to hack the students at the university to send money to women's shelters, she's agreed to help Kane and Julia with theirs, all the while being a full-time wife and mom.

I tried to tell her that she didn't have to give up her teaching assistant job. We could hire a nanny for Cohen, and I, obviously, can care for myself. But she insisted that nothing was more gratifying than taking care of her family.

"You all right?" Reese whispers in my ear.

I smile, taking in her flushed cheeks and messy hair. "I'm more than okay." I grab her hand. "Tell everyone goodbye."

We have a family to make official.

It takes several minutes for Reese and Cohen to blow eight billion kisses to all the secretaries up front, but finally, we're headed down the long hall to Enoch's chambers.

"You want to know something funny?"

I pause, turning to look at Reese. "Depends. Is it the sort of 'funny' that really means I'll be pissed off after you tell me?"

I've lived with this woman long enough to know her tells.

"Stop." She pats me lightly on the chest before stealing a kiss from Cohen. "I'm serious. I think your dairy allergy is rubbing off on me."

Surely, she knows a food allergy isn't contagious.

"As soon as I smell Cohen's milk, I feel nauseous. This morning, I even vomited."

Flutters swirl in my stomach—a lightness I've never felt before. Is this what fucking happiness feels like? "I don't think that's an allergy, Flower."

She grins. "No, I'm pretty sure society calls it morning sickness. Congratulations, Mr. Cain. Today, you've become a father of two."

If you can't wait for more Van and Reese, go to
https://geni.us/AVPbonusscene
and download a sneak peek at Tennyson's first chapter! It's a doozy!

Can't wait for Tennyson? Try a hero just as grumpy in, *The Potter*.

Dear Reader,

2023 kicked my flat butt. Everything that could go wrong, did. Releasing this book on time was one of the many things that fell by the wayside as I handled this thing called life. Through sheer will and lots of tears, I was finally able to make it happen.

I hope you guys loved Van and Reese's story of forgiveness. If you didn't, that's okay, too. But I would love and appreciate any reviews you can share on any platform. As you know, you're not supporting a big publisher with me; you're supporting a family of five whose mama appreciates you reading her stories.

And if you seriously want to know who made this book happen, these ladies below did. Give them a shout if you know them or just say an extra prayer for them for being so gracious to me and spending many long nights helping get this book into your hands.

All my love,

Kristy

ACKNOWLEDGMENTS

My teeny, little baby girls who aren't so little anymore: You two turds kept me in the game with your constant cheers and long hours at the computer, suffering with me as we read this book eleventy billion times. I guess I need to take you shopping like I promised eight weekends ago. Good thing you aren't spoiled.

Jaime: I keep thinking someone is going to talk some sense into you to stop holding my hand and bailing me out of messes. I certainly deserve it. But deep down in my exhausted heart, I know you never will. You are *that* friend, and if I have to chase your cute butt across this country and chain myself to your leg, you will never leave me. (That got dark quick, huh?) Anyway, I love you harder than Van's cock.

Valerie: Dude! You survived! Can you believe it? I felt sure you were going to run screaming after that first day, but you didn't. You are a beast, and I could have never finished this book without your many hours of help. You rock my freaking world.

Tijuana: I'd like to remind you that we have a contract, and while I'm 2000 percent sure you wanted to curse me, you didn't. That's the most supportive wife I've ever known. Thank you for always believing in me and my messages, and all the exhausting days you had to talk me off a ledge. I am grateful beyond words.

Vanessa and Colby: Without you, these stories wouldn't be half as decent as I hope they are. You're both magical.

Jessica: Do you even remember me at this point? I promise to make up for all our lost time this year. Thank you for all you do for me—especially holding down the KM fort. You are my hero.

Stacey: Maybe I can grovel publicly so you feel guilty if you run. I promise 2024 is going to be a better year. Thank you for sticking by me when you likely wanted to punch me. You are my Huckleberry.

Cat and Silver: You ladies need bodyguards—that's how freaking talented you are. Keep yourselves safe with all that amazingness and know that you made my dreams come true.

A-Team: Do we need to even repeat how amazing you are? Yeah, we do. You guys are superstars!

OTHER BOOKS BY KRISTY MARIE

The Fallen Kings of Eden
A Contemporary Series- All novels are standalone and feature different couples with crossover characters
A Vicious Proposal
AVO- Tennyson's Story
Bach's Story
Shakespeare's Story

The Hands of the Potters
A Contemporary Series- All novels are standalone and feature different couples with crossover characters
The Potter
The Refiner
The Sculptor
The Prodigal

21 Rumors Series
A Romantic Comedy Series- All novels are standalone and feature different couples with crossover characters
IOU
The Pretender
The Closer
21 Rumors Box Set

The Commander Legacies
A Second-Generation Contemporary Series- All novels are standalone and feature different couples with crossover characters
Rebellious

Commander in Briefs
A Contemporary Series- All novels are standalone and feature different couples with crossover characters
Pitcher
Commander
Gorgeous
Drifter
Interpreter
Commander in Briefs Box Set

For more information, visit www.authorkristymarie.com